J.E. CAESAR

Empyrean Earth

First edition

ISBN: 9780578345970

This book was professionally typeset on Reedsy.
Find out more at reedsy.com

Foreword

When I began reading *Empyrean Earth*, I had a flashback: ordinary-looking dorm room, average fall weather in New England, a thing called Facebook only available on slow, school-issued laptops—the one remarkable detail was the notebook sketch of a hero in robes bearing a deathly sword. Scribbled underneath were musings about a Librarian and doomed civilization and space travel. I remember thinking a seemingly banal thought, but one which (if you've ever been a teenager or young adult) has a tremendous amount of weight in a single syllable: this stuff is *cool*.

Flash forward: a mutual college friend is getting married and as a result a phone call and simple "Hey, what ever happened to that book you were writing?" turned into a yearlong journey from rough-around-the-edges manuscript to hey-I-can't-believe-it's-not-traditionally-published novel. Caesar and I reconnect, reminisce, chat, brainstorm, inspire, collaborate, go to said wedding, plan, revise, revise, revise—and execute *Empyrean Earth*. As for myself, I started 2021 with ideas of being a writer as well, but by the advent of 2022 I was obsessed with editing other people's projects—due entirely to my work on *Empyrean Earth*. The joy of working with a creative mind akin to my own is remarkable. Written stories are an amazing medium, they can take any twist and turn the writer desires, imagination is the only limiter—a limitation Caesar doesn't abide by. Sometimes I wondered if my practical side was holding him back in the revision process as he and I grappled with an innumerable amount of style choices, grammar rules, character quirks, pacing decisions, and deciding "How many people can a person kill with one sword swing?" We added chapters, removed scenes, tweaked details, clarified language, but never changed the core books-should-be-fun-to-read attitude that imbues Caesar's story. The ultimate prize: a creative work that slashes its own path, dismembers subgenre, hacks at modern society, and parries the reader's expectations and intrigue.

I feel like an uncle, I didn't raise this nephew-of-a-book, but I helped it mature into a flawless killing machine (that's what you want your kid to be, right?). If I'm losing the metaphor/my marbles, that's a good thing, dear reader, because you need to move on—your adventure on *Empyrean Earth* awaits.

-Chris Gale

Prologue:

"**E**conomists were gods. Every prediction they made, fact. In the year 2208, the gods gathered and decided that the expected and romanticized Space Age would not occur. Never in the way imagined. A 'Space Rush' would bankrupt even the richest of nations, set humanity back hundreds of years, or permanently cripple the global economy. Because no nation wished to defy their prophecy, the obvious and overdue human Space Age never matured beyond a fledgling state. The gods did not foresee the widespread psychological effects of their revelation. Their 'Cancellation of Space' created a period of political upheaval, civil unrest, and economic collapse that gods were meant to prevent.

The failed gods were cast aside.

Scientists became the new gods. Their every invention regarded as wise. In the year 2333, they unveiled a new energy source. With that, new fields of science and more gods for worship.

The new gods informed the world that a space-faring ship could be built and powered with the energy and instructed all nations to donate their top minds. They said, to save Earth—save humanity, the ship needed to be built ignoring all convention of cost.

Historic advances sprang from global cooperation. Eventually, the Endeavor 7, a space vessel unlike anything, past or future, was complete. Named after Earth's seven leading countries, it could travel the vast distances of the universe with relative ease. All who qualified for the trip—all who could fit on the ship, left Earth.

One year after successfully traveling outside the solar system, Earth lost, and never regained contact with the Endeavor 7. Despite their best effort, the mission to populate the nearest habitable planet was declared a failure. Unprecedented quantities of money, material, and optimism were exhausted by the Endeavor Project. Earth plunged into another, longer, violent age of chaos known as the Pre-Scorch.

The story within these pages takes place unknown years after the Pre-Scorch Period."

-Ido Xzaven, Empyrean Earth, First Edition, Vol. 1

Chapter 1

Moonlight bathed Span Opticon Castle, and Joan Flayr watched from a distance with a tight fist. She had stalked through the numerous settlements, fabrications, and study centers that decorated the ruins surrounding the castle's elevated base to arrive at her vantage. Her activism called her into the city-state of Virtus in the past, but never this deep.

The final leg of her trip exhausted the night. At her back, Luna cast elongated shadows across a patchwork skyline; black bandages wound tightly about a festered wound. Scarred and decrepit edifices were monuments to the city before. A real city; huge and teaming with industries, unlike the humble settlements of today. In the darkness, the towering, skeletal structures almost looked complete, as though the Scorch Period never existed.

Elder Zachariah Sandhurst, leader of the Syndicate of Valor, founder of Virtus, and Joan's mark, made it law that no Pre-Scorch buildings, regardless of condition, be removed or disturbed. Adhering to his restriction, Virtus evolved into a microcosm for life on Neo-Earth: monoliths, once in bloom, now degraded, incomplete, and overrun with smaller, simpler dwellings. Elder Sandhurst, during his conquests as a younger man, took the region specifically for its abundance of ruins.

Unchecked, Virtus' borders grew alongside its founder's influence. His ideology was the way of life for its inhabitants, and by way of his Treaty of Neo-Earth, all citizens on the planet. Joan, intending to disrupt his control, planned to assassinate the Elder.

The accepted accounts lacked detail on the how-and-why the old cities were abandoned and the Earth scorched, but they overwhelmingly pointed at war. The stories and theories suggested ancient humans, the Preneo, laid waste to precious, finite terra firma with rank and advanced warfare. When one side built a machine to bake the Earth's surface, the war ended. But the war was a draw. Areas of the world remained inhospitable, barren, and uninhabited. With humanity crippled and unlikely to recover, the survivors commissioned themselves to space-sleep for the millions of years the planet needed to be suitable for human life again.

Joan never liked the story. If Earth was scorched purposefully, why? She mused. War only sorta-kinda answered the What. It didn't satisfy the Why. Would the Preneo burn and level their townships? Deconstruct and downsize civilization to make a weapon? The Scorch felt too purposeful and intelligent to be the desperate idea of warring nations.

But that was the story—put forth and popularized by Sandhurst's Syndicate of Valor—the same story taught to school children. Like all good lies, she suspected there was enough truth to float the fantasy.

Insatiable curiosity made her an outcast, leading her into clandestine circles and underworld cabals. Circles, where she met and eventually wed an equally curious man, Paulo Flayr.

Joan and Paulo, together, challenged Neo-Earth's largest factions and gained the support to create their Boundless Movement. Their movement brought them far into the Uncharted Regions, where they lived among the Feral-men, uncovering untold artifacts, always garnering influence for their cause, and seeding an intellectual rebellion.

Paulo believed in peaceful methods. Joan was tired of pacifism. While Paulo gallivanted, Joan trained for combat. She even convinced her loyal friend and bodyguard, Grase, to provide lessons in secret. Born to the daughter of a late Seraph, she was a natural warrior and a quick study. With Grase's guidance, Joan turned her body into an inconspicuous weapon.

The rising sun would signal the seventieth anniversary of the Treaty of Neo-Earth. Releasing a breath through her teeth, Joan pushed onward towards the castle and promontory.

Chapter 2

Depot stood as the oldest and most popular jazz saloon on Neo-Earth. The Retro Bars of the Neutral Zone were an emerging trend. Built to resemble the almost mythical saloons of the Ancient West, in addition to live music, they offered what no other place could, unquestioned unanimity and loads of convincing Pre-Scorch Period-styled drinks. Located beyond the southwestern border of Virtus, in the largest Neutral Zone, Depot enjoyed an assortment of clientele.

Thick swirls of smoke clung to the air as readily as patrons clung to each other, dancing speedy jigs. From all corners of civilization, they traveled across miles to lose themselves; drawn to Depot where they escaped their sworn loyalties by transporting back to a time in history, no one was sure existed. Depot was a place, *the* place to disappear; or be reborn.

Even the Vicaarians, pious people of the cloth, were present, bouncing about waists in hands with off-duty, helmet-less Legioneers. Members of the stuffy Syndicate of Valor gathered about tables engaged in games of chance that promoted anything but integrity. The occasional Feral-man, drunk and rubbing elbows with devoted members of the Boundless

Movement. Even women of the Ars Femina came to Depot, to bury their inhibitions and mingle with the men they were sworn to oppose. The rest of the crowd was transient workers, traders, explorers, and entrepreneurs whose pilgrimages often converged on destinations like this one.

Altazar Gahren, a self-made success, owned the establishment. Altazar maintained celebrity status among the Nutes—people with no allegiance to the larger factions that lived in the Neutral Zones outside of faction territories.

"Ay, Zar! What the fuck's up?" One of Altazar's favorite customers slinked up to the service area of the bar.

"My sales," Altazar let out a booming laugh. "Ah, Keano, you sonuva ... What'll it be?"

"The usual," he rasped back loud enough to be heard over the commotion.

"One Fiya Water, coming right up!"

A master of his craft, Altazar handled any bottle of liquor with misplaced grace. The sole bartender, he displayed unfailing precision that made people wonder why he hadn't become a faction surgeon or chemist. Altazar the Alchemic was the nickname given to him by regulars. Mixing the elements of his signature drinks was his second nature. He slid the concoction down the obstacle course of the bar counter to his longtime friend. Only a few drops escaped as the cup met with the old man's outstretched palm.

Depot attracted many newcomers and retained more regulars. Keano was a regular and a regular old guy. He saw the days before the establishment of the Ars Femina or the Legioneers. He remembered the days before the Treaty of Neo-Earth when Elder Sandhurst was younger and vibrant, and just.

Altazar loved Keano's stories of the past and gave him drinks on the house in exchange for lore.

"Fuckin' incredible, these guys. Ya' like 'em?" Altazar shouted over his live musicians. Keano shook his head as enthusiastically as an eighty-five-year-old bricklayer could. He was no doubt riddled with arthritis but found the ability to animate his body to the fullest when recounting stories.

"Bartender!" a patron yelled, "Another of mead. Not a cup. A pitcher for my pals!" Slamming a pile of trusts down on the bar with one hand, they stabilized themselves with the other. Spinning, Altazar hoisted a barrel of mead onto his shoulders, lowering it, he filled up a pitcher and collected the trusts in one smooth motion.

"Alright ... What've you got for me? Unexplored and fertile patches of the earth? Ooh, or maybe, one about the Fallen? Wait, how about one of Sandhurst's rise to power? I dunno'. Just tell me a good one, will ya'?" Altazar said, returning his attention to Keano. Keano chuckled, then quickly hid his smile.

"This one's about Celeste and her girls walkin' into a bar." Keano leaned forward and whispered with elbows resting on the counter.

"Why you whispering?" Altazar, back turned to prepare a drink, shouted into a quiet room.

Keano leaned even closer, "Because *she* just walked in. And I don't want them to hear this one."

A chill landed on Altazar's back and inched up his spine. Turning slowly, he locked eyes with the leader of the Ars Femina.

She headed for the counter—directly towards Altazar. He couldn't get his mouth to open to squeak out a greeting. The drink almost escaped his balmy grasp. Celeste was massive and appeared more pissed off than usual. If Celeste remained there, no one was safe. Even Keano, with his boasts of doing and seeing it all, knew better than to keep his back to her approach. The sea of intoxicated dancers parted for, not one, but three grim harbingers.

All knew who the women were. No one was happy to encounter them. In stride, from right to left was Dezba, Celeste's chief advisor and enforcer, adorned in full Searcher armor, Celeste in the middle, carrying an unknown device, then Jelani, Celeste's second-in-command, also an enforcer, also in full Searcher regalia. Their polished chest plates, bracers, and leg guards glinted under the dimmed lighting of the saloon.

Dezba and Jelani were rarely seen apart. Celeste often sent the pair on missions too much for other Searchers, but too sensitive for her direct participation.

Wall-to-wall, every soul was transfixed. Earsplitting silence replaced the band that had only moments before controlled the exciting pulse of Depot. Walking through the forest of living statues in an inverted triangle formation, Dezba and Jelani were upfront, with Celeste lagging between them. An eternity passed before the trio made it to the bar. When Dezba and Jelani arrived, there were no vacant seats. A nervous cough from somewhere cleared three stools. Celeste sauntered up and sat like a sack of bricks in the middle stool. Her enforcers assumed positions in the remaining seats.

Once settled, Altazar probed for the nature of the visit with humor, "Ahh, Celeste! What are *you* doing *here*? Heh, you know you're bad for business."

"*Your* business *bad*? I don't think so. No, I think business is going well. So much so, you're attracting the wrong kinda company." A handful of Vicaarians crept out the entrance.

"Uh, w—well you want something? Ya' know, on the house?"

Altazar bargained.

"On the house, huh? Tempting. I do like my drink. But not on the job." Gasps and stale breaths left their homes. Altazar's knees felt strange—like mush. Standing was suddenly a task. Celeste cleared a space with her arm then cleared her throat.

Dropping the device on the counter, she addressed the congregation, "As much as I *hate* to ruin your party." She pointed and winked at a nearby table of terrified patrons. "I believe a fugitive, a person in violation of the Treaty law, is hiding in this very saloon. Now. If you all cooperate, this *could* go as smoothly as I wish it wouldn't. We do not simply extract people—we extract information to achieve the former."

Celeste surveyed the faces of the crowd intently, as though she could ensnare her elusive quarry with eyes alone. A woman in the crowd worked up enough nerve to shout, "And?"

"*And*, the next person who talks during *my* fucking time to talk might never speak again. Paulo! Paulo Flayr! I *know* you're here. If you *truly* cared about 'the people', surrender and avoid further conflict. How I *love* conflict."

Celeste paced back and forth, separating the bar counter and the petrified crowd, until finally, returning to the device, she pressed one of the many buttons and stood back expectantly. The machine hummed to life. The onlookers took one giant step back in unison. With more space for the production, Celeste widened her course. When the partially distorted image of a man appeared above the mechanism she began, "This is a hologram. 'Ooh'. 'Ahh'. 'What's a hologram?' You're thinking. More importantly, who is it a hologram of? We all know who this is, agreed?" Celeste paused, eyeing her audience sternly. No one dared respond.

"We *are* all on the same page. This man," half-turning,

she waved her hand through the image, it rippled against her motion. "Paulo Flayr was seen in this very saloon very recently. He may still be here. I'm thinking he is."

"He isn't here!" Keano offered. "I spoke with *that* man a couple of hours and a few drinks back. Said he was on his way out east, to the Greater Ruins. Rambling about scraps and salvaging this and that."

Celeste faced old Keano as he spoke, once he said his fill, she turned away satisfied, then disinterested.

"Take the old man outside. He knows more than he'll say aloud ... Don't forget the projector." Celeste exited the saloon briskly, with Jelani already grabbing at Keano, and Dezba grabbing the device.

Altazar, with no small amount of self-control, managed to keep civil throughout the shakedown. Jelani pushed Keano to the floor and began dragging him out. Altazar erupted.

"You fuckin'..." Gasps came from the background. "... You fucking, Ars Femina, Manazon, brutes. Get your spacedamned hands off him! He's an old man." Hearing the celebrity owner of the joint stand up to the Searchers, others stepped forward.

"Back off!"

"Yeah! Paulo ain't here. You heard the poor guy."

"You ladies ought to be ashamed of yourselves!"

The shouts of discontent grew in volume and frequency as inspired patrons overcame their fear. Altazar, now standing on the counter, led the chant, "Let! Him! Go!" The outbursts and protests would have escalated to a frenzy had Jelani not unholstered a particularly menacing persuader and fired at the ceiling. Altazar was stunned. The crowd returned to stone.

"We're taking him for interrogation. Anybody who tries to stop us will be assumed to be an accomplice to conspiracy to undermine the Treaty of Neo-Earth, an act punishable by immediate expiration."

Jelani spun the weapon around her trigger finger. Certain her tirade crushed the growing courage, she began pushing her way out, followed by Dezba, dragging a writhing Keano. Before the duo made it out with their haul, a voice rang out—bold and proud from within the caucus.

"Is this what it has come to? You women are nothing more than tyrants for trusts. Maidens of murder and money." Onlookers shuffled aside trying desperately to make clear it was not they who spoke.

The crowd arranged itself into two imperfect circles. One encompassed the Searchers, the other, a table with a man, enjoying what looked like his tenth Pre-Scorch spirit. His face twisted as he gulped it down then wiped his mouth with a sleeve belonging to a jacket identical to the garments Paulo Flayr wore on the hologram. Long duster, dirty and gray. A wide-brimmed Stetson hat angled on his head, so only his nose and mouth were visible. And like the hologram, his face was blanketed in stubble, eventually giving way to a crude goatee.

"Leave that man alone," the goatee spoke. "It *is* me you came for. *This* is why we fight. The factions have sliced up Neo-Earth to their liking and left us, the small fries, the little girls and guys, out. To starve or join their efforts in desperation. We of the Boundless Move—"

Jelani had already heard enough, aiming her persuader at the table and its brave occupant, she approached. His speech went on, louder now.

"We Boundless, fight for the people! We fight for the freedom of information, and equal rights, for ourselves and the 'Feralmen'. Against conformity. We fight for the right *to* fight!"

Finished, he overturned his table.

"Everybody out! This is going to get messy," he yelled from behind the makeshift cover.

Dezba unhooked her twin daggers, curved to minimize air resistance and maximize bodily trauma. Binding Keano's legs and arms, Dezba kicked him into a corner opposite the flow of exiting bodies, then joined Jelani's semi-circle orbit around the barricaded fugitive.

Depot became a ghost town of abandoned card games, smoldering cigarettes, half-empty drinks, and toppled chairs. Even the band slipped out without taking their equipment or collecting their due payment. When the doors stopped flapping, only four people were left. The Searchers, the Fugitive, and the Alchemist.

Jelani waited for her opponent's move. Dezba rolled her neck, stretching her back and arms in anticipation of the skirmish she hoped would ensue.

Shielded from view, the Fugitive fumbled with a modified crossbow. Altazar crouched out of sight, behind the bar counter with arms protecting his head. He hoped the damage to his place would be slight. Sadly, Altazar's hopes would not be fulfilled. Events had entered a grave spiral, and Depot would become as suggested: messy.

Chapter 3

Adjusting the sleeves of his robe, the neck on his silk undershirt, and the scabbard on his hip, Hiroshi Gunkimono strode into the Chamber of the Elders for the second time in his life. The first was as a child. He remembered clinging to his older brother's arm timidly. The words Saigo Gunkimono spoke next were never far from Hiroshi's mind.

"One day, you too will be a High Seraph in the Syndicate of Valor."

The day had come and gone. Currently, Hiroshi was the only active High Seraph in the Syndicate. At twenty-five years, he was the youngest to ever achieve the distinction. With a blade, he was as effective as a hundred warriors in combat.

When Elder Sandhurst required Hiroshi's abilities, a trusted aide would be sent to detail the task, or the conversation might take place through the wall-mounted communication device in his quarters. Hiroshi preferred the aides.

That day, it was neither device nor messenger, but a direct summons to the Chamber of the Elders deep within Span Opticon, for a face-to-face briefing. Hiroshi had found the sealed note slipped under his door. The wave of excitement did not fade, even as he groomed himself and prepared his finest robes.

Standing near what he assumed the center of the chamber, he adjusted his sleeve once more. Squinting, he looked around himself. The doors behind him closed, hiding the room's walls in blanket darkness. The sounds of movement and life from outside the room gone. Nothingness remained.

His heart bobbed about uneasily in his chest—thumping, thumping. He didn't move or make a noise. As Hiroshi's eyes adjusted, above him, he saw the silhouette of a woman, and three men: the Syndicate Elders.

As the decision-makers for their nation, Hiroshi was the embodiment of their will. If the Elders said 'jump', Hiroshi would fly. When they needed him to go, he was there already. If the order was to kill, Hiroshi would strike from existence. That was the way of the High Seraph, as it had been since the beginning.

"Hiroo—shiii."

A voice crawled out of the thick silence, amplified by unseen workings. It was Elder Sandhurst. Searching for his location, Hiroshi, spun slowly in place. The chamber felt darker than he had remembered as a child.

"Hirooo—sshhiii." Again, his name oozed from overhead, reverberating off the surrounding blackness.

He fought the urge to rest a hand on his sword. Why should he fear his own master?

Breathing deeply, he followed the dull-grey lights that appeared on the floor, slicing a narrow path to the room's true center. There, the path gave way to a circle of light, large enough to stand. Stopping inside the circle, the chamber came to life.

One-by-one, four pillars of light shot down from where a ceiling might be. He expected a fifth, to cut the void and illuminate himself. But he remained unlit, bathing only in the runoff luminescence of the beams and the soft light of the circle at his feet.

In each shining column, a Syndicate Elder was revealed. Each hovering in a simple, personalized throne. Moved by unseen hands, they took their posts at the four cardinal directions around Hiroshi, with Elder Sandhurst at the north.

Hiroshi examined his elder with the intensity of an insatiable pupil. He was ancient, the oldest man to have ever lived, perhaps. The one who coined the terms 'Neo-Earth' and 'Preneo', who pieced together the story of what life was like before the Scorch. That same man, sitting suspended in the air, looked unbelievably fragile. His hands were spider webs of blue veins and bone, clinging to the arms of his chair. The ragged smile smeared across his face was at home among a boon of liver spots. Wrinkles folded in on themselves, rolling up his balding head. His robe fit him as well as a man fit in at Fortress Pangaia. It looked all sorts of wrong on his body, like a skeleton draped in curtains.

Nothing about the Hero of Neo Earth's appearance showed his past or importance; nothing except his eyes, still burning with mischievous ambition; big and green, they bored into Hiroshi. Slender cuts of jade, that had seen far more than one man should have. Embers still hot, even as the surrounding fire petered out.

The throne hovered closer, and Hiroshi broke eye contact. Elder Sandhurst chuckled. The Elders followed his lead, tightening their orbits around Hiroshi.

Hiroshi's uneasiness melted away. The cool confidence

returned to his stance, and he spoke, "Elders, I am your arms. The sword in your grasp. I cut all that move against you. It is my function. Through it I realize my purpose. What is it you would have me do?"

Sandhurst waited an uncomfortable moment before responding, "Hiroshi, a woman ... was apprehended last night." Hiroshi did not react. Sandhurst continued, "She was caught snooping around our premises. Two Seraphim engaged her. She slew them ..." Hiroshi swallowed a lump in his throat. "... Quite effortlessly, it appears. I say this because she was not contained until another seven of ours were killed."

"They should have woken me."

"Of course, they should have." Elder Kanumba Lilleane agreed from the west. His black eyes shimmering with obvious sorrow. He was the kindest of the Elders, but his face was long; stretched tight by the dogged stresses of leadership. "We were not informed until early this morning when the ordeal ended. Her attack arrived swiftly—the Seraphim were unable to react in time."

"Tch, such a waste," Hiroshi muttered.

"Excuse me?" Sandhurst asked with an arched eyebrow.

"I said, have the Ars put an expiration contract on Seraphim?"

"The attacker is not one of Celeste's. No contract has been approved. The Ars Femina are smarter than that," Sandhurst said.

"Who else could kill not one, but nine Seraphim?"

"We know exactly *who* she is," Elder Eriksen Apopthis confirmed, from his southern post behind Hiroshi.

Eriksen was as enigmatic an Elder as they came. Scant known of his life before joining the Syndicate of Valor. As a close friend and confidant to Elder Sandhurst, he rose through the ranks of the organization quickly. He played his role faithfully—never openly challenging Elder Sandhurst even when he wanted to.

"She has demanded to speak to you only," Sandhurst's man rasped, wiping wisps of his long gray hair from his brow.

"I have nothing to say to one such as her."

"You *are* going to grant her wish," Elder Adeana Cherveyo entered the conversation, no fondness in her voice. Suppressing a snarl, he turned his head to the right to face her.

Elder Cherveyo had the longest and sharpest memory in the Syndicate. The fact that Hiroshi had beat out her son to become High Seraph, she would not soon forgive.

"What is it, *boy*? Did you forget? You answer to *all* of us, not just *your* Master. Look, Zach. You see his insolence. You see his contempt—the disrespect, he is too young. Too young to—"

"Enough," Elder Sandhurst whispered.

Hiroshi faced north again.

"The intruder was positively identified as Joan Flayr. Enemy to our cause and spouse of 'The Most Dangerous Man on Neo-Earth'," Elder Lilleane picked up after a brief, tense silence.

"H—how could Joan Flayr? This must be a mistake. I trained with every Seraph myself."

"That you did," Elder Cherveyo quickly agreed. Hiroshi didn't turn.

"The Ars are clever, how deeply have we checked into this? If I am just hearing of it now, how far could our scouts have traveled? What of the Feral-men? They have strong enough ties to the Boundless and their activities remain unmonitored and largely unknown."

Elder Cherveyo countered. "The Feral-men have scant knowledge of warfare. They are little more than meek scavengers—enthralled by the refuse of their ancestors. There has been no war, no open conflict in decades, approaching a full century now. If someone is out there with the ability to slaughter Seraphim, they belong to one of our rival factions. No plain's rodent could compete with the combat methodology of a Seraph."

"It should not be hastily ruled out," Hiroshi retorted flatly.

"I agree with Elder Cherveyo. But this treachery cannot be the work of the Boundless alone. The Feral-men bear no allegiances and display no loyalty or hostility to the Treaty. Hiroshi—Joan Flayr, is in Holding. Question, then kill her." Elder Sandhurst offered unflinching.

"Master?"

"Dead. She cannot be allowed to live. No one can know how she manhandled our ranks. The Syndicate of Valor has a reputation to uphold, and we will not let some maverick undermine it. And, Hiroshi ..."

"Yes, Master?"

"There is a chance we have been misdirecting our attention in search of Paulo if Joan proves to be the mastermind of the Movement."

Hiroshi wanted to say more but, under the needling glares of the other Elders, he decided against it.

"It will be as you wish." Hiroshi spun on his heels and exited the Chamber of the Elders, trying his best to hide his disapproval. The Elders waited for the massive doors to close then began to speak among themselves.

"This news is disturbing, Zachariah. An attack on Span Opticon stinks with pungent arrogance. It seems your Age of Peace may be near an end. For our sake, I hope young Hiroshi can handle this."

"Elder Lilleane, he may be green, but you know as well as I, that with Hiroshi on our side, victory is guaranteed. You have seen him with a blade. He is godly."

"God-*ly*. Not *a* God. The Legioneers have been quiet. Let us hope they are not our covert aggressors or the Treaty you have worked your whole life to install may dissolve in your grasp. If it is Amram, brave Gunkimono will need more than a sword to protect us."

"Have faith, Cherveyo. With this invisible manipulator moving against us, it is no time to doubt our instrument. He is a High Seraph in *our* Syndicate of Valor, after all."

"I am hoping that this incident remains contained. We are old, Zach. More so by the day, things aren't like they used to be. We do not have nearly enough Seraphim to go to war, let alone start one," Elder Apopthis lamented.

Elder Sandhurst was growing annoyed, not with his peers specifically but, his loss of control. "It will not come to that—ever! I have kept this miserable rock in one piece for, as of yesterday, seventy years. It is no accident. Trust our treaty, trust our syndicate, trust our High Seraph."

For a moment, Elder Sandhurst's words seemed enough to quell the obvious concerns.

"Zachariah?" Elder Cherveyo locked eyes with Sandhurst. "What will we do if the boy learns of his brother's fate?"

"All we can—pray."

Chapter 4

The skirmish started, and Altazar watched it all from the safety of behind the bar counter. The fugitive dove from behind the table hiding him from view. Managing to fire what looked like a crossbow, mid-dive, at an incoming Jelani. Expecting an arrow to whir by, she dodged and was pelted instead by a barrage of tiny arrows—dart-like and tipped with vicious barbs. Riddling her right arm, the impact knocked her off balance and she tumbled to the floor.

Altazar's mouth was open so wide his jaw ached.

Jelani grimaced in pain but fired four projectiles towards the fugitive with her left as she fell. The fugitive was on his feet, loading another salvo into his unique weapon when three of Jelani's missiles lodged into the wall behind him. The fourth entered his shoulder and exited his back painfully. He remained mobile and on the move to Depot's exit. Dezba followed closely, hooked blades in hand. Bleeding profusely from his wounds, he was losing speed.

Four small explosions rocked the bar, sending splinters and glass shards airborne. Jelani held with her injured arm a small cylinder with a red button. Releasing the button with a thumb, Jelani dragged herself to a table and managed to stand.

Dezba threw one of her curved blades at the retreating fugitive. He shot his volley at the glimmering projectile. The arrows collided with the spinning blade, changing its trajectory and robbing the attack of any lethality. But the agile Dezba closed their distance enough to bury her second blade deep into his entry wound.

Altazar cringed as the fugitive let out a blood-curdling scream. His crossbow, now empty, petered down beside him. Grave pain prevented him from retrieving or reloading it. Face to face now, Dezba slammed her forehead against his skull. Crumpling to the floor in a pool of his blood, the fugitive struggled to stay conscious. He suffered from hairline fractures and a compound persuader-dagger wound. Jelani attended to her arm, meticulously pulling each barb free. Dezba glanced at Jelani with concern.

Unsupervised for only a moment, the fugitive mustered the strength to raise his crossbow, and club Dezba in the knee. Crashing backward through a table covered with drinks, she was doused in Pre-Scorch alcohol. Dezba was back on her feet instantly. Wrestling matches, from the breast pocket of his blood-soaked duster, he lit the entire book, flinging it at the drenched Searcher. The flame hit her, rolled down her armor, then landed in a booze puddle with a meek sizzle.

"Y—You cheap piece of neowolf shit! What's the proof of these spacedamned spirits? You're watering them down now?" The fugitive shouted to Altazar.

Altazar *did* water his drinks down and if Altazar had not been a 'cheap piece of neowolf shit', the fugitive might have lived to tell a different story. Maybe he would have defeated the infamous duo and achieved his freedom. Instead, he slid backward, kicking frantically at the ground, trying to scoot himself to the swinging doors—to his escape.

Dezba retrieved her thrown blade in a somersault, landing in front of the entrance. He was trapped.

The last thing he saw was the dripping figure of Dezba slashing his eyes. The last smell, the bitter stench of Pre-Scorch liquor, and the last sound belonged to Jelani's persuader. His final sensations were something hot, penetrating the back of his head. Then a headache, like an excruciating itch, clawing up from deep within his skull.

He tried to talk—to plead—but a bloody gumbo of unintelligible noises was all he could produce. Unable to see or hear, he struggled to his feet. A proud Boundless leader reduced to a pathetic and broken sight. He stumbled as he walked and left overturned furniture in his wake.

The Searchers circled their wandering foe like two hungry, yet patient eel sharks. Never straying too far but always keeping their distance. Dezba locked eyes with a deathly serious Jelani, who holstered her persuader and fingered the detonator. Pausing for a beat, she depressed the button. The fugitive, who had bumbled away from the doors and towards the performance area, died when the back of his head exploded into a mass of blood and bone, painting the stage red.

"Who would have guessed, *your* thrift would save *my* life? Altazar. Get me a brandy. Hold the water," Dezba growled over her shoulder.

"That's how you extinguish Paulo's flare. Consider yourself expired," Jelani muttered, hovering over their quarry. Hoisting him onto her good shoulder with her bad arm, she made way to the exit.

Dezba downed her brandy, approached the bar, and reached behind for a towel to dry her face and body. Altazar was there, cowering. Looking past him, she tossed the cloth carelessly to the floor near a trash bin. Retrieving the projector and Keano, she followed Jelani out.

Chapter 5

In the twelve years of its full operation, Holding Wing became a symbol of obedience and control. The octagonal prison stood as the tallest spire of Span Opticon Castle and could be seen from almost anywhere inside Virtus. By day, the sun kissed its crude metal paneling, making it shimmer as the spire turned, and caused its outline to leap out of the static backdrop. By night, the moon poured over the structure, making it glow against the somber darkness of the skyline.

None of that mattered to High Seraph, Hiroshi Gunkimono. His daily patrol ended at Holding Wing every morning and unlike the inhabitants of Virtus, Hiroshi knew the real wonder of Holding lay not in how it looked from the outside but worked on the inside.

The pinnacle of stoicism, Hiroshi navigated the winding hallways of Span Opticon. Brick gave way to metal as he rounded the final corner, only to be surprised by two of his very own, blocking the path.

"Good day, sir!" one of the Seraphs sputtered.

"Here on your daily, I assume, sir?" the other cut in no less nervous.

Annoyed with the waste of personnel, Hiroshi dismissed

them with a wave of his hand.

"Yes, sir!"

"Of course, sir."

With voices trailing off and around the corner, they vacated their posts and entered the network of hallways leading back to the main castle grounds.

Sighing, Hiroshi stepped through a doorway and into the person-sized compartment that separated the prison from the surrounding building. He pulled a yellow knob, cleared his throat, then spoke into the Communication box.

"High Seraph Gunkimono."

Hiroshi heard rustling and static on the other side, then silence. He waited eagerly as he did every day. Then began the cacophony.

The creaking of Holding Wing's mechanisms groaned to life. Gears with gritted teeth, pulleys hauling their loads, steam pistons awakened begrudgingly amid sibilant hissing fits, levers, and switches synchronized, all in motion, working to bring the doorway of Holding into alignment with Hiroshi's compartment. The discordant orchestra finished. Silence told him to slide the metal door aside and step into Holding's interior.

Once inside the mechanized prison, he looked up. Sunlight trickled down from a single pentagonal ceiling window, illuminating the control seat at the room's center and creating obsidian shadows where the beams were obstructed. Shielding his eyes with a hand, he surveyed the cells above him, waiting for the Seraph manning the controls to make the exit disappear.

The clamor welled up and subsided again, and Hiroshi was now locked inside.

That was the genius of the prison's design. The entire

building could rotate about a central axis. Whoever sat at the controls could move the cells together, or independently; clockwise or counterclockwise.

Hiroshi thought of the decades-old dream that had inspired the design. As the story went, Elder Sandhurst once dreamed he was trapped in an inescapable prison, operated by just one guard. Twelve years ago, with Former High Seraph Donnel's help, Holding Wing became reality.

Of its fifty or so cells, only one could be opened at a time. The first floor was counterbalanced against the five above it. In the unlikely event that a prisoner managed to break free, if a cell door opened, the exit on the lower level would shift out of alignment. The building's exterior was patched together using recovered slices of rare metals—selected for their resistance to damage and manipulation. It all looked like a segmented, metal pill, some fifty or sixty scorchfeet long, turned tall and fixed to the side of Span Opticon.

After memorizing all of the archive entries on Holding Wing, he still didn't understand the details of its operation. Ignorance did little to curb his interest. He imagined the same mechanisms that could move Holding, were at work inside the hilt of his blade—on a smaller scale. They were crafted with the same metal, why should the similarities end there?

Hiroshi stepped out of his thoughts, and further into the prison. Making eye contact, he hailed the Seraph at the controls, "Afternoon, Seraph Guiles."

Shuffling to his feet and wiping his mouth, the Seraph stowed his lunch before responding, "Good afternoon, sir!"

"No need for formality. Resume your meal ... What level?" Hiroshi made his way to the personnel lift connecting Holding's floors. Hiroshi only turned around after waiting for an answer for what he felt was too long. Seraph Guiles simply stared at Hiroshi. Eventually offering, "Sir, this one ... She's got some *spirit.*"

"Spirit?" Hiroshi scoffed. "Thank you, I will not be long. What floor is she on, which cell?"

"Three. Four, sir," Seraph Guiles responded, manipulating the controls. Machinery groaned, and the third floor began to rotate, grinding to a halt when Cell Four on the third floor was aligned and ready to be opened.

Entering the lift, the safety cage came down around the High Seraph. The quaint elevator jerked into motion and began its spasmodic trip upward. Getting off on the third floor, he peeked over the railing and indicated to Seraph Guiles that he was ready with a delayed nod. Guiles noticed uneasiness in Hiroshi, but chalked it up to vertigo.

Hiroshi approached the door, preparing himself for the interrogation and execution.

Closing his eyes, he waited for the telltale click signaling an open cell. It sounded subtle but sure. Hiroshi opened his eyes then pushed the metal door open and inward.

Joan wasted not a second. Using the cell's shadows to conceal her form, she vaulted at Hiroshi from a crouch. She was much larger and far more fit than the High Seraph imagined. Momentum carried her forward, knocking Hiroshi back and pinning him between her and the rail, preventing them both from plummeting to the levels below. He understood immediately how she killed nine of his men.

Hiroshi had never seen Joan Flayr outside of archived images. Pictures did not do her justice; she was magnificent. Her black hair was wrapped up in a slapdash bun. The strands that dangled free clung to her forehead. Jagged, matte cuts of obsidian were her eyes. Her blood-stained, dirt-speckled tank top clung tightly to her musculature. She was a ferocious angel of doom, a person, unlike any Hiroshi had met prior.

Joan Flayr's knee came to rest in Hiroshi's stomach, followed up by the sobering prospect of death. High Seraph Gunkimono dropped to his knees, doubled over in agony. Joan wound up for a kick but stopped short to taunt her adversary.

"Bring me High Seraph Gunkimono and I *might* spare your life."

"Consider it as done," Hiroshi shot back, standing now. Joan looked around. "I don't see him. I want *the* High Seraph, 'The Young Wonder', 'Undefeated with a Sword'. He wears a black robe embroidered with wings from shoulder to shoulder much like you. But his wings are red where all others are gold." Joan's eyes caught sight of the red embroidering on his shoulders. "Lookit that, *your* wings *are* red, might you be ... No, no. Little, no-talent shit like you, couldn't be a High Seraph."

That was as much as Hiroshi could take. A few steps brought him inside her guard. She brought her arms up a moment too late, a flurry of fierce elbows and fists hammered her midsection. The wind left her body as a final kick launched her back into the cell. A few hops brought him close, delivering a chop to the side of the head when she landed. Fighting to stay conscious, she managed to block his next chop and countered with a kick of her own. Hiroshi dodged, easily retreating out of her range.

Blood trickled from her mouth and nose, a ringing sound reverberated inside her ear, but she could still fight. Hiroshi zeroed in. Joan flipped backward, keeping one of her legs outstretched. Smirking, Hiroshi avoided the attack. What he didn't expect, and couldn't avoid, was her arcing leg sweep when she landed. With his legs kicked forcefully to the side, he landed on the floor with a thud. The High Seraph was stunned. Joan lunged for Hiroshi's now exposed sword. With a tug his sword was hers.

She thrust the blade down, tip first, where Hiroshi's head lay a moment before. Joan was surprised by its lightness, and strength. It was the finest sword she ever held. The gem-encrusted hilt was too ostentatious for her taste, but with such fine craftsmanship, a flaw or two should be ignored. More curious than the blade's perforated edge was the black lever extending out of the sword's handguard and hilt running most of the length of the handle. She wouldn't have time to inspect any further. Pulling the blade up and free from the floor, Joan closed their gap. Hiroshi dashed about unwilling to be sliced by his own weapon.

"You even handle my weapon well. Who trained you? The same person who sent you here?" He probed, drawing Joan out of the cell slowly. Soon as she cleared the cell doorway, he leaped forward, so that he and Joan were side-by-side and facing opposite directions. Hiroshi then threw all his weight against her nearest shoulder. Joan's grip loosened enough for a strong open-fist punch to knock the sword from her grasp; but not before accidentally depressing the lever on its hilt.

A thick liquid oozed from the dozens of perforations on the blade as the sword clambered to the ground. The liquid didn't gather and pool when it touched the grates as expected. Instead, the gooey substance sizzled, bubbled, and ate jagged holes through the floor. Hiroshi snatched up the weapon and returned it to the acid-resisting sheath at his side.

"Fucking *acid*?" Joan blurted, keeping Hiroshi at a distance and taking special care not to step on any of the splotches.

"Fucking *acid*," Hiroshi mocked her tone.

"Everything okay up there, sir?" Seraph Guiles called up from the lower level.

Against her pride, Joan had to accept she was no match for the High Seraph. She couldn't hit him, and he was holding back. He wanted her to see it for herself. Painfully and slowly. If she wished to survive this duel or lay eyes on Paulo ever again, she needed a miracle. That, or some quick thinking. Even if she managed to take Hiroshi down, she would need enough energy to deal with the Seraph at the controls. Still more to find her way out and back home.

Calling upon all her training, she gathered her strength. Joan shot towards the Syndicate's champion, winding up her dominant arm. Expecting the attack, Hiroshi bounced away to safety. Or so he thought until he felt the wind from Joan's hand whirring by. Off-balance, her body twisted and continued to spin as she appeared to fall. Hiroshi lowered his guard, sensing victory. Joan lashed out with her weak hand, forming it into a brutal backhanded punch. He tried to jerk his head away. It was too late. Her attack landed in the High Seraph's eye socket. Ignoring the pain and burning of pride, Hiroshi dealt Joan two swift blows. One to her abdomen, another to her nape. She collapsed to the grating with a whimper.

Blowing a breath of exasperation, he moved to the railing. His hands still trembled from adrenaline.

"Everything is under control," Hiroshi called down to Seraph Guiles. Turning away, he hoisted an unconscious Joan onto his shoulder. "Bring me down!" he commanded, then entered the lift.

Chapter 6

Hiroshi made his way out of Span Opticon and brought Joan to a secluded area behind the castle, but still on its grounds. It seemed as good a place as any to perform an execution. The sprawling landscape of Neo-Earth was behind them. The sun peered down on the pair expectantly.

Joan Flayr fought like hell, killed nine of his men, and had given him a black eye. Nine lives lost was inexcusable—a crime easily deserving of death. But for the black eye, he was grateful. He could see things clearer.

Hiroshi couldn't bring himself to kill his prisoner. Beyond simple attraction, he could only assume his reluctance arose from a desire to understand her.

Elder Sandhurst had become callous and wasteful in his old age. If Joan could be developed, he might have her as a student; maybe, eventually, even a friend. As her assigned executioner, he grappled with the swirl of emotion.

"Hurry up and kill me, you coward. Before my husband shows up and makes you wish you had done it hours ago." Joan's outbursts shook him from his internal discourse, yanking him back to the task at hand.

"Your husband? Paulo? To defeat me and rescue you? No, I

don't think he will."

"Yeah, whatever. Do it!"

"You *wish* to die?" Hiroshi was puzzled.

"I wish to live!" Joan spat, struggling against the bonds at her arms and ankles. "In a world where you and yours can no longer treat the people as pawns."

"Pawns?" Hiroshi turned the word over with his tongue. "You are one of, if not the most influential woman on the planet. Imagine a world where you are subject to no power save for your own. Joan, I have seen your ability firsthand. With the right training, we could—"

"We? Fuck you! Don't talk to me like some child. And don't let my name grace your lips again. We aren't friends. You don't understand Neo-Earth. You've never been there. Haven't lived long enough. When I was your age, *your* late brother killed *my* family. *Your* Syndicate scorched our homes to make room for *more* study and fabrication centers. High Seraph Saigo Gunkimono was nothing more than a dog, frenzied by the taste of blood. He was elated to do the bidding of his master ... It's a joke, his younger brother is a bitch too afraid to bite."

Hiroshi drew his blade, then brought it down swiftly on the neck of a prone Joan. She neither flinched nor screamed, unknowingly earning her life anew. How could she accuse a High Seraph—his brother—of those crimes? What could she gain from lying beside a quicker death?

"I see no virtue in decapitating an unarmed woman, no matter how vile the creature. My world is simple, Mrs. Flayr. Chaos and control. That is all it is *ever* about. *Your* lies create chaos, *I* take control. I see some beauty in your chaos." Hiroshi lifted the sword off her neck, returning it to his side. "You *almost* made me kill you. Remember it. Next time I might not show so much self-control. No one speaks about the late High Seraph Saigo Gunkimono irresponsibly in my presence. No one."

The pain in Hiroshi's tone was enough to make Joan reconsider her reply. The feeling was short-lived.

"I could help you develop your talents further."

"Save your fucking pity, I have no interest in your spacedamned war games. You Seraphs are the same. High, Late, or Former. Killing—it's not valor. You say it's for the Treaty, for peace. The whole lot of you—contras of contradictions—killing for nothing more than glamour."

Hiroshi came around to face Joan, crouching in front of her before speaking, "Have your way, words. It is ... amusing. Is it always a conspiracy to you people? Does nothing ever come about by the consensual efforts of humankind? Or is everything the result of some consortium of evil geniuses? You say I am this or that. Here is the proof ... I am going to let you live, despite the wishes of my master. You *did* kill my men so there will be conditions. Understood?" Still wrenching against the confines of her bonds, she ignored him.

"You must leave here as soon as I cut you free. Not just leave, disappear. Joan Flayr is dead. Struck down by my hand, here in this place, overlooking the city. You *do* understand me?"

"Kill Me!" Joan thrashed and gnashed her teeth like a rabid neowolf.

"Do you not want to see your Paulo again? Relax, relax Mrs. Flayr ... Limit your illegal activities. I will be watching. I suggest brushing up on your combat forms ... I would be honored to kill you. But you have to earn it."

"Do what you will, Seraph. Know we are enemies. I won't show you a sliver of gratitude, a crust of respect, nor an ounce of forgiveness. To me, you're already dead. Cut me loose? You would be better off cutting your wrists!"

Hiroshi cut the ropes at her wrists, then her feet, with two strokes. Joan whirled around, pitching a grapefruit-sized stone at Hiroshi's head. He did not dodge. Tracing its trajectory with his mind's eye, the stone came to rest in two clean slices at either side of him. His sword came to rest at his hip.

He stood, paralyzed in place by a potent mixture of admiration and indignation, watching the prisoner escape. He felt a peace that had eluded him of late. In his tranquility, he was unaware of the high-ranking Syndicate member peering from a balcony high above.

Hiroshi's grip tightened around his sword as realization broke. He allowed Joan Flayr to escape. Because he could not make himself kill her. The Elders, Sandhurst, would be furious.

His mind was already concocting ways he might fix things before the Elders ever found out.

Guilt, prickly as ever, made each step back to his room stickier than the last. He was not so preoccupied that he forgot to remain unseen.

Chapter 7

Retrieving a key from his sleeve, Hiroshi locked the training facility behind himself. As he skulked inside, he felt Sandhurst's disappointment already. He needed a place to clear his mind before he faced the Elders. Hiding in his quarters proved disastrous for his nerves.

The odor of stale air and sweaty mats leaped into his nose. Under his leadership, Training Wing was transformed into equal parts gym and armory. At forty-five scorchfeet long and sixty-five scorchfeet wide, it was easily the largest open area inside the castle. Cloth partitions, drawn across its width, divided the room into three equal spaces.

In the first area, Seraphim trained in hand-to-hand combat, evasive maneuvers, first aid techniques, and meditation. Inside the second partition, both walls were adorned with a full cast of weapons. Each bringing back a formative memory as Hiroshi passed.

Long swords, short swords, bastard swords, daggers, dirks, clubs, maces, cudgels, morning stars, all manner of pole-arms, and nunchaku, staves, axes, spades, shields, and slings. There were gauntlets, cestuses, knuckle dusters, even rope; all must be mastered to achieve the distinction of High Seraph. His happiest moments clung to the walls, within reach, just out of grasp. Cracking a smile, he remembered Saigo, and the countless lessons imparted there.

Hiroshi arrived at the ultimate partition; here artists, poets, musicians, and comedians were fostered and developed as they discovered their complimentary talents.

Elder Sandhurst stressed the importance of the arts, more so than combat. Hiroshi recalled the talents of former High Seraphim, removing an easel and canvas from their home.

Former High Seraph Donnel, a savant with his hands, had taken to sculpture; the late High Seraph Zabyn, wrote songs; Elder Sandhurst, while never officially a Seraph, chose topography; Saigo was a painter. Naturally, Hiroshi picked up painting as well. Moving to his usual spot, he set up. Reaching into the depths of his robes, he brought out his brushes. Popping open the bottom rim of the easel he freed his palette. Hiroshi retreated into his thoughts as the piece came together seemingly of its own will.

Joan Flayr, with the blood of nine on her hands, was free. What would be his punishment? Might the Elders rescind his status as High Seraph? But what of her claims? Saigo was not the same after High Seraph Donnel left the Syndicate. He could have razed a village on one of his stormier days. Even if he was guilty, Saigo was already dead.

If Sandhurst gave the order, the High Seraph was to execute without question. One should not blame the sword for the action of the wielder, should they? Shaking his head, Hiroshi tried to settle his thoughts. Seconds later he caught himself wondering if and how hard Joan might train for their next bout.

Finishing the painting, his full attention returned to the canvas. A step back let him observe the completeness of the work. Objectively, his best yet. Hiroshi had unknowingly painted a portrait of Joan. Capturing her intensity, her passion, her strength, her vulnerability in a single tense moment.

"Joan Flayr," Hiroshi muttered with more admiration than he expected. "What have you gotten us into?" He continued, releasing his sword from its scabbard. His fingers pulled the lever attached at its hilt, destroying the piece with one final stroke. The canvas tattered to the floor sizzling as acid reduced Joan Flayr to nothingness at his feet.

Hiroshi disposed of the broken easel, swept up the canvas remains, and retired to his quarters. Facing the Elder would be saved for the next day.

Chapter 8

O veractivity terrorized Joan's mind. Her body raced to keep pace as a torrent of thoughts and emotions swished about in her skull. She hadn't stopped once, not even to regain her breath, since escaping High Seraph Gunkimono's custody. Her vision blurry and lungs afire, she ran further and farther from Span Opticon.

Passing study centers, restaurants, and lodges—no one paid her much mind. The occasional, curious eye would follow her before being distracted by the demands of their own life. Joan paid the Virtans little mind in return. Elbowing through the crowds of the Bazaar District, the fire in her chest raged. White splotches and multi-colored spheres populated her vision. Panting, gulping, checking over her shoulder, all the while never straying from her path out of Sandhurst's country.

Unwilling to withstand abuse any longer; her being rebelled. Her legs, finally turning against her, refused to stand. Sweaty, dehydrated, nearing delirium, Joan fell to the packed earth. Her arms ignored her plight. Her mouth sealed itself shut with crystalline saliva. Her nose stung, unsatisfied with the spurts of air it received not enough of and expelled too quickly. Her eyes turned to treachery, searing the image of

Zachariah Sandhurst's statue into her retinal cortex. The statue signifying the end of Virtus' Border. Reluctantly, her mind joined the full-bodied mutiny and shut down.

* * *

Ido Xzaven, High Librarian of the Syndicate of Valor, had watched Hiroshi cut Joan Flayr free, from a secluded window in his bedroom. Sadly, a woman with a similar build and features would have to die. Her body, and three Seraphim more loyal to himself than Hiroshi, would be needed to trick the Elders.

Obedient Hiroshi had transformed into Foolish Hiroshi, before Ido's eyes. Was he ensnared by Joan's potent aura or inextinguishable will? Or, was it the scent of that rare desert flower called love—with thorns all up its stem and along its petals, but the fragrance known to lead adventurers to stray and soldiers to desert? Grabbing fistfuls of his beard, Ido wondered these things.

As curious as Ido Xzaven was about Hiroshi's intentions or Joan's characteristics, he could not allow her to escape. Joan and Paulo Flayr possessed a cache of Pre-Scorch documents rivaling the Syndicate's archives. The information within them was worth looking beyond Hiroshi's transgression to attain. Elder Sandhurst might forgive the deception if Joan could be traced back to her hideout.

The Elders needed to remain in the dark to keep Hiroshi in the clear, and their Syndicate intact. If plans proceeded smoothly, he might spin things to appear as though Hiroshi was always in the know.

Rising from his desk in three stages, Ido navigated towering stacks of manuals and manuscripts like a careful colossus.

Arriving at the room's door, he contacted the Keep, Span Opticon's communication center, with the press of a button.

Without question, suspicion, and within an hour Ido had his requested list of Seraphim with open or closed disciplinary infractions and a list of ten Seraphim who had tried, but failed, to become High Seraph.

* * *

Awakening with a hoarse chuckle, Joan realized she was no longer where she fell. Someone had dragged her limp body into the shade of a large wooden awning. Rising to her knees, then slowly to her feet, she dusted off her tank top and slacks. Turning around she caught the name of the establishment providing the shade: *Depot*. Paulo's frequent dive, she thought, releasing a sigh of relief.

Joan and Paulo had a standing agreement to never appear there in tandem, but both of their false identities were recognizable as regulars. They knew the eccentric barkeep well. Altazar knew Joan to be a simple scavenger named Jan. Joan hovered at the door with the sun at her back, then entered.

"Jan!" Abandoning what looked, to Joan, like a massive remodeling project Altazar ran up to meet. Ignoring her extended hand, he went in for a hearty hug.

"Oh! Hey there. How are ... things? Looks like a bit of renovation?" Joan pointed to the mess with her head.

"You know it," Altazar released Joan and beckoned her over to the bar. "The Boundless had their hearts set on the old look but then my Ars patrons decided to improvise some decorating."

"Ha," Joan laughed, not just at Altazar's joke, but at the idea of Ars Searchers having off-duty drinks at a bar like Depot. She continued to laugh, realizing some Boundless loyalists might've started a fight and trashed the place.

"Well, Mr. Alchemic, lemme get something while I'm here. How about—water on the rocks?"

"You got it, Jan my gal. One H-Two-Ice coming up."

"Altazar ... *all* this is from a little bar fight?" Altazar offered his signature hardy laugh, but there was some strange seriousness to it.

"It was no fight. This was a manhunt. The Ars strolled right in, started draggin' people out and tearin' up my place."

Handing her water, he returned to sweeping up glass shards and dozens of what looked like large splinters—or small arrows. Lingering on the pile momentarily Joan took a seat at the bar. Spinning to face the door, a whiff of burnt hair passed her nostrils.

"Manhunt? It was *that* bad?" Altazar stopped moving, the broom frozen between his palms. He didn't face Joan as he spoke.

"You are thinking maybe this is a replica Bloody Mary and maybe these are bits of glass or porcelain I'm cleaning up now? Nope ... It's all Dezba and Jelani left of Paulo Flayr."

The world ended.

Joan spit out her drink, launching wet particles everywhere. Altazar turned with a raised eyebrow. "What? You've had better ... water? Is it the ice?"

Altazar's oblivious insensitivity rubbed Joan like coarse salt in a new, exposed wound—and she could not show the slightest indication. He was mistaken; Paulo couldn't be dead. She had just seen him last night, in bed, asleep. She had kissed his forehead before setting out on her trip to Virtus. Had he awakened, seen her missing, and come to the Depot to investigate?

"No, sir! Best in the Neutral Zone. I, uh, just had a tickle in my nose. I mean no offense. Heya', Zar? Not to switch the conversation on ya', but did you happen to see who dragged me into the shade?"

"Gotcha'. My eyes water a lil' bit when I sneeze too. It was me. I dragged you over," he admitted with a hangdog grin.

"Why the heck didn't you bring me inside!? I could've been robbed, or worse."

"You could've been trouble, or worse. You're my girl and all but I haven't seen you in a while. I don't know, maybe you fell in with the Boundless, maybe the Ars were hot on your trail too. A mere precaution."

Joan stared at him disapprovingly. Disappointment joined her burgeoning cast of emotions.

Paulo cannot be dead. Joan insisted to herself.

"How long was I out for?"

"Few hours. It was just after noon when I found you."

"You sure it was Paulo?" She fired back, without reloading.

"Spacedamn sure."

The Depot went silent, Altazar was no fool, and Joan barely held back her scowl. He chanced one last comment as she slammed her drink down, stalking past him to the door. "J—Jan? Be careful out there. And, just know, there's always a safe place here for you."

Joan paused in the doorway, cocking her head she replied, "Is Depot *safe*? Look around. Under the Treaty of Neo-Earth what the Ars Femina did here *is* legal. I hear the Boundless fight to expand the rights of the people against oppressive extractions and expirations. Members of the Boundless Movement are some of your most loyal patrons. The NZ is a hotbed for what they call 'anti-treaty activities'. If they had their way, there would be no Depot!" Joan gripped the door's frame tighter and tighter as she spoke. Finally overwhelmed by emotion she punched it. "Don't you get that ... spacedamnit? They're spilling blood for you. Not for glory, glamour or trusts. For freedom. Neutral means inert, inactive. How can Searchers have jurisdiction here? They shouldn't, Zar. You roll over and let them walk over us? Mow us down, lock us up? For what? So Nutes like you can have their Retro Bars and Period Saloons? No one is safe *here*, save for you!"

"Your words wound. I am a Nute and a friend, Joan. But a Nute nonetheless."

Joan stepped out into the beaming sun of the late afternoon and made her way to the closest intersecting roads. From person to person her eyes searched the busy avenue for meaning. Commuters, traders, scavengers—sheep.

Three Feral-men slinking through the crowd caught her attention. She approached them and uttered a lesser known of their many traditional greetings. Accepting her as though she were one of their own, they allowed her access and space on their caravan. As Joan had hoped, they headed out of the Neutral Zone.

Chapter 9

The High Librarian successfully gathered three Seraphim that fit his criteria. Kneeling before him in humble reverence were Seraphim Sanaji Taper, Kance Tally, and Whestley Greeves.

"Is the mission understood?" Ido's voice crept out of the voice box built into his suit of armor, reverberating off the walls of his quarters. The three nodded in unison. Ido, shifting his mass, leaned forward in a wooden chair, comically small for his size.

"What is your task, Seraph Taper?" Without a beat, she responded, "To follow Joan Flayr in complete secrecy, obtain the location of Libyrinth, engage and eliminate targets Joan Flayr, Paulo Flayr, Grase Jeffroy, and silence any persons in our way no matter faction or allegiance."

"Correct. Now Seraph Tally. Surely the peoples of Virtus would wish to know of our ensuing victory, why is it important that we maintain secrecy?" Seraph Tally calmly raised his head to answer, "High Seraph Hiroshi Gunkimono allowed the fugitive Joan Flayr to escape. Rather than embarrass our esteemed High Seraph, it has become necessary to handle these matters discreetly."

"And when you return?" Ido probed.

Whestley Greeves jumped at his chance to speak, "*If* we return. You will be briefed on all information, this Rapid Action Squad will be dissolved, and we will resume our previous duties as Seraphim. Our comrades will never know, can never know ...That it was us who answered the call and stepped up when asked."

Self-impressed, Ido could not help but to wonder why he had not assembled such a team prior for other matters. He dismissed his subjects with a wave. The three Seraphim exited as if whisked away by a shifty wind.

Chapter 10

D epot was looking like her old self again, Altazar thought as he finished cleaning. Stepping behind the patched-up counter, he bent down, grabbing a clean glass to pour himself a celebratory drink. He arose to three Seraphim in front of him, no-nonsense written across their faces.

"What is this shit? Ars Femina last night. Syndicate of Valor today," he sighed a crestfallen sigh. "How may I help you all?"

"Why was *that* woman here?" Seraph Greeves probed, little emotion in his voice.

"Wh ... What? Whom? Who are you talking about?"

"Do not jerk us around, Altazar!" Seraph Tally cut in.

"Seriously. I don't know what the fuck you're talking about. What woman?" The words left his mouth. Jan entered his mind. "Oh, you mean Jan? She's a regular, ya' know, dropping by for some water."

"What do you do for the Movement?" Greeves pressed.

"The Boundless Movement? Tch ... Everybody knows I'm a 'Nute'."

"Nobody is a Nute!" Tally spat. Altazar swallowed the boulder lodged in his throat.

Seraph Taper hopped up and over the counter. "What happened back here? Looks like blood in your mop water." Motioning to the bucket stowed conspicuously outside a utility closet. "And the air." She sniffed. "Smells like ... citrus fruits and ... black powder."

Six eyes narrowed on Altazar. Throwing his arms up in resignation, he found the closest stool and sat.

"You all *really* want to know what happened here? The Ars Femina. Celeste and her gals waltzed in here ready to acquire and expire. Shot *my* place up, insulted *my* tastes, interrogated *my* friends, then walked out with Paulo Flayr's corpse ... They did all of this." Altazar pointed to his repairs with outstretched and open palms. "Without so much as tipping. Not a hat, not a trust."

Tally snickered, rejoining his squad mates and Altazar on the other side of the bar. He spoke with a lighthearted air as if he were always getting close to the punchline of a joke, "So-lemme-get-this-straight, the Ars Femina killed Paulo Flayr? Here? Last night? And one of your regulars shows up? This morning? Poking about. The whole NZ knows what happened here by now. Everybody else avoided it like the Plains. But Jan ... What did she say? Any indication where she may be headed?"

"I have hundreds of regulars, but you lot know that," Altazar explained.

These Seraphim were different than the ones that stopped by after routine patrols for drinks, he could tell. Something about their movements and language, their silence made Altazar suspect valor had little to do with their visit. Sweat coalesced on his brow as they closed in.

"Okay, okay. Maybe, I saw her join a Feral-men scavenging caravan passing through here a little while back. They usually head south from here ... Through the Uncharted Region. That's all I know. That, and you're wasting your time. Jan is a nobody. Simple."

The Seraphim retracted, satisfied by his confession. When they were gone Altazar slinked to the floor, contemplating shutting Depot down for good.

Chapter 11

Perched over the battered corpse of Paulo Flayr lying in the center of her office, all Celeste saw was a pile of trusts. Never had the stench of the recently deceased smelled so sweet. The Ars Femina had accomplished a feat of greatness: 'The Most Wanted Man on Neo-Earth', the elusive Paulo Flayr, was dead.

Unstrapping the buckles and hooks that kept her armor pressed securely on her body, the breastplate slipped off as she pieced together the final strokes of her plan. Celeste propped up Paulo's lifeless body and danced around her office. Our time has come, she thought, bouncing about, inventing the steps of a terminal tango.

Next, independent meetings with the Syndicate of Valor, the Vicaarians, and the Legioneers would be arranged. If swift, not one, but all three astronomical bounties on Paulo Flayr's head could be collected and secured before anyone might know or interfere. Simple, lucrative, and brazen; Celeste's favorite kind of mission.

Dezba entered the office followed by Jelani. The two women engaged by conversation ignored the usual protocol of knocking and were confronted with the unusual scene.

Their leader, the living legend, Celeste, was not only hugging a corpse, but dancing and humming to the tune of madness. Noticing her enforcers, she dropped Paulo's body, embarrassed. It tumbled to the ground, rolled a bit and stopped at Jelani and Dezba's feet. Glancing at the cadaver then back at Celeste, Jelani broke the silence.

"Who was leading?"

Celeste and Dezba burst out in uproarious laughter.

"Sit down, ladies. We gotta' talk," Celeste commanded, concealing her smirk.

Jelani pulled up a swivel stool and sat. Dezba took up a post close to Celeste's desk but remained standing.

"Never mind what you just saw, heh," dismissing her mania with a laugh, "We gotta' focus on our next moves. Extractions and expirations have been declining for years. I want the Ars to become self-sufficient before those geriatrics decide they no longer need us. We'll need revenue to do so. Once we collect Paulo's bounty we will live like queens for a decade." Celeste floated to her desk and continued the briefing from a chair.

"That won't be enough. We need to be *set*. Power, we *have* … But it's purchased by running here and there, solving idiots' problems. Let them do their own enforcing. Ya' know?"

Jelani and Dezba nodded in unison.

"I wanna' know if some dumb bastard cuts me down that the Ars Femina, that Pangaia will be secure for a hundred years. I got us a plan. We are going to collect our high-profile bounty three times over. Back-to-back … to back. Set up meetings with Ecclesiel first, then Donnel, and Sandhurst last. They will give us their trusts, we will escort them out with proof of Paulo's death, and by the time any of them catch on, *if* anybody catches on, Pangaia will be secure." Celeste didn't find the enthusiasm she hoped for. "I'm seeing your faces and I get it—I do. Don't worry, I'm already calling all our girls back home. I gave the order before we ever walked into Depot."

Jelani wasn't surprised. Celeste proved, time and time again, to be a factory of endless schemes and machinations. Celeste's plan, like many before, was wily, dangerous, and the more Jelani thought, the more it sounded like a shitload of fun.

Dezba voiced no complaints. Celeste and Jelani were her friends—sisters in all but blood. She would go anywhere and do anything with, or for them.

"So what? I take it by the silence ya'll agree?"

"Of course. Sounds risky as hell, but if you want to play chicken with the Treaty ... I'm game," said Dezba.

"When're we gonna' break the news?" Jelani inquired.

"And how?" Dezba added.

"Break the news? To whom? Neo-Earth is so small someone knew Paulo was dead before *he* did. Right now, only people with trusts are in the know. Everybody else can wait."

* * *

"The General *is* glad to have any thorn from his side removed, but ... " Mr. Galtero paused, then sat back with folded arms. "The amount of trusts you are asking for is unheard of. Not even the Vicaar, with their numbers, have that amount of trust laying around. General Donnel would like to offer something else. Another unique weapon, uncovered by his Legioneers. Says it is something Celeste will especially like ... I was expecting her to be present at this meeting."

Dezba specifically disliked the man in front of her. She disliked most men, but what struck her about Mr. Galtero the

Ghost was his intonation. Laden with uninterest, it screamed that he'd rather be somewhere else. He formed words as though each was a bitter medicine. He looked and sounded bored. Dezba wanted to grab him by the neck and squeeze some interest into him.

"Really?" Dezba said, against her true feelings. "What class of weapon are we talking about here? We have plenty, most of which have no practical use." Mr. Galtero's ear twitched. "We accepted them as payment from the Legioneers in hopes that we could one day sell them."

"And?"

"And, things aren't like they used to be. There ain't much work for the Ars these days. With Paulo Flayr dead, the Boundless will fade on their own. There won't be much use for persuaders in a few short decades. But trusts, well, ya' know what they say, one can never have too many." Mr. Galtero let no time elapse before his response, Dezba noted.

"The General suggested you might not settle for the weapon alone." He yawned, then continued. "He is prepared to offer you a favor on top of the whole deal. Not just any favor, but a Donnel Favor: redeemable at any time and for anything, within resource and reason, of course."

"Is Donnel aware that this meeting, held within our walls, is a favor to him? Killing Paulo Flayr, wanted by the Legioneers, for producing, in mass, altered copies of the Donnel Manifesto and instructing people to use it to wipe shit from their asses, was a favor to him? He already owes us big. We ain't askin', we're collecting."

Jelani, having just finished her meeting with Ecclesiel the Illuminated, walked in, pulled up a chair, and took a seat on the opposite side of the simple table separating Searcher from

Ghost. Still gingerly holding her injured arm, she jumped in where her counterpart left-off, "Amram Donnel wanted Paulo dead more than anyone. Is he now unwilling to pay the price advertised?" She imitated Mr. Galtero's tone. He droned on, unaware or unaffected by the mockery.

"General Donnel had doubts that Paulo was in fact a real person. Evading capture for years, he could have been some figurehead used to push the Boundless Movement's agenda. Your team on Level 2 showed me ample proof. What was once an enigma is to be entombed. The General is just ... *surprised* by the news of Paulo's death and asks Celeste to think about what she wants in return. The trusts you are asking for take time to round up, pay cuts, terminations, liquidations, et cetera. He wants me to ensure you want nothing else first."

"Celeste is at lunch ... if you could go into further detail about this weapon before we make the decis—"

Galtero's interest finally peaked. He cut Dezba off. "It's called a Scorcher. The Preneo likely called them flamethrowers. They are as devastating as magnificent. With the ability to ignite anything you aim them at, synthetic and organic material alike. You could burn water if you wanted. The flames that spew from its nozzle are an ancient mixture, buoyant and able to burn until smothered. The General finds that Scorchers lack his signature subtlety. He could think of none other than Celeste, who might have the stomach to turn one loose."

Persuaders typically didn't impress Dezba, but the weapon the Ghost described seemed different. A handheld capable of scorching all it touched. The idea of scorching the earth was uniformly distasteful. It was little wonder the General wanted to get rid of them. But the assassin had a point; Celeste was the only person on the planet with the gravitas to wield such a thing. Jelani was coming to the same conclusion. Mr. Galtero could see it in their eyes.

"We thank you, Mr. Galtero and the General, for your trouble and we'll be in contact soon. Celeste might be interested in these Scorchers ... Prepare those trusts nonetheless."

"Thank you, Jelani ... Dezba ... For ah, having me. I'll make sure General Donnel hears of your hospitality."

Galtero was up and out of the office in a flash. Clearing his throat when he hit the hallway, Dezba called after him, "The personnel lift is to your right, then a left, you'll see the violet light take it back up to Level 1. The help will escort you out."

He was already around the corner, the gears of his mind spinning and drowning out Dezba's words. He floated away from the drab meeting.

Mr. Galtero was unattended inside Fortress Pangaia, a shame that it was diplomacy and not cunning that landed him there.

The meeting had not gone as planned.

The Ars were the Legioneers' most consistent clients. Loyal only in the fiscal sense. As council and confidante to General Donnel, Galtero was witness to shipment upon shipment of lost and new technologies beginning long journeys to Fortress Pangaia. The Ars were sure to be hiding a stockpile of advanced armaments, rare enough to make a detour worth the danger.

Galtero's obsession with Preneo technology started when he was a young man and eventually allied him with the fledgling Legioneers. Amram Donnel fed his compulsions and encouraged Galtero into a reclusive life of assassination and surveillance. His grim profession fueled his hobby until the pleasure of a new persuader and the thrill of the kill were all he enjoyed.

As an intruder, he risked unfathomable death a thousand times over at the hands of the Ars Femina. Easing into a jog, and progressing to a sprint, he made his way toward the central personnel lift. Taking the less illuminated path, he progressed until he heard women's voices trailing behind him. A glance over his shoulder caused him to collide with a man.

The man was thrown to the floor. A silver platter piled high with appetizers was knocked out of his hands into the air. Unfazed, Mr. Galtero spit a command at the servant.

"Where's the armory? *Quick*."

"Level 7, sah," he responded obediently, and beginning to rise, "but all guests have been asked to report to the Council Room, Celeste's office, or the Main Hall. All of which are on this level. You appear lost. I'll escort you ..."

Galtero opened his attaché case, removed his favorite persuader, and put the servant out of his assumed misery quickly and quietly.

He was certain no man deserved to be left to endure such humiliation at the hands of Celeste, no matter their crime. Rummaging through the expired servants' garments he found a clearance cartridge, on it written '*Chaperone: Levels 4, 6, 7*'. He was in luck, but he couldn't leave the body there. Before blood could pool, Galtero picked him up and found a lift to Level 7.

The doors of the personnel lift hissed open, and a burst of violet light spilled out, partially illuminating the foremost segment of the armory. Mr. Galtero hovered in-between the doors, using the light to survey his surroundings. The walls of the damp room were hidden, littered with weapons that had not seen the light of day in years. Flicking a switch on his briefcase, a tiny light penetrated the darkness beyond the violet haze.

Stepping off the lift, it chimed and returned to an upper level. The air was earthy but fresh. The gentle gust that touched his face and ran through his jet-black hair told him the room was far larger than he would've guessed. He dropped the limp body of the servant and was stunned by what he saw when his eyes acclimated.

The area he faced dwarfed the Legioneers' own storage room. He walked for what he estimated to be one hundred fifty scorchfeet and was met with persuaders, explosives, and armor pieces stacked in haphazard piles. Persuaders were sparse on Neo-Earth, and by the look of it, the cache around him was a reason why.

Moving to the nearest heap, he inspected it closely. There were persuaders of all makes—pistols, rifles, trench guns, and lobbers all covered in dust and cobwebs. The lack of upkeep boggled his brain.

The Ars Femina were sitting on a stockpile of weapons large enough to arm most of the inhabitants in the Holy Lands. He moved to another pile of stagnant weapons, searching through them. He wandered from pile to mound for an hour until finally a curious object caught his eye—a bouquet of flowers.

Black roses, crisp and full of life. No soot, no cobwebs, just green and purple-black roses, bound by twine, propped up against the dirt wall. Reaching out with a finger for one of the thorns adorning the rose stems, Galtero expected the familiar prick, instead his finger moved through the thorn as though no solid object was present.

"What the fuck," he muttered to himself, yanking his hand back in disbelief. He reached for the flower again, this time with a fully outstretched hand. And just like before, his hand moved through what should have been the bouquet's blossoms. Nothing, no petals. He waved his hand through the floral mirage, impressed. The image distorted more as the motion of his hand increased speed.

He had never actually seen one, but he once overheard a group of Legioneer technicians discussing something they called a Hologun. They said it was a hologram of any kind that could hide the shape of a persuader inside its projection.

He reached into the image with both hands, fishing for something within the display itself. He found a familiar shape of a grip and trigger at the base of the bundle. Certain the flowers were an illusion, he searched for a switch. Once located, he flicked it and the image of the flowers distorted with a ripple then disappeared. He flicked the switch on, and the image reappeared with a *bzzt*. Satisfied, Mr. Galtero placed his latest toy into his briefcase, made one last round, then returned to the personnel lift.

Making sure to leave the servant's body atop a dusty pile of weapons, Mr. Galtero staged a suicide before returning up to Level 1. Joining the flow of pedestrians on Pangaia's ground floor, Mr. Galtero meandered through the masses of Searchers, recruits, clients and in-house help. He thought he saw High Seraph Gunkimono of the Syndicate of Valor enter the lift he had exited minutes earlier. Deciding it was merely his eyes readjusting to sunlight, he dismissed the thought. Strolling out the main entrance of Fortress Pangaia, his mind went to the new tool in his arsenal.

Finding Benben Observatory on the eastern horizon, Mr. Galtero began his trip home to Motopia.

* * *

Hiroshi hated the damp air inside Fortress Pangaia. He learned of this place as a child, all children had. It was among the most recognizable buildings on the planet. From the outside it looked like a fortified wall standing a hundred scorchfeet tall and stretching a thousand scorchfeet across a fertile valley, from inside it could have been any dank network of winding, dimly lit hallways. Roots battled clay and stone for dominance over the ceiling. The light structures were simple bulbs dangling on a single wire, swaying back and forth against air pressure and wind. The Syndicate built a castle, the Ars built a bunker.

With ample resources, manpower, and trusts at their disposal, Hiroshi found it odd that they would leave their fortress largely unfurnished. Then again, comfort was likely the last thing on the mind of a Searcher.

Hiroshi and his two escorts exited the personnel lift on Level 4. He could only imagine the declining decor of the lower levels. Lucky for him, no Syndicate business required him to go any lower.

Elder Sandhurst had sent Hiroshi to Pangaia to verify Paulo Flayr's expiration. He didn't say he doubted their reports outright. Hiroshi suspected pride was inhibiting the aging bureaucrat from accepting Ars Femina success where the Syndicate of Valor had repeatedly failed. The incredulous tone of the mission briefing was all Hiroshi needed to investigate the matter further.

If Paulo was not dead, the meeting was a ploy. If the meeting was a ploy, then Hiroshi was the asset they meant to capture. Celeste could've stopped him at the entrance on Level 1 and taken the two duffel bags packed with trusts slung over each of his shoulders, if she wanted. But the bags were secure with locking clamps, designed by former High Seraph Donnel before his resignation, to only be opened by a High Seraph. The money was safe, but was Hiroshi?

Did Celeste know about Joan? Did Sandhurst? When he received instructions to visit Pangaia he thought Sandhurst would have asked about the execution. He didn't. The only odd activity Hiroshi noted was High Librarian Xzaven and Seraph Guiles burying a body in Span Opticon Cemetery. Nothing else. The Elders were unusually quiet.

Might Celeste and Sandhurst work together to expire a traitorous High Seraph? Or, had Celeste positioned herself to call checkmate without risking pawns?

Hiroshi's hand found the familiar butt of his blade as he reexamined his two Searcher escorts. This time he noticed the decorations and medals ornamenting their armor. Their presence felt more and more like intimidation than precaution.

The silent dialogue progressed. Spurred on by duty against anxiety and paranoia, he ventured deeper into the wall-fortress until arriving at an area built in stark contrast to packed dirt hallways leading to it.

Three metal lintels and tiled path lead up to a conspicuous door. Hiroshi's brooding was cut short by a sight that would make most men cringe: Celeste.

The embodiment of beauty and brutality, Celeste guarded the entrance to her office like an angry cherub. Her unique Searcher armor beeped and blipped, occasionally flashing yellow, blue, or green lights on her chest plate, pauldrons, and boots. Her bob with no bangs sliced an oblong border around her square face and terminated just above her shoulders in exacting edges. She stood a foot taller than Hiroshi, and made it clear by stepping so close, he strained his neck as far back as possible to address her.

"Celeste, your reputation precedes you. The honor is all mine."

Celeste did not look down or smile as a formality, she simply addressed Hiroshi's escorts who had remained with them at the door of her quarters.

"When will Hiroshi 'Sword of the Syndicate' Gunkimono, arrive? He's supposed to be here with my trusts. Soon as he gets here, send him in." Celeste turned, kicked the door of her office open, then retreated inside. Once the door swung closed, his escorts looked at each other, then at Hiroshi, then left.

Pushing the door open with one of his bags, Hiroshi cleared his throat and spoke again—all formality gone, "I officially represent Zachariah Sandhurst. You should practice the habit of addressing me as though the Elder were here, in this comparatively well-furnished room himself ... I implore you to continue this exchange by showing me the slightest bit of respect. Or you might find our organization suddenly very uninterested in the fate of one Paulo Flayr."

Hiroshi readjusted the duffel bags on his shoulder loudly.

Celeste, still refusing to meet his eyes, spun on her heels and gave Hiroshi her back. Sauntering around a gargantuan desk sporting four active display screens, Celeste spoke once there was as much space between herself and Hiroshi as physically possible given the room dimensions—a wise move, given Hiroshi's inability to be chided for long.

"You're only a child."

"Is *that* what *this* is about?" Hiroshi rolled his eyes. "You were hoping for someone closer to your age?"

"This is a matter for adults. Tell your surrogate father, Sandhurst, to send a lap dog that has gone through puberty.

You're a tyke, a tot. Do you know where you are, toddler? Pangaia is the nightmare setting of men throughout the world. Even your master sweats in my presence. General Donnel wouldn't dare threaten me. And you, a boy, come into *my* fortress, *my* quarters, in my face, and threaten me? Ha! Paulo Flayr is dead by our hands. I hold the cards. Not some teenager with a long knife." Celeste began sorting documents on her desk. "What has become of the mighty Syndicate of Valor? The Age of the High Seraph is over. Amram, defected. Saigo, dead. And you, underdeveloped. Sandhurst has succumbed to senility. Sending a kid to meet with the Devourer of Men."

With that said, Celeste looked at Hiroshi for the first time since their introduction. Her attempt to intimidate him failed. What she saw in his eyes were the perennial flames of anger and angst.

"What's to keep me from swallowing you whole?"

Hiroshi, hand on his hilt still, approached Celeste. Nothing but the desk and screens keeping the fiery souls at bay. Hiroshi, satisfied, smiled and spoke.

"Sharp teeth and sharper wits ...Very good. Be assured, I am no child. Only the most capable High Seraph the Syndicate has yet produced. I am favored among my ranks, regardless of age. Any harm to befall me will be met with excessive retribution. Your threats fall on rebellious and eager ears ... Try me and let all Neo-Earth know how a boy cut down the great Celeste Stronima."

"Ha! You have balls!" Celeste boomed.

"I am young, not a woman," Hiroshi cracked wise.

"And I am a monster, not a human. Don't wander too close to my teeth. You might find that even Syndicate steel will not be sharp enough to save you."

"I always heard the Ars Femina were man-eaters."

She boomed with laughter, "Hiroshi. Sit down. No one has got me going like this since, shit, no one gets me going like *that*."

Celeste grew partial to the youthful warrior that strode into her office of operations and demanded the kind of respect not even a two-hundred-year-old prima donna deserved. Hiroshi unknowingly gained the favor of the most powerful woman on Neo-Earth, without drawing his sword. Sandhurst would surely be pleased to hear of his success. The conversation shifted from mutual fondness to the business of trusts and proof of Paulo Flayr's death.

Chapter 12

"They have her. They fuckin' *have* her. I want them dead! Spacedamnit! What was she thinking? Grase, you hear me? Dead. Searcher or Seraph, I don't care. I want you to kill any trader who sold Syndicate weapons. I—I want General Donnel dead for—for writing bad literature. *Fuck!* They have her, and there is nothing *I* can do. I am nothing. Nothing, without her…"

Paulo's lamentation culminated with his face buried deep within his palms. Tears saturated the surface of his hands, trickling down his chin and landing in the crevice of the open book on his desk.

Grase, the Flayrs' bodyguard and confidante, sat across from him, tremulous with anger. She hated seeing Paulo upset and, in all her years of service, it was her first time witnessing him cry.

"Joan is tougher than a Collector's claw, Paul. I'm sure she's alright."

"You're sure? Have you been reading my books on mysticism? You're psychic now, that it? You know who these men are. How Seraphim … are. Have you *heard* about Hiroshi?"

"Paul …"

"Don't 'Paul' me. All it takes is Joan's temperament to excite the High Seraph's combat lust and *poof*." Paulo pantomimed an explosion with his hands, wiggling his fingers as he brought them down to simulate showering debris.

"Paulo! Joan is a political prisoner. The Syndicate of Valor is prohibited from executing her by their treaty. The Syndicate stands to gain more by keeping her alive."

"The Syndicate of Valor doesn't stand to *gain* anything. They control most of the historical documents on Neo-Earth; and the when, how, if they are revealed. Sandhurst needs nothing but absolute control, a control that we will perpetually undermine. He'll kill Joan just to lash out at us."

"Hopefully people think you're dead. You know how quickly word spreads. They don't *need* to make an example out of her. Makes more sense to just keep her locked up."

"Grase, you can be so logical. It *kills* me. Sandhurst is no fool. He won't accept rumors of my death as fact, if not pride, empiricism will keep him from simply assuming them true."

Slamming his fist down on his desk, the tears on his face had dried, creating salty distributaries. He fidgeted, more so than usual.

"I'm making a drink. You want one?" Grase asked.

"You fuckin' know it. Scotch. Please." Paulo ran his hand back through the tight curls of his black hair trying to ease his nerves.

Grase moved to the liquor cabinet hidden behind the massive door that separated the Flayrs' living area from the rest of the decrepit and aging museum the Flayrs made their base of operations. She rapped the mahogany bookshelf twice with a clenched fist. It squeaked and popped open, revealing dozens of bottles of Pre-scorch styled liquor—all at varying levels of full or empty, depending of course on the perspective and disposition of the drinker. To Grase, at the moment, all the bottles appeared almost empty.

Paulo Flayr, among rare books and artifacts, was in possession of a private collection of recovered rums, wines, gins, tequilas, and his favorite, scotches, held in one place. He could sell a half bottle of his least favorite and make enough trusts to fund their operation for a year. But as Paulo is famous for saying, "To sell a spirit is to sell a soul." So, his collection grew even as he consumed it.

Grase removed a bottle of scotch, sloppily pouring two drinks she returned to her seat with an exaggerated sigh. Paulo grasped at his glass just as sloppily and put the drink away in a gulp.

"Grase?"

The tone of Paulo's voice was grave, Grase tensed up immediately. She didn't meet his eyes as he leaned forward. She swirled her drink with one hand and peered into it as though the meaning of life was hidden within the cup. Paulo leaned closer and said again, "Grase?"

"I know," she responded sullenly. "I'll save you the trouble. You're going to say, 'I have to go get her.' I'm going to argue against it and win. Then I'm going to say, 'I'll go get her.' You're going to argue against it and lose. I'm going to get her back, then you're both giving me a raise."

Paulo was not amused. Grase produced a forced laugh and finished her drink. She stood up to leave but hovered in the doorway.

"I'll be fine," Paulo said. "Come on. I'm not 'The Most Wanted Man on Neo-Earth' because I'm an easy target. Have a little faith, Grase." She disappeared into the hall and around the corner. Paulo could hear her loudly searching for something in a neighboring storage closet. Returning, she had a satchel in her hand.

"You're pretending it's you you're worried about. That's fine. Take this," Grase said, removing an object from the bag and tossing it to Paulo.

"The heck is this? Grase, you know I don't use persuaders."

"Yeah, yeah, because a crossbow is so much of a difference … It's a flask, just a flask."

"Looks real as shit. Thanks. Grase, you're amazing."

Paulo took the realistically weighted replica and placed it in the main drawer of his desk. Grase tied a green band around her head to match her full body jumpsuit. She already had her massive spear in hand and longbow slung across her back. A draft found the moment and added to the drama by lightly fluttering Grase's garb and jostling the follicles of her pixie cut. The long tails of her headband came to rest together on her shoulder. Nodding her characteristic head bob, she saluted Paulo with two fingers then vanished out of the Flayrs' office.

The home and secret headquarters of the Flayrs' brainchild, the Boundless Movement, was called Libyrinth. Endless rows of decaying shelves containing books so fragile they would evaporate upon touch filled the main cavern of the aging museum for libraries. Crumbling pillars, rocky outcroppings, and splintered wood carved out only one safe route through the main room.

Myriad Pre-scorch artifacts, paintings, sculptures and architecture decorated the walls. Roots compromised the ceiling and bushy overgrowth speckled the interior. Structural failures siphoned strings of light into the main hall from the surface.

Grase traveled this route so frequently it was ingrained in the memory of her muscles. She dashed, vaulted, and flipped over obstacles. Sliding, spinning, and twisting through the safe nooks, gaps, and crannies, she landed at the end of the great hall without breaking a sweat and in record personal time.

The crucial architectural characteristic that saved the subterranean museum from complete destruction were stone stairs that stretched over a hundred scorchfeet into the air and reached the surface. Grase sprinted upwards, fortifying her resolve with each step along the way. Reaching the top, she slid the Libyrinth's circular stone door aside and bathed in the light of mid-day.

Lifting an arm, she shielded her eyes and gazed upon an expansive patch of land. What their Libyrinth lacked in surface security, it more than made up for with its remote location. Missing from any official map of Neo-Earth, the museum's entrance hid in a sea of ruins. Joan had uncovered the place years earlier on Feral-men information.

The Feral-men specialized in discovering and excavating structures of the Preneo. They were seasoned jacks-of-most-trades that showed little regard for the Treaty of Neo-Earth, and even less for the conformity demanded by it. Grase liked that. The Feral-men were at odds with Zachariah Sandhurst's autocratic and oppressive interpretation of peace. His open condemnation of the Preneo technology was an affront to their way of life.

The Feral-men found scraps and artifacts, which they then sold or traded to the Legioneers for equipment that allowed them to further explore the uninhabited regions. Thus, increasing the size and value of their hauls. Though not contractually bound to the Treaty of Neo-Earth, the Feral-men were an integral but undervalued part of its economy.

Grase, herself, was the child of an Ars Femina dissenter and the renowned Feral-men leader Adiraja Jeffroy. She inherited the durability and size of the people of the Perennial Plains, and the honed combat skills of her mother's training.

Politics had influenced her mother's decision to abandon her. Celeste would not accept an Ars recruit born to a Feral-man as prominent as Adiraja. As a final blow against the perceived treachery, Celeste ordered Grase's mother to kill Adiraja to prove her loyalty or be banished and expelled from the order. Adiraja died by the hand of his loving wife without a fight.

Grase, at the Ars Femina naming-age of five, watched as her mother took her own life. Left with no faction or parent to claim her, Grase wandered Neo-Earth's Uncharted Regions for years.

At the age of twelve, she met and saved a young, ambitious explorer named Joan Flayr from a pack of wild dogs. That day Joan made Grase a promise, "As long as I am alive. You will never have to worry about where your next meal will come from. You will always have a roof over your head. And you will always have somebody to depend on." Joan's words continued to resonate in Grase's head as she moved through the ruins, away from Libyrinth and towards her imprisoned friend.

Joan never broke her promise. Not as Grase grew in age or spirit. Or when it became painfully obvious that Grase was falling deeply in love with Paulo. Despite Joan's suspicions, they maintained their bond as close as sisters.

Grase trudged on, being careful to travel in the shadows of the massive structures that made up the desert graveyard. As far from civilization as she was, the sun would be her biggest enemy; it beamed down relentlessly, baking the earth for miles ahead. It was nigh impossible for a traveler with no water to make it to Virtus on foot; another advantage of Libyrinth's location.

On the move and hopping from shadow to shadow, Grase reached an out of place bundle of shrubs. She pushed a shroud aside to reveal her Tri-Bike. Mounting her motorized transport, she revved the engine once, twice, thrice and it whirred to life like a sleeping beast roused from slumber.

"Hell yah! Yah!" Grase let out a call appropriate for an iron steed. Shifting her weight back on the bike, the front wheels took to the air spinning in anticipation of their use, the larger back tire dug into the sand, kicking dirt up ferociously. Grase's hands wrapped around the handlebars. Leaning into the throttle, the three-wheeled motorcycle jerked forward, and began to carve a trail through the sand.

At top speed, Grase estimated it would take a few hours to reach the satellite settlements surrounding Virtus. Glancing down at the fuel gauge located between the handlebars, there was more than enough to get her back, but Grase already accepted it might be a one-way trip.

Nightfall hid Grase's approach and the roaring wind kept the fumes from her Tri-Bike out of her face. She had arrived in Virtus minutes earlier. With her sights on Span Opticon, she sped through the city up onto the overlook.

Her destination was the same large, rounded wooden doors of Span Opticon Castle's outer bailey that Joan arrived at a day prior. Two, the usual number of Seraphim, stood guard, engrossed in conversation.

"Hey—hey, shithead. You see High Seraph Gunkimono at all today?"

"Nope. Haven't seen him. Don't want to. Heard he's not too

happy with how things went down."

"Shit man, no one is."

"Seraph Chapen's best friend was killed by that *bitch.*"

"Easy. Seraph Garsone's ole gal got killed too. One hell of a day, huh?"

"An actual attack on *our* HQ. It's madness. Kinda' exciting though, ya' know?"

"Keep it down, you idiot."

"No, no I'm just saying ..."

"Yeah, and I'm just saying that excitement you're talking about got people killed. Lower your voice."

A faint alien murmur grew from the distance.

"You hear that?"

"Of course. It's you bumping your gums."

The noise grew in amplitude.

"No ... Serious, it sounds like. I think it's a vehicle."

"It's getting closer ... I think it's coming up here?"

"Can't be. Not this close to Span Opticon."

The whir of the approaching Tri-Bike increased to a roar.

Rushing to the railing that prevented a fatal fall from the castle grounds, one of the guards retrieved the magnocle from within his robes and peered through the tool at five times magnification. He surveyed the snaking, cliffside path, connecting the city below up to their fortress.

"Oh shit," were his last words. A piece of searing metal shattered the lens of his magnocle and came to rest directly behind his retina.

The remaining Seraph went prone and freed his blade. The motorbike was upon him. Rolling sideways, he narrowly missed the murderous tires and treads as a Tri-Bike with a female rider blew past him, crashing straight into the outer bailey doors. The explosion sent fire and sediment high into the air. Emergency bells sounded loud and in unison.

The Seraph, still on his stomach, crawled to his downed companion who still jerked and convulsed violently, releasing gas and fecal matter as his body lost system control.

"Seraphim on alert! An explosion has punctured the outer wall. I repeat we are under attack. An unidentified woman at outer bailey. It looks like a suicide attack." He shouted into the commlink still hitched to his comrade's waist. The communication channel went silent for a beat. "We read you. All available Seraphim to the outer main gate! What is your status, Seraph Jervais? Are you hurt?"

"Seraph Marley is down! I'm fine, but she got him."

Jervais wasn't fine. The attacker, bailing and surviving the crash, had doubled back to clean up. His grip on the communication device tightened as a shadow fell over him. He turned to face a giant with madness and dirt smeared on her face.

"Why?" Jervais whimpered. She did not respond. Holding her battle worn cutlass in one hand and pressing the barrel of an advanced persuader to Jervais' forehead with the other, Grase's mind wandered.

Grase made one stop after leaving Libyrinth and its sea of ruins—a brief meeting with a Boundless sympathizer and friend that worked for the Ars Femina. The clandestine affair occurred in a study center on the outskirts of Virtus near its border. The centers doubled as rooms for rent, for those with the trusts to spare, and boasted limited access to Syndicate archives.

The hum of the unknown technology that made remote access to the Archives possible droned in the background as the two women casually discussed a major breach of the Treaty.

"Grase, I know we're tight and all ... But *this* shit is excessive. Sandhurst and Ecclesiel might be onto something about all this junk, ya' know. Whatever you're planning is going to prove them right."

Grase chuckled, peering into her friend's eyes blankly. Sa-Rah had dutifully completed extractions for the Ars Femina for years. A particularly unsavory assignment left her questioning her loyalty to Celeste. After bumping into Grase during a saloon brawl and handing a rowdy party an ass-kicking to forget, the two were close ever since.

"Uh, hello. Neo-Earth to Grase. You hear me? You think any good can come of all this crap."

Grase began strapping the munitions and weapons provided to her back and waist.

"Damn it all to space! You think you can contact me out the blue, borrow an arsenal of super illegal shit, *and* pull that brooding, introspective crap. I won't let you just walk outta' here with an atrocity fixed to your back."

Grase finished arming herself despite Sa-Rah's protest. It was not until Grase made motions to exit that Sa-Rah grabbed her arm sternly.

"Wait."

"What?"

"What? What *exactly* are you going to do with that persuader? My neck is out on this one. Celeste will feed me to the help if she finds out ... That or she'd be proud, but I really doubt it. I wanna' know why, or who, or what the fuck?"

"They have Joan."

Sa-Rah's stomach dropped and continued to plummet as she pieced together the many shards of information held within those three words.

Even Sa-Rah knew Grase would burn all of Span Opticon down for Paulo, and Paulo would burn all of Virtus down for Joan. By the transitive property of love, Grase would destroy the planet to reunite Joan with Paulo.

"I am fucking ruined," Sa-Rah said. Knowing it was too late to talk her friend down, she regretted ever meeting Grase.

"You're really gonna screw me on this one. You're gonna fuck everything up, the Treaty, *your* life, *my* life, everything. Just go home."

Grase left.

Sa-Rah was angry, but she would never talk. She was already an accomplice to conspiracy to murder, trespassing, illegal sale and use of persuaders. The more crimes the quieter the contact. Conversely, Sa-Rah would have nothing to worry about from Grase. Dead women don't give up their co-conspirators.

Returning from reverie, Grase pulled the trigger. Seraph Jervais rejoined Seraph Marley in the afterlife.

Grase caught sight of the group of Seraphim exiting the smoldering gate. Leaving the door locked, they poured out of the hole created by her Tri-Bike crash. Ducking down and out of eye-line she created a plan.

The Seraphim arrived at a scene of three bodies displayed grimly in the dirt. The squad of ten encircled the bodies, closing in for inspection. The captain of the group, Seraph Luther, used his commlink to report three bodies to the Keep—two Seraphim and the deceased attacker.

"The attacker is down? Can you confirm the attacker is deceased?" the Keep answered back.

Grase reached for the handle of her battle-ax placed tactically with its head submersed in a near and still burning fire. The giant ax eviscerated five unsuspecting Seraphim who lingered too close to her assumed corpse, with a wide, arcing swing. The remaining Seraphim were alert and on the offensive. Grase repelled their numerous, relentless attacks from the ground with the handle and broad side of her ax. Making it to her feet, she split a Seraph in half. The ax dug into the ground with a thunk as the Seraph peeled away in either direction.

Four remaining Seraphim danced around her, daring to obstruct her mission. Nine more of Sandhurst's soldiers squeezed out the charred, cracked doors eager to join the fight. More squads stood ready inside, if needed, to wear her down with sheering numbers.

Seraph Luther stepped forward to face Grase alone. His squad mingled with the arriving nine, swelling their numbers to fourteen ready warriors, forming a circle in preparation of the likely duel.

"What do you expect to gain from this?" Luther asked calmly, making gentle cuts into the air with his katana-styled long sword. Grase bounced from foot to foot sprightly, even with her mobile armory. The advanced persuader dangled from her hip, glimmering menacingly in the glow of the still burning Tri-Bike wreckage.

"I'm looking for a prisoner. Joan ... Joan Flayr."

Luther planted himself.

"Terminated. I *am* sorry. Unprovoked attacks are against the Treaty, and, you know as well as I, punishable by death."

Hearing this, Grase was injured for the first time since her assault on Span Opticon began. She had feared an execution but hoped she could prevent it. If Elder Sandhurst wished to make an example with Joan, Grase would make an example of her own.

"Luther! Call off your friends." Ten Seraphim arrived and reinforced their ranks. "Your number is twenty-four now, including yourself. Send out Hiroshi Gunkimono, no one else has to die."

"High Seraph Gunkimono is away—dealing with *official* Syndicate of Valor business."

"Well, that's a real fuckin' shame. You boys aren't gonna like what happens next ... here we go!"

A puff of dust at her feet signaled her approach. Luther held his ground until Grase was a breath away. Adjusting her grip on the battle ax so the head faced down she swung it like a staff, their weapons clashed with a pang. The wide-bodied Luther pushed Grase off balance, stepping in with a swipe. Grase blocked the blow with her persuader by holding it up and across her chest. Syndicate steel sparked bright against the distressed metal of the persuader. Anchoring the butt of her ax into the ground, she steadied herself and fired.

A torrent of bullets flung from the barrel toward Luther. He dove sideways and met the ground with an oof. Locking eyes with Luther, she aimed the persuader at him again, then to the onlooking Seraphim. Determined to save his men, Luther regained his footing and unleashed a flurry of sword strokes. Grase dodged his manic attempts to connect and fired her automatic weapon anyway. The magazine emptied into the surrounding crowd. Six Seraphim lay dead, leaking from multiple fatal wounds.

She loved to fight Seraphim. They were so disciplined and unimaginative.

Luther gathered air into defeated breaths, toiling to match Grase's movements as she reloaded her persuader with fresh ammunition from the bandoleers slung over her shoulders.

Seraph Luther was inside her guard in an instant. Lunging forward, he slashed her forearm. Grase took a knee, cradling the wound with her free hand. Her other hand released the ax.

As the ax leaned to totter over, Luther thought he saw the end of their duel. He was right; however, it did not arrive in the form of his devastating, overhead, downward thrust but as a drawn cutlass from Grase's freed hand. The ax hit the ground and Grase's sword embedded in Luther's gut. His innards bubbled and tumbled out from the site of impalement. Pulling the blade free, she cleaned her cutlass with his ceremonial robes, reloaded her persuader, then engaged the nearest combatant.

It was a woman. Her sword was short, broad, sharp, but raised too late. Grase's cutlass made tassels of her throat. Kicking the woman's body at the legs of another Seraph, the second warrior tripped. Sliding sword-first, Grase caught the falling Seraph on the tip. He came to rest with a basket-hilt on his chest and the blade clean through his spine. Yanking her cutlass free, the body rolled off. A sword blade struck the dirt where Grase stood a moment before. The automatic persuader fired and turned the attacker's head to mush.

Twenty Seraphim remained. Aiming at a group of her attackers, she held the trigger until the weapon burned hot in her hands. The steamy heap of gore increased by four. Pulling more bullets from her twin bandoleers crisscrossing her body, she refreshed the advanced persuader then holstered it.

Reinforcements popped out of the gates. Thirty fresh soldiers swarmed her position. The alarm bleated out in the background and beads of sweat weighed on Grase's brow. She reached onto her back, freeing her longbow and spear-arrow.

The longbow was Grase's favorite weapon. She had fashioned it out of scraps as a child. The spear-arrow was her own personal touch. She fit the elongated arrow into the bow and aimed it at the chink in the main gate.

The projectile flew from her bow, an excited missile, impaling three Seraphim as they exited—the tipped end completely embedded in the stone wall behind them. With ax and sword Grase hacked a path to retrieve the spear-arrow. Slipping through the splintered nook, she breached Span Opticon's outer wall. She knew she would not easily evade her enemies, but the confined quarters of the castle halls might afford her time to catch a breath and calculate a plan.

* * *

Paulo Flayr erupted with pure ecstasy as a weathered, weary Joan stumbled down the front steps of Libyrinth. He was in their study smoking, drinking and reading, when he heard the relieving grind of the circular stone.

Joan was back. He didn't care how. He wouldn't ask—just yet. He skated across their book-littered living room and caught Joan in his eager arms, spinning her playfully.

"Hey, handsome. How ya' been," Joan giggled. Paulo's muffled response was lost in her neck. Kissing her from chest to chin, he tasted the sweat and grit of her trip—the grime of her turbulent odyssey. Joan pulled Paulo in for a longer kiss. Joan's fatigue melted.

"Joan, my love ... My life. My prologue, plot, and twist. I've been sick—just a wreck without you. Don't ever, ever do that to me again," Paulo tried to sound stern, but relief showed through.

"I'm sorry. I am so sorry," she whispered, biting his ear. He hoisted her up and moved to their bed. She didn't think to ask about Grase. The two founders of the Boundless Movement reunited in the comfort of each other's intimate company leaving the multiplying chaos of Neo-Earth to progress without them.

* * *

Panting, Grase darted through the raw marble corridors of Span Opticon. Her destination was the Keep. There, she might learn the location of the Syndicate's Elders during emergencies.

The deaths of dozens were on her hands. Grase was past her peak, and she knew it. If she stopped, stopped moving, stopped caring, stopped killing—she would die. Her body lent strength in an exchange she could never repay. Her wounds bled, mixing with the gore of the vanquished that clung to her like brambles. She did not move like a woman a rest away from doom, rather like a Valkyrie incensed and fueled by unnatural vengeance.

The alarms pestered the headache radiating from a gash on her forehead. Her face felt like a mask. Blood dripped into her eyes, obscuring her vision of the words chiseled into the wall at intersecting hallways. Rubbing the blood away with a bloodier hand, the sign read: *the Keep, keep right.*

Enraged shouts bounced off the walls and into the hallways around her. The indifferent stones betrayed her pursuers, showing their positions with detailed echoes. It sounded like multiple Seraphim squads on her trail.

She put distance between pursuers and herself amid the confusion and carnage. When Luther informed that Hiroshi was off-site, Grase had hoped it was a lie. It was not. Hiroshi was well outside Virtus by now, meeting with the very same woman who had banished Grase's mother.

Following the wall-signs, brought Grase to an elegant anteroom. The room was about the size of a football field. The Keep, at the end, was just fifty scorchfeet away. The typical two Seraphim stood guard at its entrance even during her assault.

Sticking to the shadows, she dropped her weapons with the exception of her long bow and spear-arrow in the nearest corner. Hiding behind one of the large potted plants running the room's length, she inched closer to the communication center. By the voices that spilled out of the Keep, she estimated fifteen people inside. They bustled about in between making reports and orders.

Stopping momentarily, she felt death making its move. Slow and purposeful, gradual and certain. She coughed and spat blood onto the smooth marble floor.

"Well, Grase. Here you are. On your last leg and you didn't even get to kill that rotten Celeste."

Erupting from the shadows, bow on her back, and spear-arrow extended tip first at the nearest Seraph. The feathered spear entered his head at the temple, traveled through his skull, and out the other side only to pierce the chest of the second guard. It was a precise and quiet attack. Or it would have been had the spear-arrowhead gone deeper. The second guard dropped to his knees fixed to the weapon and released a shrill scream. Her pursuers arrived, flooding the anteroom and creating a bottleneck at the entrance.

A tug returned her spear-arrow. Waving it in front of her and side to side, she kept the encroaching Seraphim away. Their display of swords showed no intention of letting her pass.

Accepting death as the only retreat, she attacked. Any Seraphim within her reach met quick and unfortunate ends.

Notching her bow with the spear-arrow she tried to clear a path. Leaping from the longbow, the spear killed many. Recognizing its threat, the Seraphim swarmed where it landed and broke the shaft in two.

Grase grabbed a Seraph and broke him similarly. Using her fists as escorts she hammered her way toward her weapon stash. The swirling sea of Seraphim solidified around her. Two skulls, slammed one against the other, cleared her final obstacle. She grabbed her cutlass as a series of swords slashed and gnashed at her back. Grase could barely turn to face her attackers. A fatal blow was deflected away. Its owner was cut down in swift retaliation. Grase raised her arms again, but no strength belonged to the motion. The Seraphim parted.

The image her eyes captured merged with one she had seen many times before in her head. She blurted her thoughts out loud, "Ido? Ido Xzaven, High Librarian of the Syndicate of Valor? Ido Xzaven, the Historian of Neo-Earth?"

Ido Xzaven was a monster built atop the frame of a man. His suit of armor could have been some grotesque prototype of a Legioneer Alpha. It did not shine like that of an Ars Searcher, instead sporting a dull, metallic polish. To Grase, Ido Xzaven looked like a hybrid network of pipes and wires twisted around a bloated set of knight's armor.

Ido Xzaven's beaked helmet scraped the top of the doorway as he lumbered forward out of the Keep. The mechanized ogre pushed the comparatively tiny Seraphs aside.

She caught the awe-inspired stares they gave him, mixed with the looks of hatred aimed at her. They wanted to keep fighting, but respect for the Librarian was too great. They shuffled out of his way, bemoaning.

"Grase? Previously thought to be deceased? Dishonored

child of decorated Ars Femina Searcher, Senora Witney and Feral-man leader, Adiraja Jeffroy, was it? Are you Grase Jeffroy?" The artificially enhanced voice trickled from his helmet with perfect annunciation and otherworldly grace.

Hearing her parents' names left her stunned. Her cutlass quivered in grasp. Thousands of questions hurled themselves at the dam of curiosity in her mind, threatening to break through and spill over to her mouth. There was so much she wished to know, and the man with the answers was in front of her.

Grase burst into tears.

The behemoth waved his arm, dismissing all lingering on-lookers. The sweaty and alert Seraphim filed out, making visible signs of disapproval. Even the curious Seraphim that had left their stations inside the Keep returned to their various tasks, muttering objections under their breaths.

Exhilaration slowed death's progression. Did Ido Xzaven, the Historian of Neo-Earth, really mean to duel? She didn't want to fight, and her opponent was unarmed, save for a giant tome under his arm. Wiping blood out of her eyes, she squinted to inspect the words written on the book's spine—*History of the Fallen*. At last, she collapsed, unable to stay conscious.

Chapter 13

The stone door of Libyrinth sounded its usual unhinge and grind across the gravelly doorway. The Flayrs knew it wasn't Grase. Whoever rolled back the stone fumbled with it, moving it in short, unsure intervals. Not knowing just how far to pull or push. When they did figure it out, Joan and Paulo had already sealed their living quarters behind them and hidden among the shelves of their ancient museum; enacting a plan they practiced often.

Seraphim Taper, Tally, and Greeves pushed Libyrinth's door open wide enough for them to scurry in and begin a cautious descent down its central stairway. They paused, surveying the Boundless Movement's fabled hideout. Sunlight beamed in from dozens of translucent sky wells in the ceiling, or ground depending on the point of reference.

Seraph Greeves took the lead once his eyes adjusted from the brightness of the desert. Whoever built the library was not ashamed to show their influence. Decrepit, imitation Egyptian arches and obelisks, shelves shaped in the likeness of Nubian and Mesoamerican pyramids. Greek arches, miniature Chinese pavilions, and Etruscan bridges, all interspersed the cavernous main hall.

Seraph Taper saw a garden in one of Libyrinth's back corners. It was incredible. The Boundless Movement possessed what would be the most important archaeological discovery on Neo-Earth. A gallery of the past, each work of art a window through time.

Seraph Taper could not believe ancient humans would compile so much information in one building. One little match. One flicked cigarette could burn away history in a snap. The Boundless Movement found this place and hid it from the world; disgusting, she thought.

To Seraph Tally, aesthetics were secondary. Where his companions saw history, he saw hiding spots. Where they saw beauty, he saw booby traps. While they searched for silent words to describe the monuments and nostalgia, he searched for any movement or noise.

Paulo and Joan watched from an enclosure as the trio approached the base of the central stairway. They reached bottom level, still looking around in awe but maintaining a tight formation. The Seraphim were surrounded by rows upon rows of packed bookshelves, stuffed with dusty archives, encyclopedias, magazines, and pamphlets. The occasional light pillar stabbed down from cracks in the ceiling illuminating slices of the library-museum around them.

"It's bigger than the Archives," Seraph Greeves stated aloud what they all thought. Seraph Taper held a vertical finger to her lips. Both Greeves and Tally nodded in agreement. They moved forward in a rotating circle formation.

"Shh ..." Paulo shushed just loud enough for the intruders to overhear. The Seraphim locked eyes, then triangulated on the position of his voice. When they arrived, Paulo was gone.

"Over here ..." This time Joan set the bait. Again, the

Seraphim surrounded its source. Again, the Flayrs scurried on.

"That was most certainly Jan—Joan. Can't place the male voice though," Taper whispered to Tally and Greeves.

"If we hear it again, it's a trap. We should stay here and wait for them," Greeves answered.

"I think we lost 'em," Joan whispered again. Seraph Tally almost laughed. They didn't investigate. Instead, they fanned out, backs to the shelves, to inspect their immediate surroundings.

"It's not working, babe," Joan said into Paulo's ear.

"They're just poking around, I think. They'll eventually stumble into something," Paulo responded in the same manner. Joan nodded, then moved to his ear to respond.

A loud snap preceded by a muffled rumbling, cut their whispering short.

"My fuckin' leg! It's crushed. I'm, I'm done!" Tally screamed out; all the decorum of a Seraphim was gone from his voice.

The Flayrs exchanged an excited high-five as Seraph Taper and Greeves rushed to Tally's aid. They each took one look at his leg and knew there wasn't a physician on Neo-Earth that could save his life, let alone his leg. He was losing too much blood. Visible, his bones jutted out at odd angles. Blood pooled.

"Is it bad?" Tally asked frantically, ignoring what their faces made obvious. "I mean, I don't *need* a leg. I just want to *live*. Come on, help me up. I am not going out like this. A fuckin' bookshelf ..."

It was worse than he knew in his shocked-fueled delirium. The Flayrs' mechanism was meant to trip whoever stepped on the pressure plate and drop a nearby massive shelf on their lower torso. For Seraph Tally the machine worked without a hitch, pulverizing his lower body. Greeves and Seraph Taper did not speak. Syndicate Seraphim were quite tough in fact.

"Oh, thanks guys. See, I told you I'm fine ... Wow, I feel great. It's like I can fly. Look I can see Joan and Paulo right there, *look*!"

He pantomimed his morbid delusions from the floor. His pulverized lower torso rendered him otherwise immobile. The Flayrs, unable to see Seraph Tally, assumed his rambling true and moved in to finish the job. Two mahogany shelves loose from their weakened roosts, came tumbling down from opposite sides of the aisle.

The rumbling settled and Libyrinth was silent. No one dared betray their location. Joan and Paulo retreated from their devastation. Taper and Greeves, evading the attack had looped around to neighboring aisles and positioned themselves between Paulo, Joan, and Libyrinth's elevated egress. Using the dust in the air as cover, Seraph Taper sneaked within inches of Joan and prepared to strike.

Grase's training saved Joan's life. The tip of Taper's blade struck parchment instead of flesh. Paulo slinked out from behind a tilted shelf and threw himself onto Seraph Taper's back.

"Joan, *run*!" Paulo shouted. Greeves was there, prying Paulo from Taper's shoulders. Joan scurried away, disappearing between the rows of shelves around them.

Paulo fumbled at his pockets as he and Seraph Whestley Greeves wrestled. Seraph Taper aimed her sword at the distracted Paulo and slashed out in hopes of a fatal blow. What her blade found was the firm two palm grip of a protective Joan, who only pretended to retreat.

Seraph Taper's look of utter surprise was met with a firm punch. She was smaller than Joan and had no time to brace herself. The force of the punch blasted Taper into one of Libyrinth's many stone columns.

Paulo and Seraph Greeves fought each other to the floor; with the Seraph desperately and nearly reaching his blade and Paulo madly trying to prevent him, whilst still reaching for his pockets. The thud of Seraph Taper hitting the column and collapsing, stopped the men. Both peered over, astonished. Joan had defeated the unit's veteran with a single punch.

Rolling her shoulders, she loosened up for her next opponent. Paulo finally reached the gas pellet in his pocket and, in one smooth movement, covered his nose and mouth and smashed the pellet across the Seraph's skull.

The pellets' outer membranes didn't rupture. The gas didn't release. But a stunned Seraph Greeves did release his grasp just enough for Paulo to shimmy free. He ran to Joan's side panting as Whestley Greeves rose to his feet.

"We should run!" Paulo suggested, grabbing hold of Joan's wrist as the Seraph approached, dueling sword out and ready. Joan shook Paulo's hand free.

"I got this. Stay back," she said just loud enough for him to hear.

"What's that?" Seraph Greeves taunted, slashing at shelves to either side of him as he neared.

"I was just telling my man that I got this. I fought hand-to-hand with Hiroshi Gunkimono and lived, no way some regular Seraph's gonna take me. You've seen what I can do."

That was the first time Paulo heard the story told in that manner.

Seraph Greeves knew instantly Joan Flayr wasn't boasting.

The way she stood, the look in her eyes, told the truth. Shaking the thoughts away he assumed a battle stance.

"Maybe you did face him ... But this isn't hand-to-hand."

No retort. Joan closed in, never taking her eyes off of his blade. Seraph Greeves swiped at the air incessantly, testing her speed. She didn't dodge, knowing the attacks to be feints and flairs. His sword whistled, heckling her as it darted through the air, eagerly awaiting blood. Back, forth, up, down, no discernible pattern to his strokes. One extravagant display of dexterity and stamina after the next.

Joan moved closer, leaning back to stay out of his flurries' reach. The barrage stopped suddenly. Switching stances, the Seraph stepped in for a thrusting lunge. She wasn't wearing armor and Seraph Greeves knew he didn't need much power to pierce her shirt, even with a dueling sword. She dodged the strike with a pivot, counterattacking with a side kick.

The kick impacted his left obliques, most certainly breaking a rib. Catching her leg with a wince, he stabbed out again with his sword.

No strike landed. Joan dodged with grace, putting all her body weight into her leg. Seraph Greeves couldn't attack and keep her leg captive, not for long, not with fractured ribs. He let her go, retreating a few paces to check the severity of his injury. Slipping a hand underneath his robes, he felt no protruding bone.

Joan gave him little chance to check thoroughly. A downward fist smacked his hand free and an open palm to his chest pushed him back up against a shelf. The exhilaration of battle stirred in her gut. Joan felt as Hiroshi must have during their fight in Holding—in control.

Recovering, he shot at her like a primed spring, sword tip

first. It bore into her shoulder, twisting cloth, and tore through her shoulder blade. He pulled the blade free, transitioning into his signature flurry of blade strokes.

Joan circled the Seraph, ignoring the searing pain. Focusing only on his whipping slashes and the dueling sword's tip.

Two more well placed punches, one at his shoulder and one at his elbow joint, forced him to drop his weapon. Before its patter subsided, a kick and four rapid knocks to the jaw pummeled an overwhelmed Seraph Greeves. His knees almost gave out. A head-butt from Greeves to Joan bought him time to bring his hands up for defense.

The distinctive sound of Seraph Tally's death throes interrupted Greeves and Joan's bout. Paulo, never one to waste an opportunity, released the realistically weighted, replica persuader from his pocket. Before Greeves could return his attention to Joan, Paulo cracked the flask across the back of his skull. Seraph Greeves joined his squad mates on the floor.

"I could have taken him," Joan said, between breaths.

"I know. But *I* had to pull my weight too."

After disposing of Seraph Tally's body, the Flayrs bound, gagged, and isolated Seraphim Taper and Greeves in opposing storage spaces. Both Seraphim remained unconscious as Joan and Paulo decided their next moves.

"What are we gonna do with them?" Paulo asked, avoiding the unpleasant subtext of his question. They were in their shared office. He tapped a cabinet and their minibar appeared from its hidden compartment. He poured them both a drink.

"Whaddayamean, what are we gonna do? We have to kill them. They came here to kill us. They've been following us! And who knows for how long?" Joan reasoned, scrunching up her face. She retrieved her drink and emptied the glass.

"Oh, so we're just gonna exterminate two unarmed people because they followed us?" Paulo said, his voice laden with sarcastic curiosity. "Following someone is not a crime punishable by death." His drink disappeared down his throat.

"Paulo!" Joan snapped. "This is no fuckin' time for moralistic philosophy or legalism. Shit is getting out of hand. We have to update our rule book."

"You went behind my back and tried to start a fuckin' war! You went on a *suicide* mission. You could have died, and I wouldn't know how, where, *why*, Joan. You risked everything we've built over the years for what?"

"To make a point!"

"Yeah? Make a point. What point? That you can be such a sneak and a liar? Manipulate Grase into teaching you how to fight? Then you get captured, escape and lead the Syndicate right back here? *That* point? Point proven!"

"That's what this is about, Paul. You're mad I did something and didn't ask you first? Sorry, Daddy. You're mad I went and learned something you didn't want me to learn. You're mad you don't control me, or Grase. That we do whatever the fuck we want when we want? You sound like fuckin' Sandhurst."

Paulo had abandoned pouring the drinks and simply began drinking from the bottle. Big dramatic swigs as he paced back and forth.

"Sure. Maybe walking up to Span Opticon and defeating a few of their elite soldiers single-handedly made a point. Showed our strength. Showed those Syndicate bureaucrats that shit isn't calm anymore. Joan, I get it. I *do*. But you got caught. It's luck they didn't kill you then, luck they haven't killed us yet. Doesn't seem like they're gonna stop."

"How is that any different from a few days ago? We've had a price on our heads for years. What's changed?" Joan demanded with two open palms and a shrug.

"What's different? Well, for one we only killed in self-defense. You're just going around killing fuckin' everybody. This isn't what we agreed on. They know where we live, Joan. I—I had to send *Grase* to save you."

Something in the way Paulo pronounced Grase's name sent Joan into inconsolable rage. She tore and kicked at any and every object in the room as she railed.

"Did you have to send *her*? Look, I'm back, where's Grase? For all you know, she died! I made it out alive Paulo, I can *fight* Seraphim. Grase taught me how. We don't need her to be our errand girl, we don't need her to protect us anymore, we don't need her. I can do it. You just have to let me show you."

"Show me without murdering two unarmed humans. Show me without sacrificing your life on a whim."

Paulo got up from the tiny desk in the corner of their bedroom, bumping his knees and knocking a small bust to the floor. Picking up the bust, he found a seat on the edge of their bed. Joan leaned with her back against their bedroom door, knee up and arms folded. He examined the shoddy statue of the former leader of the Ars Femina, Shirley the First. It was a cheap trinket but served its purpose as a paperweight. Paulo collected his thoughts.

"Joan. You're my world. It's wrong, but I fight, I fight for Neo-Earth because it's *your* home. It is easy for me to do the right thing with you in mind. I always imagine what *you* would do, or how I want someone to act if it were you. You don't have to prove anything to me. You're already the toughest, sharpest woman on the planet in my eyes. Nothing short of murder will change *that*." Paulo paused, head down and eyes darting back and forth, looking up for a moment as if to make an admission, he shook away the thought before continuing. "Had you gotten caught and High Seraph Gunkimono and Elder Sandhurst were having a similar conversation I'd hope they make the same decision."

"Well, they didn't, Paulo. I'm sorry I didn't tell you the truth sooner. I crept into Virtus, walked up to Span Opticon, started some shit—a few guys later I was unconscious. I woke up inside a cell in Holding. When Hiroshi came to talk to me, he told me his orders were to kill me unless I talked. I told him to go fuck himself. We fought. He beat me, unconscious again. I woke up and said a lot more shit to him, Paulo." She laughed. "I don't think he was ready for it. It threw him off and instead of killing me he freed me and said he'd be back to finish it at some point. I was scared, babe, but I ran. All the way home."

"They were gonna just *kill* you?"

"I mean, I think I killed a few of those guys. I imagine Sandhurst is pretty pissed. Probably wanted to make an example of me or something."

"He just let you go? And you didn't think it might be a trap? You essentially led them directly back here."

Joan's temper flashed, "They were gonna find us eventually! What, you're gonna blame me for this? If something happens to Grase, blame me for that as well? What isn't my fault right now, Paul?"

"Spacedamnit, Joan! I don't want to fight!"

"Yeah, I know, I heard. My husband 'The Whiniest Man on Neo-Earth'. Are we going to change the world hiding underground in an old museum for libraries our whole lives? How long has it been since we found this place? Ten, fifteen years? Sure, we have the Boundless Movement. A network of fuckin' anonymous people who give us food and trusts, help us copy books, let us sleep in their basements and sheds when we're on the road."

"People ready to die for us, at the drop of a hat," Paulo added, thinking he had delivered the coup de grace. But Joan was ready with a rebuttal.

"Exactly my point, love, we can't have people laying down their lives for us if we aren't equally willing to do the same. I'm not saying what I did was the most well-thought-out approach. I'm not sure we can be pacifists if our followers are dying so *we* don't have to fight. I'd rather it be me standing up to the Ars in bars, not sweethearts like Flayo Paul ...Yeah that's who actually died at Depot. Who Celeste *really* killed. If I'm right, Paulo, things are gonna get hairy when they find out you're not dead. The Treaty is in jeopardy. Shit's gonna go *down* and I want to make sure the Boundless Movement is the most prepared and ready to react."

"You're not wrong, Joan. It's just, I wish we could've just talked about this before it all went this far."

"I wish I were just as good as Grase in a fight. I wish I didn't have to kill these sneaky fucks that we've dedicated our lives to defeating. But ... We've released Syndicate secrets, destroyed sensitive documents, framed members of their organization—all actions that have gotten people killed, directly or indirectly. I'm not saying I *want* to kill them. Or that killing them justifies past actions. I know I was wrong going in alone. I had to prove it to myself. If I really wanted to put pacifism to rest, I might as well start a fight that mattered ..."

Paulo sat elbows on his knees, hands clasped beneath his chin, watching the love of his life make murder sound pragmatic. He feared she was right. He wasn't afraid to be wrong. He was afraid of the world in which Joan had to be right. Things were no longer as simple as they were when they had first met. He always believed in the good in the world, the good in himself. It was becoming harder to find as of late. He was drinking more, Grase had become distant, and was likely dead. Joan was always off on her own adventures meeting so-and-so, wherever. He knew Grase only taught Joan to fight out of guilt and spite. Two things he was full of. He was clinging to pacifism as desperately as he clung to Joan. Even as time tensed their bond. When he and Joan had met, they were free spirits flying in the same direction. As time passed, he learned there was no spirit freer than hers. She would fly away some day, any day, leaving him behind to soar the skies alone.

"... Not to mention we built fatal booby traps to guard Libyrinth. It's cool to kill Seraphim like mice? But not when we're protecting the secrecy of our home? Some half-scorched idea we agreed upon the better half of twenty years ago? We no longer have the privilege to not kill, there are people dying for our ideas."

Their happiness hid his sadness for so long it became unrecognizable. Arguing less often wouldn't make Joan stay with him. Nothing could make Joan do anything against her will. Not even High Seraph Gunkimono. What a person—what an awesome human, he thought as she spoke. Joan was correct. The intruders needed to be killed to protect the Boundless Movement.

Joan had already won. She convinced Paulo, beyond a shadow of a doubt, that the Syndicate of Valor assassins must die.

"You're right," Paulo spoke for the first time in a few minutes. "We have to kill them."

"Oh, so I'm just right all of a sudden," Joan replied indignantly. He couldn't explain all his thoughts at that moment, settling for what he thought was the logical approach.

"It's just what you said about Flayo Paul. I mean, yeah, that guy was a wildcard ... and a little bit obsessive, but he gave his life for the Movement. More than I have ever done. It's selfish to think I don't have to get my hands dirty. What's the alternative? We let these guys go and they kill more people to find us again. Here's the thing, if we kill them; *I* do it, and *my* way. That, I won't move on. You have had enough action for today."

Happy to have convinced Paulo, Joan rushed him, giving him a huge, exaggerated kiss on his cheek.

"Sorry for everything, my love," Joan said. "I'm sorry those Seraphim have to die."

Paulo Flayr approached the storage room. Joan was close behind, her shoulder bandaged and in a makeshift sling. Seraph Taper could be heard cursing. He took a deep breath, unlocked the door, slipped into the room, and locked it back behind him.

The room was quaint, not large enough to lie down comfortably in any direction. Paulo faced a shelf, three walls, and a chair. In the chair was Seraph Taper.

"You done yelling? If so, you can have a drink." Seraph Taper immediately ceased yelling profanities and eyeballed the bottle of Pre-Scorch liquor Paulo dangled in front of her.

"One glass?" Seraph Taper pointed out, suspicious. "This my last drink, that it?"

Paulo sighed and turned a nearby stack of books into a stool. He looked into Seraph Taper's eyes and spoke with sincerity.

"It's like this, my wife is gonna kill you *and* your partner ..."

95

Seraph Taper jerked forward and bit at Paulo, the restraints that held her stretched, cutting deep into her wrist and arms as she leaned away from them.

"Whoa! Listen, I'm gonna need you to calm down … See, like I was saying, Joan has to kill you both. I personally don't think it's necessary. Joan's always been better at this stuff than me, but that doesn't mean you can't enjoy a fine glass before you go." Seraph Taper identified the bottle to be genuine.

"What if I don't drink? What if I'm an alcoholic? Or a diabetic? Do I get to choose my last drink? Does it have to be a drink? Don't suppose you lot have some Pre-Scorch meat down here, huh? Maybe like a three-thousand-year-old beef fillet? Any plains mix?"

"What would any of that matter now?" Paulo responded, popping the cork with his mouth and pouring her last. "You're taking this much better than I imagined. You don't fear death?"

"I knew I was dead as soon as your wife beat me. Not sure why you tied us up. Should've killed us while we were out." Tally motioned out of the room with her head. "What if I got loose? And where's Greeves? What if he got loose? Joan is either stupid or cocky. Either way, it's gonna get a little twerp like yourself killed. Now gimme the damn drink, then send your wife to finish the job like a man."

Hiding his scorn, Paulo lifted the glass to her lips. She nudged it with her chin and swallowed the spirit in three gulps. A bit dribbled from her mouth.

His tone shifted, much more serious, empathy coating his every word.

"Seraph, still your tongue. Maybe you have some information. Maybe you can prove some use to us, and Joan won't have to come in here."

Soon the poison would take hold.

"See, the Boundless Movement started as a nonviolent movement. Our first rally, we were young then, held right outside of a study center in Virtus. You know what happened? General Donnel, he was a High Seraph. You remember? Him and a few of his Seraphim walked right up and started beating the piss out of anybody brave enough not to move. Donnel punched my teeth out," Paulo grinned, "These are veneers. One of 'em broke Joan's collar bone. We were only kids back then. I was in so much pain, and humiliated, I made Joan promise to me that we'd never be like them, the factions, using violence for their own gain."

"And now you think every Seraph is the same," Seraph Taper quipped her last remark before a deluge of blood and bile burst from her mouth and nose. Her eyes became blood-stricken and jaundiced. Her veins, once invisible and oxygen rich, were now deep cerulean estuaries flowing full of toxins. The Seraph's face twisted and contorted in fiery agony.

Paulo looked away, burying his face in his elbow holding in a gag; only turning back once the choking and gurgling subsided. Untying her hands, he lay her face down then refilled the glass. Paulo paused at the door to the storage room, stealing a moment to recapture his composure. A few deep breaths returned him to center. Joan waited for him just on the other side.

"One down. One to go," Paulo muttered, defeated as he exited. He closed the door behind him briskly. Joan's hand brushed his arm as he passed. Cradling the glass to ensure it wouldn't spill, he didn't stop. His eyes remained locked on the door down the hall. The door containing his next task.

* * *

Grase was broken, bleeding, and sprawled out on Ido Xzaven's bed. Her labored breaths came at longer and longer intervals. A part of Ido pitied her, a part loathed her, and another part of the Librarian, envious.

Amram Donnel had outfitted Ido's armor, his life suit, with a feature capable of monitoring human vital signs. Within his helmet he could see if someone nearby was injured or near death. A green glow signaled a healthy person, yellow meant unconscious or sleeping, and red aura meant critical condition. No glow of course meant dead.

Most of Grase's body glowed red, but her belly pulsed green. A healthy baby hid underneath her jumpsuit. In all his years, travels, and relationships, Ido never fathered children.

"Here I lie. Ready to tell the truth. I love Paulo Flayr more than the stars love to shine," she paused, barely enough life left in her to speak. "I'm sorry Joan—I made it hard for him. He *is* a good man."

Grase's confession revealed all the High Librarian needed to know about the curious story unfolding in front of him. Paulo Flayr, 'Scoundrel of the Boundless', impregnated his wife's best friend.

Ido was now a major player in their grim production. His co-stars bumbled about giving it their best dramatic performances; to be expected from actors ignorant to key elements of the plot.

Grase turned to Ido, finding what she could only assume was his gaze, then spoke, "Ido Xzaven, don't let my baby die."

Grase Jeffroy was still. Ido wouldn't cry. He would respect her dying wish but shedding tears for an enemy was too much.

The alarm inside Pangaia had long subsided. Details of her attack had likely reached Elder Sandhurst. Being the Elder's oldest friend and closest comrade, Ido had nothing to fear. Zach, as he affectionately referred to him, would not interfere. There was no shortage of trust between the two.

Seraph Augustine was the best physician in Virtus and Seraph Babatunji the most talented surgeon; if they were summoned to Pangaia immediately the child could be saved. A giant armored first slammed a comm link. A buzz then a response, "The Keep here. Everything smooth up there, sir?"

"Xzaven. All is calm. Summon Seraph Caprice Augustine and Seraph Slaid Babatunji. The enemy has integral information, and they are dying. This matter is of extreme importance."

"Got it, sir. On it, sir."

Forgetting his mission and rapid action squad, Ido devoted his consummate knowledge and careful attention to saving the child curiously delivered to his care.

Chapter 14

G eneral Donnel gazed at his life's work through a large bay window in his command hall. Behind him a prospective Alpha Ace prepared their recital.

"When *it* comes into question. *It* being completely unavoidable combat, we as free men will be over-equipped in anticipation of victory and longevity of life. The geriatrics of the Syndicate have sworn me their enemy. The very same Syndicate that fostered and trained me. Their ways are ancient and effective. But *they* exist to contain change. To curb technological advancements at every juncture. *We* exist to usher in a new age.

"Neo-Earth. We have been given a second chance. No one exactly knows why ... We are going to rebuild, making sure to perfect and surpass our careless ancestors. How can we, who know the Preneo possessed capability and technology of unequaled proportion and possibility, do otherwise? The Legioneers will be free people, not meant to live as slaves, barbarians or as pets. The geriatrics deal in taboos and superstitions. Join my ranks and become part of the machine that will rise on its own and forge a Neo-Earth comparable to the paradise days of yore.

"It won't be easy. Vicaarism is an acid of non-truths that burns the eyes, leaving behind the blind and helpless. At first, I accused them of ignorance. Then I saw that it was worse. Religion was being used to lash out, against logic and reason. Against history and facts. Against the artifacts of the Pre-Scorch days. Always, against. Against. *Against.*"

Reaching an emotional crescendo, Geeza Londo stomped his foot three times. Donnel mouthed every word from underneath his helmet, nary unfolding his arms from behind his back or averting his gaze from the window he faced. Londo stepped closer to Donnel and his L-shaped seat. His voice, louder and steadier.

"Hypocrites! They rely on which they decry. Ecclesiel broadcasts his slippery sermons over the Wave weekly. Schools teach children that science and technology are the cause of our current plight? Yet, without either, we humans would be extinct. I use my resources to provide haven for women and men who wish to improve their relationships with the neglected arts. Technology, taboo? How could we accept this most preposterous premise? But we *will* change their minds. We will change the world!"

Spinning to face Geeza, as he moved onto the next segment of the infamous manifesto, Donnel swelled with pride. He eyed the man before him and judged him worthy to ascend to the highest rank of Alpha Ace.

"When on board with the Legioneer vehicle, there is no stepping off. Our secrets are more important than the lives of deserters. To pledge allegiance to me is to enlist as a member in the most technologically advanced faction on Neo-Earth.

"The Syndicate will despise our existence but will never attack us outright. Existing in a world of bureaucrats and diplomacy and commodities and trade, our value to Neo-Earth will not be might.

"Instead, we will make ourselves integral to the Treaty, thus shielding ourselves from conflict. Working from within, until the very idea of going against us invokes images of destruction and decimation of resources."

The General tightened his fists, allowing himself to feel the emotions he first felt years ago. Still mouthing along through a nostalgic smile, he took note of Geeza's demeanor.

The Alpha was not holding back. Often Legioneers seeking promotion would stand stiffly by and recite the Manifesto to robotic perfection. Geeza Londo hit the cadences and rhythms, leaned into the emotional highs, added the inflections signifying rhetorical questions. More than a display of memory, he felt the words.

"We will be peddlers of information and intimidation. Using fear to become enigmas among the people of the world. Free to pass as we wish, viewed as wizards or devils. Their superstitions will be used to propel our agenda.

"We will trade our skills for the right price. When I say price, I do not mean trusts, I mean favors—labors, errands and tasks. Possessing the important fabrication manuals and the talent needed to bring their secrets to life, we are in a position of power once reserved only for Zachariah Sandhurst alone."

The General found the edge of his seat and sat.

"If the Ars Femina needs a new Tri-Bike model, we will produce or procure the designs. If the practitioners of Vicaarism need a personnel lift installed at some harrowing peak, we will install or invent the solution. If a group of Nute's need the means to till a patch of fertile land, we will give with gratuity. We will not become so entangled in the web of the Syndicate's fabricated global economy. This way, we are protected from the inevitable failure of Sandhurst's Treaty. Trusts are inconsequential to shadows. Our craft makes us rich."

Geeza Londo paused, adjusted his Alpha armor, centered the L-shaped insignia on his breastplate, and stood up straight before delivering the last line. "Join me, sisters, brothers! And we will enjoy everlasting victory!"

Donnel let silence rule the room for close to a minute before he ended its reign. "I could not have said it better myself." General Donnel rose from his ornate seat, designed to take the shape of the letter 'L' when viewed from any carnal direction. He towered over his subject. Examining the man, he wondered if the Alpha's were getting smaller by the year.

Geeza Londo was the latest of his Beta Phalanx reviewed for promotion to Alpha. A promotion offered only to Legioneer loyalists so familiar with his impassioned words they committed it to memory. If the manifesto is quoted word for word, the individual then presents the General with an innovation improving the lives of Legioneers. As one of his favorite prospects, Donnel eagerly awaited Geeza's presentation.

"And these, I call Stun-chucks. They're a reimagining of the batons used by our ACOs."

"I see," Donnel said then beckoned Geeza closer with a hand.

"You may have noticed." Geeza demonstrated the stances and maneuvers he had prepared. "By styling them after an ancient Preneo weapon, I was able to increase their offensive abilities. I believe the lethality has been upped by forty percent. Unfortunately, the skill required to wield them has increased disproportionately. These aren't something that can be rolled out immediately. They could make for an excellent training tool, and eventually a dedicated unit.

"I'll try them out now," Donnel said, rising. Geeza plopped the prototype in his open palm. "What exactly does one do?"

Stifling a laugh, Geeza responded, "The most important thing is to not hit yourself with the conjoined sticks. Especially not their tips, which contain the incapacitating mechanism."

Donnel, rising, took the Stun-chucks and tightened them between outstretched fists. "Okay. Let's see the potential of your invention. Did you bring another pair?"

"I did," Geeza said with pride, "In case the first pair failed."

"Perfect. Your first act as a newly promoted Alpha Ace will be our friendly duel. I was long convinced you are deserving of distinction. Now, you must show me your weapons are deserving as well."

Geeza Londo released another pair of Stun-chucks from his waist and prepared to face General Donnel.

Chapter 15

Amram Donnel never left Motopia. All he needed lay comfortably suspended 1,700 scorchfeet above Neo-Earth's surface. Back when the city was first hoisted into the air, he boasted never to let his feet contact the ground again. Over a decade later, he held his word. Motopia grew to represent every difference between Zachariah Sandhurst and Amram Donnel.

Lifting buildings and the technology making the act possible, were in direct violation of Article Two of the Treaty of Neo-Earth. "A floating city?" his detractors balked. "Impossible!" they exclaimed. "Illegal!" others warned. His rivals had no shortage of doubts, but here he sat at the center of his Legioneer industrial capital, defying both gravity and convention with unapologetic prominence.

His engineers achieved the feat by repurposing and recycling the machine fragments long discarded by the Preneo.

Before abdicating his post as a High Seraph, Amram spent most of his waking hours between study centers and the Archives. He, one day, stumbled upon a grouping of old entries, all containing cryptic maps and images that suggested the existence of vessels capable of leaving the planet. With that knowledge, Amram Donnel assembled a bipartisan team of Seraphim and Feral-men and embarked on a secret expedition.

What he found during that trip sparked the schism between master and subservient. Returning, Amram had been eager, proud even to share his discoveries with Elder Sandhurst. Instead of the expected praise, Elder Sandhurst met High Seraph Donnel's discoveries with anger.

General Donnel peered out the wide windows of Central, his command hall. Watching Motopia from Central's elevated, centermost position, he replayed the heated argument in his mind as though it happened moments earlier.

"How did you discover this place?" Elder Sandhurst had demanded. Donnel had to catch his breath before responding. He had burst into Elder Sandhurst's hidden study, accessible only by a trapdoor located in the Antechamber of the Elders.

"You mean your true office? Or the site of the Great Wreckage?"

"Th—the Great Wreckage? What is this nonsense?" Elder Sandhurst backed away from Amram nervously.

"Master—Zach, we are like brothers. And I find out you are keeping *this* kind of shit from me? *Me?* I am *your* guy, remember?" It was not the first time they had argued but it was a new high for his insolence. Cornering his older comrade, they stood face to face.

"Yes, we are friends. But you are my subject first and foremost. As my High Seraph, it is not your place to question my judgment, but to enact my will," Sandhurst had said.

"Space travel!" Donnel pierced the air with a finger pointed at the ceiling

"The information in those files is unsubstantiated! Trust me. I have spent my life chasing the very same ghosts. Only when I set my sights on something more tangible, did the world know peace."

"Save it, Zach."

"My peace was fifteen years strong by the time you were born. This was done not by revealing the bitter natures of our past but by showing people a simple way. The people of Neo Earth know what is needed, what is sacrificed to maintain peace. Tch, you know this, High Seraph Donnel. More so than most."

"We can fly, Zach. What. The. Fuck? That is not exactly something we keep to ourselves. These show the locations of all the vessels that seeded Neo-Earth. They show how they were built. Information on the technology that made them go to space. It's all there."

"Drop this, at once. Look, Amram. The Preneo were capable of all manner of destruction. Their problem was everything they created was a weapon. No matter how much they tried to create something else. It was impossible. That's why we don't follow their footsteps. We leave their ruins in the sand, because they are just that, ruins lost to the sand of eons."

"I'm not dropping this!" Donnel insisted, his heart pounding then and now.

"You *will*! *We* will, because I demand it. What more do you want of me? You ask for digital archives, I grant your wish. You ask for remote study centers, now they are a reality. You ask to make a suit of armor to help keep our aging friend alive. Look at him now. Can he *even* die? I expanded my vision at every juncture to incorporate your irreverent gadgetry. This is how you repay me? By ambushing me in my private study, assaulting me with accusations?"

Sandhurst poked Donnel's chest with his index finger to drive each point home. "I have entertained this outburst just long enough. High Seraph Donnel, the information you have shared today is to remain inaccessible from the study centers. And I want you to remove these entries from the Archive."

The exhilaration of his duel with Geeza Londo still coursed through his body as General Donnel reflected on the day he finally departed the Syndicate of Valor. It wasn't the same day he and Sandhurst had argued, but soon after he stormed out of Span Opticon with a group sympathetic to his ambitions. It was the beginning of his Legioneers. Reminiscing on his final moments with his former master, leader, and friend usually stirred in him a foul mood; today, it brought him joy.

* * *

Miles across Neo-Earth, Elder Sandhurst turned over his own unsettled musings. A lot occurred in the past few days and his aging mind grappled to make sense of it. With frail arms clasped at his front, he searched the massive map of Neo-Earth covering the back wall of his private office for answers.

Joan Flayr was dead by High Seraph Gunkimono's hand. Paulo Flayr, expired by the Ars. Grase Jeffroy, lay dying in Ido's custody. Elder Sandhurst knew he should be celebrating. But a pesky thing prodded him. A persisting paranoia grew at the edge of all his thoughts, preventing any jubilation. Things were unfolding all too fast. Countless hours, myriad resources, and dozens of lives had been lost over the almost twenty-year search for Paulo Flayr; and in just four days, the top three members of the Boundless Movement were killed or captured. One shot down in a popular bar and the others marched right up to the gates of Span Opticon. Joan murdered nine Seraphim during her assault, with dozens killed just as callously by Grase.

It pained the Elder deeply when Syndicate members died, but what troubled him most was the succession of the attacks—their brazenness. The Boundless Movement was not known for violence. There was the string of bombings seven years ago, he admitted, but those acts were proven to be executed by a smaller, more radical element, from within the Boundless.

But these newer events, coming on the anniversary of the Treaty, were worrisome. Senseless bloodshed on a day meant to symbolize peace, violating the seventy calm years since he realized his lifelong dream of uniting the people of Earth. It disgusted him.

The Movement meant to send a message. It was a call to arms, Sandhurst reasoned. He turned away from the replica map on his wall and to the small table at the center of the office.

He was halfway through an audio log when the alarms had sounded at Grase Jeffroy's arrival. Pressing the pause button on the sound box he let the lecture play again. It was an old recording of a speech given by a scholar long before the days of the Treaty. The subject was a rational appeal to Monarchy. Sandhurst found that it soothed his mind during trying times.

When he was younger, he agreed with the speaker's points wholeheartedly. The audio log had been a major inspiration for the founding of the Syndicate of Valor. As years passed, he began to identify the flaws in the argument. He had become so accustomed to the speaker's speech patterns, the only joy he found came simply from the familiarity of the sounds. The appeal droned on in the background. Sandhurst inched over to the table and sat. And when he thought he might achieve a moment free from the responsibilities of his post, his mind slid back to the Boundless Movement.

It would appear they were a peaceful organization no more and its leaders would lay down their lives for their new cause. Elder Sandhurst had to now accept that ordering the death of Joan Flayr may have been a grave mistake.

"Wise Hiroshi," he muttered to himself jokingly. Mobilized and incensed Boundless sympathizers now had not one warrior-martyr, but three. He imagined Joan, Paulo, and Grase as three heads of the mythological Hydra. With the main heads severed, its body writhed and wriggled in panicked pain. He feared their exponential resurgence. But that was just a story from ages upon ages ago, he resolved. It was more likely their body would wither and die without their heroes to head them.

He found the thought as comforting as the audio log and just as problematic. The speech was almost over. Sandhurst paused the sound box again.

He would not hastily revel in their fleeting victory. Gathering his strength to stand, he shuffled off to find his aides. He had another mission for High Seraph Gunkimono.

Chapter 16

Hiroshi's paranoia blossomed from fledgling bud to blooming stalk. Three days had passed with no mention of Joan. Even when he returned from his meeting with Celeste and presented Paulo's crossbow and duster to the Elders, they said nothing. No rebuke—only praise.

After the briefing, Hiroshi paid a visit to the new plot in Span Opticon's cemetery. The hasty message on the suspicious headstone read: Joan Flayr. Underneath, the dates of her birth and death. At the bottom a final line: *Executed by High Seraph.*

When Hiroshi approached Seraph Guiles, the Holding operator explained that Ido Xzaven, himself, confirmed Joan's death. Guiles elaborated by telling Hiroshi that the High Librarian asked for his eyewitness testimony and assistance with burying the body. Guiles had eagerly agreed.

Ido was covering Hiroshi's tracks.

His secret was out. Skipping his normal routines, Hiroshi confined himself to his quarters. Watching the ceiling fan spin, he waited for a Seraph to come and escort him to Holding for treason. He even guessed at who it might be. Seraph Rogelle, or Cherveyo, or Taper perhaps. Any of them would be happy to see him go.

The buzzing, signaling new orders from the Keep, sounded from the communication device near the room's door. Hiroshi rose from his bed and moved toward the machine.

"High Seraph Gunkimono."

"Keep, sir. New orders in." Hiroshi mouthed the words as the operator said them.

"Elders have asked that you attend this week's Wave. If the remnants of the Boundless Movement are planning anything, the Elders are betting it will be there. And, sir ... I heard you got Joan. Someone close to me died because of her. I just want to say thank you."

"I am sorry. You do not need to thank me," Hiroshi said, thinking of the fresh plot in the cemetery.

"Well anyway, good luck at the Wave, sir."

Hiroshi slinked from the door to the wall-mounted mirror in his room and put on his High Seraph garb layer by layer. Getting a good look at himself, he thought about the assignment.

The Elders' reasoning was sound. As the only event recorded in public and broadcast to display screens around Neo-Earth, Ecclesiel's Wave would be a high-priority target for desperate sympathizers and loyalists. The Flayrs' deaths further increased the chance of a vengeful disturbance. The Elders' wanted Hiroshi there as a precaution.

Even if the Boundless didn't show up, there was a chance Joan might. Hiroshi smiled and turned away from the mirror.

Fastening his sword and sheath to his waist, he stepped into the dull light of Span Opticon's hallways and began his trip to the mountainside settlements of Holy Lands. He would have to hurry if he wanted to catch the day's ferry. The subterranean riverway connecting the NZ to Holy Lands would be packed with boats making the same journey.

Chapter 17

The sleek vessel sliced a path down the middle of the subterranean river. If the size of the boat caused any lack in agility it was not obvious to Paulo, Joan or any other passengers. The elongated skiff weaved in between taxi and fishing boats with ease. The river's current encouraged its forward progress with unwavering enthusiasm.

The boatmen operating the ferry called back and forth to one another over the spray of the dual water jets propelling the boat. They took turns keeping the pressure high inside of the large pump required to turn the river itself into a kind of fuel.

The coordination needed for the crew to keep the ferry moving was made possible by the chemical light of the cave's resident fungus. The segments of the subterranean river network where no natural light could reach were seeded with the cultivars chosen for their size and luminosity. The achieved effect was similar to the sunlight of an overcast morning.

Watching the lantern mushrooms pass and the boatmen at work, Joan's mind was elsewhere. Vicaarian legends claimed the river once flowed west out of the mountain range, that the arrival of their Fallen is why it flows east into Holy Lands. The arms that found the small of her back then connected around her waist were swiftly rebuffed.

"Don't think you're off the hook so easily," Joan said, moving away from Paulo and making space for him at the same time. Filling the spot next to her, they leaned over the railing meant to keep passengers from spilling into the churning water of the basin. The water, protesting its captivity, splashed loud and turbulent, drowning out the conversation to any would-be eavesdropper.

"You're still mad at me?"

"No, but we have to stay in character. We aren't traveling to the Holy Lands as a couple, remember?"

"How could I forget? It was your idea."

"What's that supposed to mean?" Joan said, looking Paulo head to toe.

"Maybe we have a romantic fling on the river and break up before we land," Paulo said.

"You would like that, wouldn't you? There's only an hour or two left. Do you think that's enough time for a proper romantic fling and fallout?"

"Oh, yeah. That's right. The fallout. I didn't estimate that. You might be right. Maybe we don't have the time for any fun."

"We can still have fun." Joan bumped Paulo's hips with her own. "Why don't we skip to the courtship phase of your little ruse, and you can buy me one of those trinkets, or some flowers? Or has your status as a general ruffian made you forget how to treat a lady?"

Paulo turned to see the trinkets to which Joan referred.

"Babe, you aren't serious. You don't want any of that macabre junk ... Do you see that mother there? She's sitting a few rows up."

"Who?" Joan, maintaining her discretion, surveyed the rows

of seats at the front of the ferry, then at the back.

"Right next to the guy in the robes, the one with their hood up. Three rows back, can you see what her daughter is wearing?"

"I think so," Joan said, following Paulo's eyes to a child and mother. The child was adorned with a necklace beaded with brass caskets.

"That's about as dark as it gets. *Three* coffin charms on one baby's neck." Paulo's joke didn't elicit the laughter he expected. Joan turned her back to the basin and gave her elbows to the rail.

"Why don't we have kids?" Joan asked Paulo as much as herself. Paulo took a flask out of his breast pocket. When his lips parted with it, he responded.

"It's not too late," Paulo said, turning his gaze to the basin and crew.

"I know, Paulo. But, I mean, why don't we have one already, or two? Why didn't we make time?"

"We were off saving the world. Before our movement, Nute was a dirty word. The Neutral Zones are three times larger now than when we started. That is no accident."

"You make it sound so simple ...You don't want children, do you?"

"What? No. I mean, yes. I do. That's not what I said."

"I guess you didn't have to. We would have one if we wanted them."

"You're simplifying things."

"The vendor is walking this way. He has more than coffins. Look sharp."

A small and sturdy man approached Paulo and Joan. His sea legs developed to such a degree that his knees bent and braced automatically with and against the bobbing of the speeding boat. While others wisely chose to sit or support themselves against railings, the vendor made his rounds with a duffel of wares as though the vessel were never in motion.

"You look like a trusted pair of Nutes," the vendor said, greeting them from a few scorchfeet away and talking the whole time as he neared. "I know just the thing for pilgrims like yourselves. Her dress and sling." He pointed to Joan's outfit and shoulder. "Says, 'I've been to the Holy Lands before and know I'm not leaving with a husband.' Your sky-blue ascot." He pointed to Paulo's necktie. "Says, 'New to this, but I know there's more to life than trusts.' Am I right? You don't have to tell me. It's our secret."

The vendor was forward and confident, things Paulo normally enjoyed in others when they weren't used to separate him from trusts. Swinging his bag of trinkets around from back to his chest, the vendor unzipped it and revealed separate compartments for his various goods.

In no loyal order were circlets, earrings, chaplets, finger rings, belts, and anklets all with assorted engravings or pendants displaying Vicaarian's unique addition to the rich history of religious symbols: the Casket Trey. The bag contained moon, star, haloed planet, anchor, ankh, and ohm charms too; but the three coffins theme dominated the vendor's selection, clarifying the local preference. Blue bundles wrapped in twine were tucked beside single flowers of various colors which themselves poked out of their compartments above, glimmering tokens, and shining beads.

Clearing his throat the vendor said, "I can tell by those expressions you need a little help. Here." He handed them each a bundle of blue. "You're gonna need these if you're headed to the Wave."

"What are they?" Joan asked, tossing the tightly rolled cloth between her palms.

"Hood and half cape, in Vicaarian blue and water resistant in case it rains," the vendor explained.

"Thank you," said Paulo. "I'd like three flowers as well. Is that a book of matches?"

"Of course, to ignite torches for the Lighting Ceremony," said the vendor. Paulo reached into his breast pocket. His fist returned plush with trusts.

"Okay, so three flowers, three capes, and a novel of matches. What do we owe you?"

The vendor bobbed his head from side to side as if the act itself were lowering his prices.

"The Vicaarian blues are two for twenty, fifteen for the third. Flowers. Are three each, and the matches—the matches you can have on the house."

"Thanks," Joan said, stuffing the caped and hooded poncho into a pocket with her good arm.

"No, thank you. It's good to see newcomers and first timers in our fine country. Our borders are open to all and Ecclesiel welcomes larger and larger crowds each week." Delivering a cocked-head bow, the merchant left to continue his rounds.

When it was safe to converse again, Joan asked, "Who are the extra blues for?"

"Grase," Paulo said. Joan didn't immediately respond. "We haven't heard from her. But she knows the plan, she'll be there." Knowing her friend would fight fang and fist to avoid capture, Joan was unconvinced by Paulo's optimism.

Before setting out for the Wave, Joan and Paulo held a brief meeting with Boundless loyalists in NZ Minor, the smallest Neutral Zone located east of Virtus and west of Holy Lands.

117

There they learned of the far-reaching and disastrous impact the rumor of their deaths wreaked on their movement. The importance of their journey to the Wave was solidified. If the attempt to hijack Ecclesiel's broadcast failed, the Boundless network would continue to shrivel and eventually collapse without the scaffold of its primary leaders and strategists. After the affirmation of her and Paulo's quest, their NZ Minor contacts also confirmed that no reports, be they sights or sounds, included Grase's whereabouts since her explosive arrival in Virtus two days prior.

"Paulo ..."

"She's easily the toughest woman we know. It won't just be her either, you'll see others will show up."

"Paulo!" Joan said louder than she should have and slammed the basin rail for emphasis. "You heard what they said. 'No sight or sound.' I hope she's headed here, babe, I really do. I just think we should plan for the event that she doesn't show up, that she won't be back at Libyrinth waiting for us. That she's still at Span Opticon, or even worse. Dead."

"She's not fuckin' dead! Even if she was, she gave her life to see you free. And you are free."

"We should go get her. Everyone thinks we're dead already anyway. If you say we ride this boat back to the Neutral Zone, make our way to Virtus, find or bust Grase out, I will do it. Just ask me to."

"You know that's not fair," Paulo said, removing a joint from the cigarette pack in his breast pocket and lighting it. Paulo took a drag. The smoke turned over in his mouth and between his teeth before being released from his nose like a glowering bull to the constant wind of their forward motion. "Love, we agreed this was the best way. We decided that getting word out to our network over the Wave was our best chance to save this thing we dedicated our lives to, Grase included."

"She risked everything for me. I owe her the same in return."

"We owe her more than reciprocation. We owe her assurance that loyalty to our cause meant something, and still means something. Killing can't be the only way to show people on this spacedamned rock a better way."

"You say Grase wouldn't let you come after me, that you tried. Could be. Could be you're a coward. Scared to do what is right, so you're running."

"Everything looks like a nail to you, Joan. I don't know what you want from me. I'm just the tool who married a hammer." Paulo abandoned their posts at the basin and retreated to an empty seat at the back of the ferry.

After protracted minutes Joan left the basin and its dutiful crew to find Paulo. She found him, sucking away at a cigarette, or joint, she wasn't sure. Ignoring the open seats to either side of Paulo, Joan took a seat in the row in front of him. Leaning over the back of her seat with an outstretched arm she assumed the role of her disguise.

"Quit hoggin' that thing, will ya'. Lemme get a hit," Joan said. Hesitating, Paulo inhaled one last time before passing it to Joan.

"It's just a cigarette."

"All the same," Joan said and puffed away.

The ferry slid out of the subterranean riverway and found its usual docking place underneath Holy Lands' main hub. The mouth of the cave formed like hands that wished to clasp; one on the ceiling, the other mostly submerged in water with only its clawed fingertips above the surface. Held between each finger was enough space for the ferry and another boat to squeeze comfortably through. The river continued on without its hitchers deeper into the inaccessible depth of the earth.

The vendor, the mother, her daughter, the Flayrs with their disguises, and all the other passengers shuffled off the vessel. The boatmen crew remained at the dock to prepare for the return trip as the others continued their venture.

Joan entered the crowd first. Paulo, never allowing more than two people between them, sulked behind her. Moving like a fabrication center conveyor belt, the pilgrims made their spasmodic ascent to ground level up a tight staircase, dyed green at its base by algae.

The amphitheater stage that hosted the Wave was hidden amid the towering peaks of the mountain range and tucked away in an elevated valley made accessible by a maze of stone burrows.

A cobbled switchback led to the loading area where three personnel lifts, reinforced and modified to carry dozens at once, went up full, came down empty, then repeated the process. Joan and Paulo were separated at the lifts but found each other inside the rolling crowd as it inched through the mountain caves.

The roar of a thousand voices and four times as many hands and feet, all babbling, clapping, and stomping in feverish excitement signaled the end of their journey. The sounds echoed through the tunnel and intensified near it's exit.

The evening sunlight revealed the enormousness of the gathering as the tunnel emptied its occupants into the packed seating area of the Holy Land's Amphitheater. The broadcast would start as soon as Ecclesiel, who was nowhere to be seen, took the stage.

Chapter 18

Before the three stone coffins of the Fallen, sealed long before he inherited the title Illumined One, Ecclesiel cleared his mind. Approaching the middle sarcophagus ceremoniously, he knelt; clasping his hands together he rested his elbow on the cold stone coffin, closed his eyes, then began to pray.

It was here, at the top level of Benben Observatory, prior to every sermon he came to practice, pray or just be alone with his thoughts. The mausoleum was humble and bare. Large enough to fit twenty or thirty people inside but containing nothing but the coffins and a large blue candle.

A cadre of robed holy men, insisting on accompanying him, stood guard outside the mausoleum. Shuffling about noisily and nervously—making it harder for Ecclesiel to focus.

The Illuminated harbored no ill will, for they were his trusted Inner Circle, a skittish and apprehensive bunch of his top advisors. On the other side of the heavy velvet tarp the Vicaarians used as doors, huddled together in debate were Girabaldi Growsch, Master of Politics, Barwyn Micah, Master of Religions, Opal Danfreet, Master of History, Jewells Folami, Master of Philosophy and Nadir Ming, Master of

Logistics. Without them, the current operation at Holy Lands was impossible. With them, concentrating was currently impossible.

Ecclesiel ambled to his feet and pressed his ears up against the velvet. They were bickering, back and forth shushing and hushing each other only when the topic or volume threatened to get too loud.

The anniversary of the Treaty had always been a time of excitement, but with the rumors of attacks on Span Opticon and the death of Paulo Flayr circulating, this year proved to be enough to drive his already apprehensive aides to the edge of paranoia.

"We shouldn't all be gathered in one place," Nadir said, talking over whatever petty debate was taking place.

"It's best we stick together," Opal Danfreet countered in a much quieter voice, meant to set an example for the others. "Just imagine what a threat that could harm us as a group would do to us individually ... It's a risk, but a calculated one."

"It makes no difference. If there exists a threat that could strike us all, one by one, it wouldn't be deterred in the slightest if we remain together. Our only hope ... is to hope no all-encompassing danger approaches. And to pray that the Fallen protect us." Barwyn Micah said.

"Hopes and prayers will do us no better than a rope made from sand, you know this, Barwyn," said Nadir Ming.

"In time, all ropes are sand," Opal added quietly.

"That is how you feel? Maybe you should just go right in there and tell the Illumined One how *little* you value his prayers," Barwyn said, goading Nadir.

"No, I—I only meant ..."

"What *did* you mean?" Jewells Folami pried.

Pushing the folds aside Ecclesiel stuck out his head. "Am I interrupting a fruitful debate?"

"Of course not, Father, what fruits could compare to those which spring from the fertile spirit of man?" Barwin Micah answered before anyone else could—simultaneously extending his arm to assist Ecclesiel down the stairs that led to the amphitheater below. The other advisors shot the Master of Religion various looks of mild annoyance to visible irritation—all making sure Ecclesiel did not notice. Even if they argued about the extent of their faith and its usefulness in the day to day, they all observed devout silence as they made the symbolic trip from the top of the crystalline mausoleum.

Benben Observatory loomed over the Holy Lands. Carved from a single, gargantuan piece of quartz crystal, it was erected in the time of the Fall atop the highest peak by a group of secretive mystics—the same group of mystics credited with the founding of Vicaarism.

Some say they built the quartz observatory at the direct request of the Fallen, others say inspired by the Fallen's sacrifice, the monument is a gesture of appreciation, and still, others claim it was erected by the Fallen themselves as a beacon, marking the landing spot of their ultimate descent.

Older Vicaarians said the crystal had been excavated from deep within the earth. Younger Vicaarians claimed the crystal could only have come from the vastness of space. The specific reasons for the observatory's construction were lost to time, but the associated traditions endured.

Twelve times a year the candle at the top was lit. The subtle imperfections in a crystal of that size and clarity exaggerated the energetic dance of flames resulting in a magnification of the flickering candle across Neo-Earth. On a clear night, the jumping flames could be seen as far east as Virtus. Other credible sightings claimed the candlelight of Benben Observatory reached past the Walls of Pangaia into the forests beyond. The Lighting ritual was performed once a month, every month, since the founding of the Holy Lands.

Ecclesiel could move mountains with his words but the idea of climbing the steps, not once but twice in one day, weighed heavily on his spirit. He was no longer a young man, already older than his predecessor from whom he inherited his title. The Aging One would have been an equally appropriate name, he chuckled to himself. If he could make the infernal trip once a month, twelve times a year, for just three more years, he would be the longest serving Illumine on record. He didn't want the accolade for himself, instead he wanted his people to be a part of something special—wanted them to spread his word and uphold his legacy, not just with humility in their actions but pride in their hearts. The people of the Holy Lands loved Ecclesiel, and he adored them in return. 'Beloved by his people' wasn't the only superlative that mattered to him. Ecclesiel truly meant to be a role model to Vicaarians and others. Even for the beloved it was not easy.

As much as he leaned into, even enjoyed the power and pageantry of his station, he endeavored to embody its importance. He reminded himself daily that he was only a man, a physical medium by which Vicaarism could touch more and more lives. His post was a temporary one and would be fulfilled by another just like him. That which made the Illumined a pillar among the people belonged to the people and not the man who held the post. Ecclesiel remembered how much they loved the previous Illumined One, and all his advisors agreed that he was loved far more. The size of their congregation was the evidence.

Under Ecclesiel, the Vicaar became the largest faction on Neo-Earth, their numbers swelled two to three times beyond that of his predecessor Godfrey the Enlightened. True, he owed much of his success to the Legioneers making it possible for his sermons to touch people all over the globe. But the Wave only made accessible what was already good, and the values of the Vicaar owed nothing to Amram's lot. Quelling the thoughts, Ecclesiel reassured himself of his independence.

Growsch, Micah, Danfreet, Folami, and Ming hovered close to their aging leader as he slowly made his way down. Each one watched for any sign of weakness, fatigue or affliction to be the one to offer an arm, shoulder, or drink of water as assistance. When they reached ground level and exited through the reinforced velvet tarps, Danfreet and Nadir began to bicker.

"We should have just kept the height of this place in feet," Danfreet grumbled, resting on a railing with one arm.

"Feet, scorchfeet the distance remains the same," Folami tried to douse any argument with reason.

"Our understanding of the world expands throughout the years. Why not our measurement?" Ming defended the system.

"I'm just saying, the place was built in feet. If a scorchfoot is one and one-half foot, then this place was shorter when they built it. If I could snap my finger and revert it back, we'd be back on the ground already."

"Fallen, catch us," Barwyn Micah said. Smiling to himself, Ecclesiel knew Danfreet's argument was facetious at best and nonsensical at worst. But that did not stop the aging leader from wishing it true.

Exiting the base of the observatory, the advisers formed a protective clump around the Illumined. Their formation shuffled off to the Holy Land's Amphitheater to begin preparations for the commemorative Wave.

Chapter 19

Ecclesiel the Illuminated was the epitome of magnetism. He could coerce and conduct the crowd with any gesture or movement. Sunspots adorned his leathery face and gentle innocence emanated in his eyes. Gaunt, chiseled, and stern, he always kept his head front-facing. Where he looked, his body followed. Ecclesiel the Illuminated, Keeper of the History of the Fallen, beloved leader and savior of the Vicaarians. Milking an exaggerated hunch, Ecclesiel shuffled forward, steady, but never too fast.

Entering stage right, he assumed his position at the stone podium centered at the staging area of Holy Amphitheater. It was here, every week, once a week for over 1,560 weeks straight, he preached. It was here tens of thousands of souls gathered for their exaltation. His sermon was their directive.

He cleared his throat into the voice capturing compartment of the podium and the undulating seas of followers stilled like frosty blades of grass. Rows upon rows of silent souls all adorned in blue shoulder hoods and half-capes. Some held hands, others interlocked elbows. The most devout lifted hands above their heads, surrendering all to their prophet.

Three figures continued their course through the eager mass.

With hoods hiding their faces and several devout Vicaarians between them, Paulo trailed Joan. Identifying a woman that matched Joan's profile and an unknown assailant, Hiroshi pursued unseen.

Joan moved from pocket to pocket, waiting for Paulo to close the distance, but never risking a glance back. If anyone saw them before they reached the podium, their plan would be foiled and their pilgrimage for naught.

Ecclesiel began. "Another week. Another toil, sisters, brothers, never foiled." The crowd exploded into shouts of adulation. Joan elbowed her way onward, a bit faster now, using the moment of unfettered passion as cover. With Paulo never far behind, they raced to arrive before Ecclesiel concluded.

He continued. "My, my, it's been an eventful week, hasn't it?" he asked no one in particular, pausing to let his people respond. More adulation. The Flayrs increased speed, parting the mass with withering regard. Camouflaged by the crowded sea, Hiroshi stalked their wake like a patient eel shark.

"You all have likely been hearing rumors. I'll address them. Yes, a wicked bunch *did* attack Span Opticon, twice. That wicked bunch has been brought to justice. The fugitives Joan Flayr, Paulo Flayr, and Grase Jeffroy. Guilty of illegal reproductions of our holy documents and defamation of the Fallen, have ascended to their first homes. The Flayrs at the hands of the Ars Femina and Grase by the Seraphim of the Syndicate. The Boundless Movement has been gutted—stricken grave by a mortal blow. The Fallen have answered our wishes again. Further proof that our labor goes not in vain. With 'the Blasphemous Movement' in tatters their members will need new homes—open arms and hearts ready to show them the way. Your arms and hearts. They need you now as I need you every day. Heal their troubled, misguided souls with forgiveness and grace."

The rabble swayed and shook with every beat. They offered up unquestioning loyalty with silent reverence or sporadic shouts. Energized by Ecclesiel's radiance, the fervor grew to a feverish pitch.

Joan jogged. Behind her, Paulo trotted. Behind him, Hiroshi closed in.

Ecclesiel was getting comfortable. He adjusted his weight and placed both hands on the podium. A scuffle, erupting on stage to the left of the Illumined One, caught Joan's attention. She slowed her approach. Paulo, not seeing what was happening ahead, sped up to meet her.

Ecclesiel, noticing the commotion, held a hand over his eyes to get a better look. Hiroshi, ignoring all of this, zeroed in on Joan's pursuer. Ecclesiel, flashing a smile and seeing a bouquet of flowers, waved over to the man who started the scuffle.

"These are for you!" the man cried with genuine excitement.

"Who the hell are you?" Hiroshi whispered into the ear of Joan's follower, blade tip at their back.

"He just wants to give me flowers," Ecclesiel said to the crowd, still smiling. The man with the bouquet moved to center stage.

"I'm—I'm," Paulo stammered. Forgoing his alias, he fished for the replica persuader in his pocket. Joan's eyes stayed fixed ahead, watching what everyone else watched.

Three persuader shots rang out. The entire mass descended into utter chaos. Ecclesiel's smile turned to a frown. The bouquet rippled and flickered in the light, two more shots split the air, carried by the perfect acoustics of the stone amphitheater. The man caught Ecclesiel in his arms and held him close. The bouquet shivered one last time, directing Ecclesiel's brain matter to exit stage left.

Hiroshi, hearing shots, stabbed his quarry clean through. The man with the bouquet disappeared into the crowd like a ghost. Ecclesiel laid out, leaking at center stage. His people ran everywhere but towards the podium. Fear overwrote their senses.

Paulo's hand fell from within his cloak, still clutching a flask made to resemble a persuader. Joan turned to see Hiroshi wipe Paulo's blood on her husband's corpse. Flicking the flask away with his sword, Hiroshi nodded at his score and smiled an expectant half-smile. Joan met his gaze with a look of incurable horror married with rending sadness. Even with the sky falling around them, everything became clear. Looking down, Hiroshi realized who he had killed.

He retreated into the crowd. Shame burned him to his very core, threatening to melt away his very being. Hiroshi fled. He fled from Joan, from Paulo, from Sandhurst. He ran, following the frantic crowds deeper in the caverns of the Holy Lands.

Paulo did not crawl or twitch. There was little blood. His face displayed no final grimace of vengeance or sublime expression, just blankness. An individual known for his boldness and vigor passed plainly, a blue hooded figure amid blue hooded figures. Paulo Flayr 'the Most Wanted Man on Neo-Earth' had died days earlier at Depot. Paulo Flayr, the Loyal and Loving Husband to Joan Flayr died that day, right before the eyes of his widow, killed by her guardian angel of death, in a case of mistaken identity.

Joan lied down next to Paulo and cried.

Vicaarians gathered their courage and returned to the stage.

Healers were among them. Ecclesiel the Illuminated was scooped onto a gurney and swooped away to a secluded area. His people would try, but no intervention would succeed; resurrection lived only in the realm of their parables and myths. Ecclesiel's light was extinguished.

Another group moved toward Joan and Paulo and collected the inseparable pair. When the Vicaarians explained their customary burial rights to Joan, she insisted on being present every step of the way, but she did not argue. Their plan had failed. The Boundless Movement was presumed shattered. Joan lacked the manpower and the energy to bring Paulo to an NZ, so he was to be buried far from home in the peaks of the Holy Lands.

Chapter 20

The Holy Lands were afire with panicked excitement and chaos. Those who called the branching network of apartments and meeting areas carved directly into the mountain range home, rushed to their respective pockets of safety. Others who had only ventured to the region to hear Ecclesiel speak in person, made their way out as quickly as possible. The confused jumble of faces and shoulders brushing past one another, too nervous to give a greeting or ask directions, packed into the narrow tunnels designed for the single file religious processions of the Vicaarians; ill fit for emergency egress.

Hiroshi watched a group of Nutes head for an exit then became their shadow. Shuffling along the tunnelway, he followed the somber crowd until it split at a forking segment.

One tunnel led back home to Span Opticon, the other to the Perennial Plains and Motopia. Hiroshi chose the path with fewer travelers and hoped to remain unrecognized. An arrow above the word *Ferry* written into the tunnel wall ahead signaled the exit. He quickened his pace.

Before Hiroshi reached the mouth of the tunnel, something stopped his progress. It was no physical object hindering him, but a flash of motion caught by his eye. A hand reached from the shadows, landing squarely and firmly on his shoulder. At the same time, Hiroshi's own hand landed on the hilt of his sword.

"Hiro, wait." A mouth belonging to the unknown hand whispered, "It's me, your brother." A body connected to the mouth stepped out of the darkness hiding its form. With a finger over his mouth, Saigo Gunkimono beckoned Hiroshi into the shade. "We need to talk."

Slipping into a secluded passage, the elder led the younger to a nook hidden from view and far enough away from the main tunnel to soften their voices. At its center, a pool fed on water dripping from a crevice in the ceiling. Two seats, worn directly into the wall, were present at either side of the pool.

Satisfied with their privacy, Hiroshi attacked. The men wrestled, tumbling about the confines of the alcove. A hip throw carried Hiroshi into the air. When his back impacted the ground and the breath rushed from his trunk there was no mistaking the identity of his opponent. The contest came to a brief pause when Saigo Gunkimono dragged the High Seraph along the ground and to the edge of the pool. With his neck and head held in place Hiroshi was forced to look at the reflecting image.

"Look at yourself. You're soft as shit. Are the stories of your combat prowess simply myth? We are still brothers, but I see things aren't as before. We stand now on opposite shores. Watching the ebbing, flowing tides of war."

Catching his brother by surprise, Hiroshi reversed the hold and their positions. With Saigo's face pressed close to the water's surface, Hiroshi said, "A decade has passed since we last met, when you cast me aside, making me believe I have been alone this whole time. I need to know one thing, Sai. Not where have you been or why? I just want to know, what did I do to make you leave?"

Cloudy droplets of saline tumbling down Hiroshi's cheek disturbed the reflecting image of the two brothers. The ripples mixed and intensified. The effect transported Saigo back in time. As his mouth moved, as he explained away his absence to his younger brother, he was already in the past.

He had just returned from a covert mission bestowed upon him from inside the Chamber of the Elders. The operation had required travel far, wide, and fast; so, he was tired. But the briefcase he had recovered contained secrets with implications that would keep him up all night. He remembered thinking that the contents would please Elder Sandhurst; instead, the Elder was furious. Sandhurst demanded that the briefcase and all within be removed from Virtus then destroyed, that no one was to know of what had been discovered, not even his fellow Elders.

"I asked you to find the location of past cities, instead you bring me a case full of persuaders and artifacts," Sandhurst had said. "I asked for knowledge of our past and you bring the fruits of our blunders. Blueprints and doodles of those infernal machines I wish to rid the planet of. I asked you to shine light on our origins and you bring back tools to darken our future." Those were Zachariah Sandhurst's exact words, untarnished by the temporal bias of memory.

Never showing his anger or embarrassment, Saigo recalled returning to his room. The emotions he bottled then threatened to well up in the present. Calming himself and continuing his story, he returned to his reverie. He was in bed when the power of his curiosity, the magnetic tug from the back of his mind, had finally caused him to reopen and thoroughly examine the case.

Removing the weapons, it was like he could feel them again, even as he watched himself place them aside. Underneath the persuaders lay an assortment of papers; old and fragile and yellow like Elder Sandhurst's skin, like the documents deep within the heart of the Archives, like ancient bones lathered in ceremonial ocher. The documents were blueprints of a gigantesque machine.

The points of interest had been conveniently circled in red by the Feral-men guides that aided in the discovery. One page in particular stood out then and stayed fresh in Saigo's mind as time progressed.

On the page, four crimson ovals around four bulbous constructs were located at the posterior edges of the machine. Each labeled: *Engine.* On the reverse side of the page were four smaller pictures. The first picture showed people walking inside the machine. The second, dust gathered about the four engines. The third, light bursting from the engines, appeared to lift the machine into the air. The last image on the page showed it floating among the stars.

The Feral-men guides that had helped find the briefcase claimed to know the location of similar engines, and that they regularly sold pieces of them to General Donnel. Learning of the existence of spacefaring ships was groundbreaking, but it was what the Feral-men told him before they went separate ways that would define his transformation.

They told him the weapon in the case was a persuader; as a High Seraph, he knew that already. Though he never held a real one prior, he saw many different models in History class as a child. The Feral-men told him the persuader was special, different from what they were used to uncovering, that the long cylindrical attachment fixed at the weapons tip was likely a sound suppressor, saying only that, they had said enough.

Once his guides left, he fired the weapon. There was no sound but his beating heart. Reliving the exhilaration of falling in love, he remembered easily understanding how and why a High Seraph like Amram Donnel left the Syndicate. He recalled coddling the persuader, running his fingers down what he would later learn was the weapon's barrel.

"My choice seemed so simple back then, the saber or the persuader. The Syndicate or dishonor. The allure, the power. It was inebriating. I made the decision right then and there. It was the easiest thing I had ever done," Mr. Galtero said.

Hiroshi held his brother no longer. He had backed away minutes earlier, and his expression remained the same since. He shook his head from side to side as if the act alone could alter reality and change the truth about the man in front of him, the man who gazed into the pool, his brother.

"I visited you that night as you slept," Mr. Galtero said, with his back to Hiroshi. Rising slowly, but never averting his gaze from the water, he went on. "Sneaking in and out of your room was the hard part. Damn me to space, if I didn't want to wake you up to say goodbye. You were so passionate, even then, you would have insisted on coming along or killed me for trying to leave the Syndicate. I could accept neither. Hoping you would come find me, I left my blade atop a neatly folded stack of clothes at the foot of your bed. You never did seek me out." A single bead of liquid salt joined his brothers in the shimmering pond. "That's how I knew Sandhurst had gotten to you somehow. He was all too eager to groom you in my place. It was only months later when the rumors of disappearance and death landed on my fugitive ears. I created Mr. Galtero to escape my past, but I became the Ghost to keep you safe. To keep the complications of the real world and the ramifications of my actions away from you for as long as possible."

"You? *You* are the *fucking* assassin!" Hiroshi said, all but spitting. "That is why you look like *this*! Are you wearing a mask of skin?"

"They're prosthetics for my disguises."

"Look at yourself, Former High Seraph Saigo Gunkimono. You do not need a mask. You have walked so far from the light, you are unrecognizable."

"It's Mr. Galtero."

Hiroshi released the sword and scabbard from his hip and examined it between his hands.

"If you left this sword for me, Sandhurst made sure to intercept it. *His* decision is what determined when I ultimately received it."

Turning in place, Mr. Galtero cocked his head and said, "The name of the blade is Cordis Adolesco. Did Sandhurst tell you *that*? It means a lot of things. Mostly, Bleeding Heart. I drafted the design myself. Ido gave me unsupervised access to the Archives while I worked. Combining what I learned there, with what High Seraph Donnel taught me before his departure, allowed me to finish the sword ahead of schedule. I hid it. Afraid to lose unrestricted access to all that knowledge. It was in my time spent trolling the Archives of the Syndicate that I first began to see the inconsistencies in what was taught to me as a child and what the Preneo felt it important for us to know. To remember."

"Well—I ... It does not matter now, does it?" Hiroshi said, throwing Cordis Adolesco to the ground between them. "You make your reasons seem justified, like you left to pursue the truth, or you stayed away to protect me, maybe. But I just saw you kill a man, possibly one of the few good guys left. You lured him in under pretense of praise then snuffed him out with a persuader. What logic is this?"

"Are you listening to me? Forget Ecclesiel. The information in Virtus' study centers is incomplete. Check for yourself, if Ido will let you. These omissions are Sandhurst's doing. Ideas he wishes to stay hidden within the myriad rows of the Archives. Concepts created in this world, but long ago, that make his peace impossible. Notions that contradict what we've been taught, told, or sold. Sandhurst has the Ars Femina poised to kill or suppress any enemies of the Treaty. *His* treaty. That's what the Syndicate of Valor is about. If you want to know the true function of a High Seraph, imagine yourself as a padlock on the gate of a great corral, never anything more than an object unflinching, unthinking, unwavering in its dedication to duty. Inside the corral is truth, outside of it bleating and begging to be sheared are Sandhurst's sheep."

Mr. Galtero, never taking his eyes off his younger brother, crouched to retrieve the sword. Fondling the weapon with familiarity, he wrapped his fist around the hilt, assuming his old stance.

"Well spoken, Ghost. You sound like my brother. You hold the stance of a Seraph, but there's no valor in your life, *assassin*. Worse than a Nute who chooses nothing, you choose wrong."

"Oh? And you're the enlightened voice of reason, right? Says who? *Your* authority is that of an ancient bureaucrat that exploits your talents for personal gain."

"I walk the path of a High Seraph! I practice the ways of valor taught to me by Zachariah Sandhurst. The same man who took you in. Took me in. Sandhurst raised me, you left. You turned your back on me, Sandhurst opened his arms. He is my master as he was yours, and his wishes are my will. Obedience, Loyalty, Valor, the virtues of a High Seraph." Mr. Galtero's sly smile took on a sinister quality.

"But I have your sword. I disarmed you with mere words. Yet, my words fail to convince you. Could be I've taken the wrong approach. I will clarify the situation. If you walk away from this cave alive it's because I've allowed it. If you get back to Span Opticon and report what I've told you, it will have been because I let you leave. You call me an *assassin*. But death is exactly what I wish to avoid."

"Why not pull a persuader on me? I hear you can be quite convincing with one of those."

"I didn't have to. You gave me your weapon. *My* weapon. I don't have time to waste, so listen up. Elder Sandhurst manipulates you. He sees in you exactly what he saw in me, uncommon potential. Sandhurst isn't loyal to you, Hiroshi. He needs you. The Syndicate of Valor is nothing without its Seraphim, the Seraphim stymied without their High Seraph. When there are no more blind subjects to obstruct access to the Archives, the information within will be free again. If you walk away, the General and I can take care of the rest. Think of the lives we could save, the lives we could improve."

"We do not simply protect the Archives. We safeguard all knowledge and insure its preservation in history." Hiroshi batted at the air as he spoke. "You know this better than any. We live in this age of reconstruction because the wars of the Preneo destroyed the previous and once numerous repositories of knowledge, not because of Elder Sandhurst. You cannot throw the ills of the world at his feet."

"That's the thing, Hiro," Mr. Galtero said, then sucked his teeth. "I know it feels like that, looks like that, but perception is not reality. Sandhurst is no monster. I would never leave you with a monster." Cordis Adolesco wavered in Galtero's grasp. "The Treaty of Neo-Earth ended an era of warlords and wanton violence, true. Sandhurst conceived the Syndicate of Valor from sweat alone and built its foundations upon his two shoulders, true again. He is a powerful man, too powerful, like an opportunistic fungus he chokes, smothers, and feeds on anything outside of Virtus with control, censorship, and secrecy. Sandhurst's society exists within a culture that has elevated him to a status safe from criticism. If he were an overt villain, easily deposed, I would have returned to kill him years ago."

"I never would have allowed it," Hiroshi said, crossing his arms and stepping closer to Cordis Adolesco, Galtero, and the pond behind him.

"It is bigger than you, or I. Sandhurst even."

"What is? What are you talking about? The reason you killed Ecclesiel?" Hiroshi said, shortening the distance between their feet.

"Stay right there, kid. Don't step any closer to me. Ecclesiel was a favor for a friend."

"General Donnel?"

Releasing a sigh through his teeth. "You think he's my master, don't you? Not even the General controls me. I answer only to the shadows. In return, I've been given my unique per-spective. Control, not peace. Power, not preservation. Those are the true forms of the Syndicate. Sandhurst knows, *we* don't. With that imbalance, he intends to create infinite inequality. These aren't just matters of theory and conversation, the truth

I deliver begs urgency, begs conviction."

"Tell me. Help me connect the dots."

"War is coming, Hiroshi. Not combat—war—just like the bad old days. And no matter what Ecclesiel or Sandhurst said or say, shunning technology will not save us from it. I'm not asking you to forgive what I have done. I'm asking you to come to Motopia and see for yourself why I did it."

"I refuse. Until I speak with Sandhurst and the Elders myself, I stand by the Syndicate."

"With my sword so close to your throat, I want you to really think about what I'm saying: If you go back to Span Opticon there may never be another opportunity like this one for us."

"Opportunity? What is the point of this? You leave then say, 'I had to.' You reappear, and all you have to say is 'because.' When I ask 'why?', you speak vaguely. I've walked this earth for over two decades and then some, and encountered multiplying mysteries, but murder being wrong is not one of them. It is cut as clear as day."

"It's not about mysteries at all," Galtero said. Cordis Adolesco balanced on its tip between the ground and the Ghost's two palms. "We can fly. The Floating City of Motopia isn't chained to its post to keep it up, the chains keep it anchored down. Humans of the Pre-Scorch Period were once so knowledgeable of your so-called mysteries they could travel the stars as easily as you walk the roads of Virtus."

Hiroshi said nothing.

"I need to get going," Mr. Galtero said. Still balancing the sword, he slid his hand up his wrist and glanced at a watch. "If I were you, I wouldn't take too long to think about what I said here. Once you do, find me at Motopia, and I'll show you everything I couldn't tell you from there ... If I hear you following me *now*, I will shoot, so don't."

Cordis Adolesco careened through the air and plopped into the shallow puddle with a splash—Mr. Galtero, gone. Hiroshi didn't follow his brother. Retrieving Cordis Adolesco, Hiroshi found the edge of a stone seat. With his sword on his hip, his head in his hands, and elbows on knees, the High Seraph sat unmoving.

Chapter 21

Mountains shrank at Hiroshi's back as his despair grew ever larger before him. There seemed no distance great enough between the amphitheater and he to evade the dismal truth. He had unwittingly and unmistakably killed Paulo Flayr, impaling him with all the sloppiness and intention of a knee-jerk reflex. The dried blood smeared and speckled on his sleeves was a constant reminder.

Bewilderment and sorrow were his companions in the isolation of the plains. Word of Paulo Flayr's death had reached Span Opticon a days ago. He thought Paulo deceased before journeying to Pangaia or pursuing Joan to the Holy Lands.

Guilt drove Hiroshi out of the Holy Lands. Curiosity drew him towards Motopia. He was in no hurry to face what waited for him back at Span Opticon. Joan was at large and Ecclesiel was dead.

The Syndicate had paid a false bounty. Whoever died at Depot was not Paulo Flayr. Who in space was it? Did it matter? Hiroshi asked himself, stopping for a moment to admire the sight of the Perennial Plains sprawled out before him.

Grass, bushels of plants, a tree here and there, tufts of brush, flowery patches, and on the western horizon, a metallic column of black rose from the verdant flatlands. Undisturbed nature, serene and innocent, then the Flying City of Motopia, the Legioneers' hovering citadel and Hiroshi's destination.

Clouds gathered and stirred, spilling across the sky towards the ominous pillar, wrapping it in a silver, velvet blanket. He had been briefed with detailed drawings of the stronghold, from outside and within. The artist, though talented, was unable to fully capture in full Motopia's peculiarity.

The Perennial Plains, though exceedingly beautiful, were rife with danger. Wildlife and scavengers alike made the plains their home and protected them fiercely. The precautionary call of a dust hawk set the tone.

Faction members rarely ventured this far east. Everything between the Holy Lands' Mountain range and the ocean was accepted as Feral-men territory, even if not specifically defined in the Treaty of Neo-Earth. Ignorance and fear seemed reason enough to keep people west of the Holy Lands. Even the Nutes, experienced with and knowledgeable of Neo-Earth's landscape, avoided the area.

Here, General Donnel erected his city. Only a brave soul or a fool would wander this far away from civilization without excessive protection or clandestine knowledge. Hiroshi had neither. The High Seraph scanned the grasslands for movement, laying a restless hand on the levered hilt of Cordis Adolesco. No collectors, neowolves, or giant monitor lizards. No dusk foxes, or man-eaters to be seen, just a herd of demi-bison, grazing in the distance.

Hiroshi removed his shoes, still stained with Paulo's blood, and walked straight for hours. Straight towards Motopia. Straight towards his estranged brother and strange secrets.

Chapter 22

The cool crunch, the tiny pokes and pinches of twigs and brush at his feet distracted Hiroshi from his weighty thoughts, even if only for tiny moments. When it seemed he had finally reached a state free of musings and worries, the ground rumbled; churning at his feet, it formed a turbulent, choppy dimple. Soot and stone, siphoned into the earthy cyclone growing at the dimple's center, then ejected up into the air.

Stumbling backward and shielding his eyes from the falling debris with one hand, Hiroshi thought he saw something moving just below the surface of the dirt, eyes maybe—beady, sinister eyes. An ovoid crest of disturbed soil encircled Hiroshi. The dimple swelled up into a small mound with him atop.

The bewildered High Seraph surveyed his surroundings again, this time seeing the unmistakable metallic shine of collectors scurrying towards him. He recalled the pictures from the Archives and the short entry below: '*Collector: See king collector. Greater Plain Scavengers. Little to no domesticity. Isolated in the plains, their broods have little competition for metal scraps. Fossil records suggested collectors survived the Scorch Period and have eked out an existence for thousands of years.*

Fiercely territorial and more intelligent than their coastal relatives.'

The collectors swarmed closer. A precise backflip landed Hiroshi away from the swell, as clumps of sediment fell away from the mound like chiseled stone, revealing the menacing sculpture underneath.

It was a king collector. No drawings had been available, and Hiroshi doubted any image could capture the elegance and might of such a thing. Fully emerged, the creature stood nearly five scorchfeet tall with a six scorchfoot diameter. All varieties of metal weapons and flattened scraps were fused to its carapace. The species was known for reinforcing its natural armor through clever and unnatural means, but this beast was exceptional. It had become a living battle wagon. Where its shell showed through were horny protrusions and rough bristles of hair.

The king stared back at Hiroshi with those beady eyes, intelligence radiating from every subtle movement.

Looking over his shoulder, the other, smaller collectors had arrived, with similar but shabbier enhancements. They formed a circle around himself and their ruler.

Hiroshi wondered again, how exactly had they accomplished such a feat; metallurgy, in a land crab species? Whomever wrote their Archive entry apparently had not known either.

The king collector shook any remaining dirt from its armor. Blocking Hiroshi's

path to Motopia, the monster perched on eight legs with two enormous claws folded up into resting positions on either side of its armored shell. One claw was elongated and sharp, the other was round, larger, and reinforced with a thicker exoskeleton. The larger claw unfurled and slammed the earth. Hiroshi no longer occupied that spot. Soot sprayed the air. A mighty gust of wind followed the attack, but that was it, wind. The High Seraph was far too nimble for the Collector's hammer.

Three similar blows struck more dirt as Hiroshi danced about the irritated crab who, undeterred by his failures, kept slamming away.

When the strikes began to wane in intensity and speed, Hiroshi made his move. A hand at his waist set loose his sword. A hop and a quick kick off launched him high up into the air. Hiroshi positioned himself for a downward, piercing thrust. The king collector smacked Hiroshi out of the air with the quicker, sharper claw before he could complete the action. Hiroshi hit the ground. The collector scurried forth, stabbing at him furiously. The burst of stabs whirred through the air, drilled the green carpet of the plains, and Hiroshi's sword, on the occasion he wasn't quick enough to dodge. Giving up on avoiding the claw, Hiroshi tried instead to meet each strike with a swipe of his own.

Clang! *Pang*! *Ping*! He fought back, matching the crab's intensity and speed. Blow for blow they fenced, neither showing the other fatigue. Hiroshi felt the snip at his ankle of a smaller collector that had grown brave and used its king as a diversion. The massive crustacean lumbered forward, on eight creeping legs, callously trampling its smaller comrade. The other collectors stood by, holding tight, cautious orbits, making sure not to meet similar fates.

The sharp claw didn't relent. Unlike the hammer-claw, the collector king's long-claw did not slow. It was speeding up. Hiroshi's arm throbbed, decimated by the aggressive vibrations of his defensive swats. As if it sensed Hiroshi's thoughts, the king collector rotated its body sideways, lashing out with its hammer-claw then long-claw in alternating attacks. The hammer-claw pummeled Cordis Adolesco, held lengthwise above Hiroshi's head. Gritting his teeth, he hopped about expecting the next strike. The long-claw appeared, and shot for High Seraph Gunkimono's feet. Hiroshi jumped. Predicting where he might land, the sharp claw returned, piercing the High Seraph's shoulder.

His blood met the dried jewels of Paulo's as it dribbled down his robes onto his shoes. Hiroshi screamed in pain before being smacked aside with the hammer-claw. Landing in a cloud of dust he wobbled to his feet. The king collector encroached, encouraged by the sight of fresh blood.

The beast gathered and spat a stringy, wet substance from its gnawing mouth. Two tiny claws located at either side of its mouth caught and weaved the string, manipulating its trajectory midair. Whipping the string towards his sword, it wrapped around the hilt. Wrenching Cordis Adolesco out of his grasp, the nimble arm-like claws reeled in its sticky line.

Astonished, Hiroshi dove for his blade and caught a face full of sediment instead. The king had already retrieved his sword and begun the bizarre process of incorporating the weapon into its armor. Hiroshi didn't intervene, at first, out of sheer curiosity.

The collector spat up another gooier substance and rolled it into a ball. Attaching the glob to the tip of the sword and them both to its string, the king swung the blade onto its back.

Finding a free space among the metal scraps that covered the shell, Cordis Adolesco landed tip down at first, then flopped over onto its side, fixed in place by the goop.

The stringy spittle dissolved. The gooey substance on its back liquefied and softened the surrounding shell as Cordis Adolesco began to descend and fuse into the creature's body.

The shell hardened quickly again.

In that brief time, Hiroshi observed the collector king's folly. The creature should have swallowed the sword whole or pitched it far off into the grassland. Focused on disarming its opponent and fortifying defense, it failed to completely absorb the sword. Just enough of the hilt's lever was exposed. It was only a small segment, but if Hiroshi could reach it, he might activate the mechanism inside.

Hiroshi's thoughts were cut short of a plan. The hammer-claw flattened him into a High Seraph flapjack. The wind abandoned his lungs, and a muffled grunt escaped his throat. Lifting its claw to confirm the kill, Hiroshi released an unfortunate and dusty sigh.

The long-claw flurry began anew. Hiroshi rolled to one side or the other with every plunge. The collector's chitinous legs kneaded the earth energetically trying to catch its rolling quarry. Hiroshi fought back dizziness, rolling close enough to a tiny collector to inspect its armor's adornments. This one had managed to fuse a small dagger to its shell. The hilt gone and only a chipped broken blade remained. Using his feet for leverage, Hiroshi ripped the blade free, tearing a hole in the collector's back. The generous creature was repaid with a swift death as an enterprising pair rushed over to consume their weakened comrade alive. Picking at its innards through the convenient hole, they stuffed clumps of fresh crab meat into greedy mouths.

The collector swarm grew increasingly restless, pinching and nipping at each other over drops of Hiroshi blood in the surrounding grass.

The king collector was unmoved. The two tiny claws at its mouth worked double time as it produced another load of stringy spittle.

Hiroshi wasn't amazed anymore. He had seen enough. Dive-rolling underneath and inside the reach of the hammer-claw had the desired effect. The collector king lurched back, lashing out with the long-claw reflexively. Hiroshi was ready. The claw missed its mark, twice, by wide margins. Hiroshi stayed inside the larger claw's reach. The collector stood its ground, slamming both claws down in a show of force as much as frustration. Exploiting the narrow window when the weight of its claws left the creature off balance and momentarily defenseless, a sliding Hiroshi passed under its belly on his knees and emerged at the collector's rear. From this new vantage, he eyed the embedded sword; watching as the lever's position shifted with the animal's every movement.

The collector spun in place trying to locate its prey. It found him, arm cocked back, broken dagger in throwing position.

The dagger left his hand with all the strength the tiring High Seraph could gather. Catching the glint of the approaching missile with gleaming eyes, it swiped at the airborne blade, missing and inadvertently moving Cordis Adolesco into the dagger's trajectory.

Bullseye.

Hiroshi made his mark. Pelting a hunk of metal, inches away from the newly adorned sword, the dagger ricocheted towards the exposed lever tip, activating it with an airy ting.

The creature froze, unsure of what happened. It wasn't until its shell began to bubble and Cordis Adolesco fell from its back through its body, carrying bloody innards out onto the ground between its legs, that the crab descended into full frantic panic.

Hiroshi backed away, leaving the king to writhe in agony. The potently formulated acid spread across the collector's shell, eliminating its metallic and chitinous defenses. Any material it touched was liquefied and cooked in the annihilating chemical reaction.

The legs and arms of the enormous crab flexed uncontrol-lably as the acid made its way from posterior to anterior. With its back legs all but gone, the collector collapsed onto its face, evaporating like a cigarette in the wind.

The smaller collectors could wait no longer, the smell of siz-zling flesh drew them. They nipped unsuccessfully at the pieces of their king as they melted and plopped away from its core. The king crab soup was still too hot for swarming collectors to shovel the steamy clumps of their former alpha into their industrious and compact mouths. The multiplying acid made short work of them too. Bloody, sweating, and surrounded by bubbling puddles of mud grass and collector chitterlings, Hiroshi dropped to his knees in exhausted triumph. An hour passed.

He did not move.

The world sped along above him. The clouds shuffled by casting ever changing patterns over the stoic High Seraph, who hadn't stopped to rest since leaving Span Opticon, not even on the ferry ride underneath the Neutral Zone. He had remained awake, plagued by visions of his first encounter with Joan.

Moist pits of flesh and failed cannibalism were all that remained of the decapod attack. No other wildlife dared venture close for investigation.

Knees bent, chest straight, and hands propped on his thighs, Hiroshi perched until finally he fell asleep. When day transi-tioned to night Hiroshi pulled his robes protectively over his body and transitioned from kneeling to prone.

Hiroshi awoke to Joan Flayr towering over him.

The moon was rising above her left cheek and the sun setting below her right. He reached out for her hand, where their hands would meet, his passed through hers. Alarmed, he reexamined Joan. All that made her strong and feminine. From the simple way she styled her hair to her antiquated garb. Then a transformation washed over her like flash showers over the plains. The moon was now bloody and full. The sun melted, trickling down her face like molten tears. He felt the warmth as she changed. Joan was now Mr. Galtero; in black Preneo suit and red tie. The briefcase at his side was darker than usual—the deepest night he had ever seen; and bursting at its seams with searching tentacles.

Hiroshi jerked away, trying to retreat, but his feet had become shoots rooted into the ground. Mr. Galtero moved closer without aid from his legs. He opened his mouth wide, revealing countless rows of blood-stained teeth. He spoke without once closing his mouth.

"You are soft. And ripe. So soft and ripe. Soft. Ripe. Soft—Ri—" Mr. Galtero repeated, pinning Hiroshi down, he began to eat him. Mr. Galtero tore chunks of Hiroshi's flesh away callously gobbling up his kin. Hiroshi felt no pain until Mr. Galtero was done eating. He was no longer his brother but the visage of General Amram Donnel.

Amram thanked Hiroshi for the meal by patting his swollen stomach, innards and viscera still smeared sloppily on his face and mouth. The General was now inside Span Opticon sitting at a table with Elder Sandhurst.

"See, my apprentice was absolutely delicious, wasn't he? A bit undercooked but the flavor kept, no?"

Aware of the dream, it began to fade away into Hiroshi's

subconscious. Nuzzled into his ceremonial robes, he found a more comfortable position to sleep, and a newer, forgettable dream began.

Chapter 23

Celeste turned off the display screen and slowly moved towards her weapon cabinet; pausing for a moment to remember the combination to the lock. The combination returned to her mind. Opening the cabinet, she removed her most effective and favorite tool: a persuader modified to spot and eliminate targets at great distances.

She received the weapon from Shirley the First, the previous leader of the Ars Femina, as a principal expiration gift. She named the weapon Cinder and began her lifelong pursuit of its mastery. Seeing the persuader one day, General Donnel assured her it was unique; informing her the Preneo that trained with similar weapons were known as Snipers.

Through rigorous practice Celeste achieved perfect accuracy. Honed by experience, her reflexes remained unhindered by age. Celeste never missed, not a shot, not a mark, not a detail. Celeste's marksmanship had propelled her to the top of the list for leader of the Ars Femina once interim leader Maw Leah's term ended.

With Cinder in her clutch, gripped firmly to her chest, she was finally ready to process what she had just watched. Ecclesiel was dead. Someone, her hunch was a Legioneer hitman or

Nute bounty hunter, brazenly assassinated the Illumined One. It was fucking crazy, she told herself. Everyone knew, beneath the banalities and mutual benefits of the Treaty of Neo Earth, festered deep-seated enmity. The factions teetered on the edge of war for decades; that was the nature of peace. Political peace, she concluded.

Celeste envisioned that ripping-off three factions at once might be the match to ignite the fire that would burn Zachariah Sandhurst's Treaty of Neo-Earth to ashes, not Ecclesiel's death. She imagined a house of cards, not just falling, but simultaneously being shuffled mid-air by some devious hand.

She replayed the assassination in the theater of her mind's eye. A bouquet of flowers, black roses. Shots fired. Ecclesiel falls lifelessly. Then again from the beginning. This time slower and with more focus. The persuader used in the assassination resembled a weapon General Donnel traded to the Ars some years back for a successful extraction. They accepted the tiny persuader that could project a hologram after the General, as he often did, went to great lengths to assure them that there was no other persuader like it.

Slinging Cinder over her shoulder, Celeste exited her office.

Dezba, then Jelani, stepped off the personnel lift into the violet light of Pangaia Fortress' Level 7 Armory. Celeste was propped up, leaning against a foyer wall, arms folded and Death in persuader form slung over her shoulder. The dramatic lighting made her no-nonsense expression particularly grim.

Dezba's eyes widened, landing on Cinder. She didn't stare—a silly superstition convinced her, and Jelani to a lesser extent, that just looking at Celeste's weapon could shorten the time to its eventual use.

"We goin' to war?" Jelani asked, putting into words what Dezba wondered, motioning to Cinder with her chin. "Haven't seen *that* thing in a bit," she continued.

"We have a problem. Not a small one. A *huge* fuckin' problem," Celeste said, showing just how big with her hands then returning them to folded position.

"You mean the whole triple bounty thing? We're waiting it out, right? See who comes a knockin'?" Jelani said, stepping further into the armory and closer to Celeste. Dezba followed.

"Take it ya'll didn't see today's Wave?"

"You know I don't watch that shite," Dezba answered.

"I barely even know how to turn on a display screen if I tried. When I get it on, I can never manage to actually sit in front of the blasted thing," said Jelani.

"Bet if it was a persuader, you'd figure out how to get it working," Celeste said in jest.

"Never anything good on, anyway. It's always the Light this, or the Return of the Fallen that," Jelani finished.

"You don't need to worry about that anymore. Ecclesiel's light is gone. He joined his Fallen today." Neither Jelani nor Dezba laughed. Celeste continued her report.

"Someone shot Ecclesiel to death with some serious gear. A persuader that looked a lot like something we *had* down here." Her close confidants' body language shifted from curious to concerned. "Remember that persuader?"

Dezba and Jelani's faces begged "Which?"

"The bouquet of—what are those plants called? Anyway, it could create a hologram," Celeste explained.

Jostling her head to jog her memories, Jelani spoke first, "Oh, yeah. I think I do. It was a bouquet of flowers?"

Snapping her finger, Dezba said, "Roses, right?"

"Yesss. That one. It's not here. I thought I saw it on the Wave, so I came down and looked. Then I checked again. I scoured the logs for any withdrawals or special requisitions. Nothing there either. One of our girls took it without asking, or someone definitely just killed Ecclesiel with it."

"What. The. Fuck." Dezba enunciated while running both her hands back through the thick curls of her short afro. Celeste nodded.

"But that's not all. There's a body down here. Death by persuader. Professional. One shot to the heart. Haven't heard any reports of shots within Pangaia and the body's only a few days old. Whoever did this has access to a silent persuader."

"Mr. Galtero," Jelani and Dezba delivered the Ghost's name in unison.

"Thinking the same thing myself," Celeste confirmed, hoisting herself off the wall, leading her enforcers to the place of the corpse in question.

"It's one of the help." Jelani knelt to inspect the victim thoroughly.

"An escort by the looks of his clothes. Suicide isn't uncommon among their caste. Then again, his access pass is missing."

"That, and I couldn't find the persuader. This shit is not exactly itemized but I would have definitely noticed some flowers down here."

"So, what? The General knew something was awry with the bounty and ordered Mr. Galtero to frame us?" Dezba said, giving the corpse at her feet a mindful once-over.

"Maybe he didn't care." Jelani dusting her knees off before standing. "This might have nothing to do with Paulo Flayr. We can assume whoever wanted Ecclesiel dead was going to assassinate him today no matter our plan."

"This could actually be good for us."

Meeting Dezba's eyes Celeste nodded and spoke, "That is unusually optimistic of you. I accepted the money by default, it's my nature. If I had only known he was going to put Mr. Galtero up to killing faction heads, I might've just accepted the scorchers."

"So. Ecclesiel. Over the Wave. No doubt word is spilling across Neo-Earth," Jelani said.

The weight of their predicament was present in the pronunciation of Jelani's every word. The three women were silent as the corpse at their feet.

"Upside is, a lot of this is still theoretical. We have some facts. One, the person we expired is not Paulo Flayr. Two, Ecclesiel is dead, I've never seen a person survive such shots, not at that distance." Celeste shook her head side to side before holding up three fingers. "Third, the Treaty of Neo Earth is moot, for now. Once all non-essential Searchers are home safely, we lock down Pangaia, and prepare for the indefinite collapse of peace."

"Not much different from what we had planned if they found out about the multiple bounties," Jelani said.

"There *is* one major change," Celeste admitted. Dezba raised her eyebrows. "I'm sending you two after High Seraph Hiroshi Gunkimono. Bring him here, to me—and try not to kill him."

"I knew you liked the kid," Dezba chided.

"I'm undecided. I *do* know that while I flirted with violating the Treaty, Donnel went ahead and started a war. The time for courtly love is over. Faction leaders are getting knocked off. This isn't going to be fun, but you do get to fuck with the Syndicate's errand boy a bit. Take care, he's gifted."

"What? We contain the High Seraph and presto changeo Span Opticon comes crumbling to the ground?" said Jelani, rolling her eyes.

"Not abracadabra, but he's the best fighter outside of our ranks. There's no one anywhere near Hiroshi's level of combat skills within the Legioneers. I would know. With the Last High Seraph out of the picture, we will storm Span Opticon, and cut up Virtus to our liking."

"The kid is *that* good?" Jelani asked

"He's smart. You've seen that much yourself. He beat Naydeen without drawing his sword. I don't need to bring up how either of you two fared against Naydeen in the Cage."

"Why storm Virtus?" Dezba cracked her knuckles and changed the topic.

"If Hiroshi is the Last High Seraph, then Sandhurst is the Last Patriarch. The ultimate symbol of those old days, when men were given free reign over the planet. As long as he lives, there can be order, not freedom. Not for us. That's why Shirley the First founded the Ars Femina: 'So, no woman shall ever again come second to a man.' To Zachariah Sandhurst, all people are second to his ambitions. Man or woman."

"We should look for that persuader. Give the armory a quick pass together before we head up," Jelani offered, peering deeper into their vast, walk-in gun closet. Dezba shrugged and Celeste nodded in agreement. Moving from mound to pile, from stack to bundle, they searched for the missing persuader.

"It was always too good to be true," Celeste began, "The Treaty. It felt like peace, but we knew at what cost: extractions and expirations, trusts upfront, and few questions asked. I don't believe this is what Shirley the First envisioned." Celeste kissed her teeth as though the thought were lodged between.

"Nah. This—this is all a bastardization of *their* world. *They* said we were weak, *we* made ourselves tougher than a collector's claw. *They* said we were good only for preparing food, tilling land, and having babies. Now, they serve *us* on platters, work *our* land, seed and nurture *our* young. They said we were dependent, we shut ourselves off from society. They claimed us below them, today we regard them as mere pests. It's been *fun*. Power always is." Celeste released a lengthy sigh. "But. We can do more. Pangaia can be a haven of equity and forward-thinking. We can leave our daughters more than a pillar of weapons. We *are* warriors and women, but women first. Somewhere along our journey we became the hyper-realization of *their* ideals—became the dragon in order to slay it. I see my part in this, but just know, I would never put the Ars Femina in any *real* danger over a few trusts. I need you *both* to understand that. Contingency plans were placed before I ever came up with the idea to collect *all* the bounties. I knew the risks and did it anyway. It's time for change. I need you with me on this, for now, and for what comes after. Because the biggest fact of all is, we already got paid. With no treaty, no Sandhurst, and Ecclesiel out of the picture, Pangaia becomes the de facto capital city of the world."

Deep tension that had been building in Celeste's shoulders finally unwound.

"You put some thought into this, huh."

"I mean, I *did* search all these piles before I summoned you and Dezba," Celeste said as they looped back to the lift.

"Shit. I was beginning to think trusts and Tri-Bikes are all you care about. I'm with you—been with you. 'Til the end. Even if you *did* just want to burn it all Scorch Period Two-style. I'd still be right there." Dezba revealed her rare smile.

"Duh, I'm with you, boss. You gotta' work on your speeches, but I'm with you. We capture Hiroshi, bring back the character, not the corpse, then prepare for war. Sounds simple enough," Jelani confirmed.

"Help me move the body and let's get out of here." Celeste gave the order in her subtle way.

Finishing their unsuccessful search, Celeste, Dezba, and Jelani returned to the foyer. Jelani, with her persuader and detonator bobbing at her hip, and Dezba, with the pair of curved daggers bouncing at hers, shuffled awkwardly with the dead weight of the help between them. Celeste called the lift by elbowing the up-button.

The lift arrived with a stutter. Once inside they dropped the deceased and the small elevator responded with a jolt. A few moments later they reached the surface.

"I'm leaving Maya in charge while we're gone," Celeste said, stopping the door from closing.

"We?" Jelani asked, jerking her neck to meet Celeste's eyes.

"Yeah, where are you going?"

Celeste tightened the straps across her breastplate, straightened the unique persuader on her back, then tossed her hair over her shoulder in an exaggerated but accurate display of confidence.

"Me? I'm going to Virtus. As much as I love a fight, too many lives will be lost if we go to war. Donnel started this mess, but Sandhurst will certainly try and finish it. You take care of Hiroshi. I'll take care of the Elder."

"Blast. We're exploiting the situation to kill Sandhurst? Probably what the General wants," Jelani said.

"It's not an exploit. It's more like aggressive defense."

"Aggressive defense, huh?" Dezba let out a rarer laugh. "I

like it. That's where *we* come in, I imagine?"

"Correct! If we're swift and smart, we could actually prevent war."

"You don't think the no-war option died with Ecclesiel?" Jelani asked hopefully and rhetorically.

"Maybe it did. Now we know the Vicaarians won't come here asking for their money back. We know for spacedamn sure Donnel won't leave Motopia. Shit, Mr. Galtero was here just a few days ago and didn't try to kill me. He stole. That's to be expected from a rodent. It's Sandhurst's Treaty that was killed, he'll be the one to retaliate. Plus, Donnel already owes us a favor. He won't attack Pangaia."

"You think he'll keep his word?"

"Of course, he will, Jelani. A man is nothing without his word."

The trio exited the personnel lift. Stopping to prop its door open with her foot, Celeste beckoned to the nearest helper. He hurried over. Immediately understanding his task, he grabbed his colleague's ankles and dragged him off towards their morgue.

"Maya's a good choice. She almost beat Dezba during the Trials and she's a Botany Biologist," Celeste continued, not missing a beat.

"Maybe you should send me and Maya to find Hiroshi instead," Jelani said, elbowing Dezba as they whisked through the hallways of Pangaia Fortress.

"Alright, you two. Get your heads in the game. Hiroshi is no pushover."

"Yeah, yeah—How in hell do we find him?" Dezba probed.

"I have good information that placed him in route to Holy Lands before the assassination. If he's half as smart as I think he is, he'll be heading to Motopia to get answers. That's what I would do if I was just at *that* Wave. Take two Tri-Bikes from the Hangarage. Fucking Seraphim love to walk, you'll find him."

Jelani and Dezba jogged toward Pangaia's garage and Celeste pushed on to the fortress entrance, where she was met by a Tri-Bike and loyal attendant. Tossing Celeste a helmet, the attendee disappeared back inside the walled fortress. Celeste mounted her custom Tri-Bike and set off towards Virtus.

Chapter 24

The sun peered over the horizon, extending its ethereal tendrils across Neo-Earth. First, dragging them through the vastness of the Uncharted Regions, then the East Ocean of Virtue, and finally raking them through the outer boundaries of the Perennial Plains.

The solar arms inched towards the sleeping Seraph. Smelling the simple heat of the approaching sun, Hiroshi rolled and gave his back to the arriving light. The terminator cut across his body, bathing his back in warmth. Hiroshi let out a relieved sigh and pulled his robe tightly about himself, not once opening his eyes.

Continuing their expansion, the beams ricocheted off the reflective metal of Motopia, casting a winking glint that could be seen by a keen eye as far west as Fortress Pangaia.

The rising sun revealed the landscape, showing soupy remains of the collectors around him. He could not remember the last time he had rested so productively. Stretching, he paid close attention to diminished or increased pain of any injury.

The layer of silk beneath his robe was cultivated for strength and woven to neutralize most of the damage from the king collector's sharp claw. It had barely pierced his shoulder when it should have easily skewered it. Rolling onto his back, he opened his eyes. The sky scrolled by. An intermittent cloud would block the sun from time to time, casting ever-changing shapes on his face.

Another sigh.

His shoulder had stopped bleeding and the makeshift bandage fashioned from a strip of cloth off his scabbard was held tight. Things were, for the High Seraph, peaceful.

Hiroshi's stomach tightened into a braided knot. Something wasn't right. The wind carried a familiar scent of dirt and metal. He was not alone and hadn't been since night. Saying goodbye to serenity, he sat up.

It was true, he had picked up two companions. Two infamous, merciless, and deadly companions. Companions considered unlucky to meet. Hiroshi had met them once already and felt terrible about his chances of surviving another encounter.

"G'morning, Hiroshi," Jelani's voice came from three scorchfeet away on his left side. Her Searcher armor glistened menacingly in the morning light. She was almost glowing. Her persuader drawn, aimed at his center of mass.

"Sleep well?" Dezba added. Her voice came from three scorchfeet away on his right side. Dezba scowled, with crescent daggers in each hand. Her armor shined similarly to Jelani's but embossed and emblazoned onto the chest plate was a scene of two clashing warriors, those warriors also scowling.

"Sloppy, right? You fell asleep during the blasted war. Not very *High* Seraph of you. Then again, you *are* the youngest High Seraph," Jelani teased, tilting her persuader sideways as she paused. Hiroshi kept his silence. "Or is it they just don't make 'em like they used to?" she continued, grinning.

"No, Jelani. It's not that. He actually wants to die. Look at him. Covered in blood and on the run."

"I am *not* on the run!" Hiroshi snapped back.

"Then what *are* you on? A bender? A high horse? A warpath? What the blast brings you out here, to 'No Woman's Land'?"

"Nice," Hiroshi said, nodding emphatically and sarcastically. "Good to see that Ars trusts are going towards better comedy writing. No. I am a sober man, a humble man, and a man of peace." Saying his piece, he folded his hands in his lap and lowered his head. Dezba put her blades away. Jelani's persuader remained, unwavering.

"But a man nonetheless," Jelani quipped.

"Peace?" Dezba wondered in his direction aloud.

"You call the execution—without trial—of two Neo-Earth inhabitants, peace?" Jelani scoffed.

Looking up at Jelani, hands still folded, Hiroshi spoke softly, "I guess you guys tracked me here with a brand-new moral compass? Came looking for a Seraph but found your conscience first?"

"I found mine lying on the ground. Just waiting to get stepped on, *just like you.*" Dezba punched her palm with her fist then made a motion to move.

"Easy," Jelani said. Dezba held her position.

"Celeste said bring him back alive, she didn't say bring him back *pretty.*" Dezba stepped forward.

"Now look!" Hiroshi boomed. "I have entertained your nonsense. Why did you come here? I will gladly debate philosophy or politics, but if either of you try to impede my progression you will find no mercy in return."

The wind plucked the strings of tension with a sudden gust. Hiroshi stood. He tried to hide the wince as pain shot from his shoulder and trickled down into his weary vessel. "This is ridiculous. There must be some error. Why have I, High Seraph Hiroshi Gunkimono of the Syndicate of Valor, been selected for extraction? I demand you show me my bounty papers."

"Listen, bud. Someone just filled the Illumined One with holes during the Wave. And you stuck Paulo like a rabid neowolf. Yeah, we've heard. The Treaty? It's tassels. And guess which 'Little Golden Boy' Celeste sent us to extract to prevent a war?"

Chuckling and straightening his robes he looked to Dezba and then Jelani. "Celeste thought you two alone could bring me back?"

"Not alone," Jelani said, persuader out and up.

"Together," said Dezba, arms flexed and folded across her chest.

His bluff failed. They were fully prepared and quite capable of bringing him back. He was now in a worst-case scenario. One he couldn't have imagined, not even in the dreamscape-like Perennial Plains. Hiroshi might easily defeat one of Celeste's legendary enforcers, but not both. That's why they mocked him and approached so confidently. His choices were to become their prisoner or to die in combat.

"He gets it now," Jelani pointed out, lowering her persuader.

"Be a good boy and come to Pangaia with us. We'll teach you some parlor tricks for entertainment until this shit blows over," Dezba offered, nearing Hiroshi's right.

There was something almost comical about their synchronicity, Hiroshi thought while analyzing their body language, facial expressions, words, and inflections. He hoped to discover some detail to create an opening and save himself.

One breathed out and the other in, theirs was no typical war bond. No, they operated with a complementary familiarity. More than just comrades. Friends in a deeper sense than he was initially aware of.

"Hands on your head," Dezba commanded.

The sun chiseled perfect silhouette statues of the infamous Searchers.

"I never said I was coming with you. No. I have a counter-ask. If you two come with me to Motopia I will happily go back to Pangaia with you. I must speak to the General."

Jelani couldn't contain her laughter. "*Ha!* Okay. What else? You want a massage as well?" Finding Jelani's eyes, Hiroshi spoke again, this time with the tone and posture of a High Seraph in the Syndicate of Valor, "When we fight, will you laugh like that if I kill Dezba and not you?"

His words cut Jelani's fit of laughter with a razor. Before Dezba could react or respond, he glared at her grimly.

"And you?" Hiroshi said. "What if I don't put my hands on my head? What if I cut Jelani in half instead? I can do that; you both know it. Are you willing to take *that* chance?"

They divided silence between their trio for over a minute.

"I get it. Do not think I do not." Hiroshi paused to adjust his robes and stretch again. "Either one of you is prepared to die for the other, but neither prepared to live without. That's the only reason you will both live."

Hiroshi allowed them time to mull over the implications and limitations of their forced union.

"Seraph?" Jelani asked after a long while.

"Searcher?"

"You would throw your life to keep us apart?"

He pondered her question, answering deliberately, "I would. Would you risk war and disobey Celeste to save a friend?"

"I would," Dezba and Jelani answered in unison.

There was nothing else to be said. Hiroshi defeated his

captors and gained followers without drawing his sword. He resumed walking towards Motopia.

Its cloudy covers were pulled back for the moment, revealing 'the Floating City' in all its glory. To Hiroshi, it looked like a flattened top or a bloated version of the mushroom cap abodes of Virtus.

"You're just gonna walk off, your Highness? After all that!" Dezba shouted after him.

"Blast, Celeste was right. That little fucker got us. Should've just tied him up while he slept," Jelani said, muttering to herself.

"Not our style," Dezba answered

"It should be."

"As I said, we are all going to Motopia, or two out of three of us will die!" Hiroshi shouted back.

"We have a trike!" Jelani yelled after him

Hiroshi stopped in his tracks. Excitement welled in his belly.

He spun around and followed Jelani and Dezba to an unsuspecting boulder. A tug of tarp revealed their hidden, motorized inverted tricycle. Two treaded wheels in the front connected two seats to a large wheel in the back of the vehicle. Yellow Ars Femina graffiti and stickers speckled their matte black mount.

"There are only two seats," Hiroshi pointed out, confused and disappointed in equal parts.

"We should've run back to the Tri-Bike and left as soon as he started with all that shit," Jelani was still muttering to herself as she hopped into the driver's seat. Assuming the shotgun role, Dezba jumped onto the passenger's seat.

Hiroshi, watching Jelani's hands closely, saw her insert a key somewhere near the handlebars then twist. The bike coughed black smoke out of aerated exhausted pipes and shivered itself awake. Purring, it began to crawl. Jelani stepped heavily on the accelerator with a mind to leave the trailing Hiroshi behind. Hiroshi caught the back lip of the bike and hoisted himself atop the accelerating vehicle.

"Nice try," he yelled to Jelani, finding some semblance of comfort and safety in the cargo basket as the Tri-Bike ripped across the plains.

Chapter 25

"Are we just going to sit behind these shrubs all day?" Dezba inquired, breaking the pencil thin tension of the calm.

High Seraph Gunkimono and Searchers Jelani and Dezba had arrived at the base of one of the god-sized Chains of Motopia. Tens of dozens of links each taller than Hiroshi, and weighing a half ton, stretched high up into a cloudy vanishing point. The chains and the equally large rock bolts anchoring them into the ground were the only man-made objects visible for miles. The spot where the chains met the ground was bordered off by a rectangular wall of plants. Along one of the longer walls was a gate.

Nothing terribly fancy or secure. A wire fence with a latch. The unlikely trio waited and watched for any sign of motion. Infiltrating the outer row of green, they confronted a shorter inner wall of foliage. From there they spied a small hut, control panel inside, presumably used to call an elevator down from a platform above.

There it was, 'the Floating City', suspended above them. The Chains of Motopia were shooting sprouts, extended from the ground through the center of the city where, at the top of

Motopia, the chains met the middle support beam. There the links fanned out into eight smaller chains, each sewn through massive ring clamps positioned at Motopia's north, northeast, east, southeast, south, southwest, west, and northwest points.

Motopia was a doughnut-chandelier of metal, held in the air by the tension of the chains that supported it. To Hiroshi, the whole system was as awe-inspiring as it was unnecessary.

The nearest chain links disappeared into the clouds far to the left of the hut and console. Two people stood outside.

Hiroshi, finally looking at Dezba, rolled his eyes and responded, "We're waiting for a change in guards. Mr. Galtero could not have beat you here by much, even if he has a Tri-Bike of his own. We just need an opening, or a sign, or something. Keep your voice down. And these are bushes—not shrubs."

"Bushes, huh? *Bull shit.* Lookit the upkeep on these things!" Dezba said in a spiteful whisper.

"They are *clearly* bushes. These are too tall to be shrubs," Hiroshi shot back.

"And you're too short to use that argument. These are damn near trees compared to you," Dezba fired.

At this point Dezba and Hiroshi had inched over to one another. Smoldering, they continued their semantic showdown nose to nose. Hiroshi's wrinkled brow told all as his mounting frustration threatened to blow their limited cover.

"To the small-minded, shrubs can appear larger than actual," he said.

Jelani could barely hold in her laughter. Dezba at her full height was still hidden by the group of outcropping plants in question. "Listen close, Seraph. Do you see any other plants like this? Anywhere? They're only here. In a human-made pattern. They're shrubs."

Hiroshi standing now as well, met Dezba's intensity. "What do Searchers know of horticulture? There is not one tended plant in front of Pangaia for a mile."

"Yeah, we wouldn't want a Syndicate sneak-thief to have something to hide behind—just like this!" Dezba gestured to the plant as she huffed. "And it's not what is in front of the Wall it's what lies behind it that matters!"

"*Shhh*! You two are gonna get us blasting captured. It's not going to matter whether it is a shrub or bush if we become the fertilizer," Jelani chimed in, finally able to suppress her laughter. A glowering Hiroshi backed down from a glaring Dezba and resumed his self-appointed position as their lookout.

"Whaddya' see?" Jelani asked, taking up a crouching position next to him.

"Guards. Same ones. They don't look like Alpha's to me. Maybe we just put them down and take the lift up?"

"No dummy, that's why we're waiting here. What if we call it down and they aren't expecting anybody up? Raise all the alarms," Dezba countered with all the latent contempt of their previous conversation.

Hiroshi glanced her way then addressed Jelani directly, "Have you actually gotten into a fight with a Legioneer Alpha before?"

"A fight, no, not exactly. Encounters, sure. They're armored but sleek. They used some kind of hovering ability. They use it to cushion falls or increase movement speed. But they're just men; cocky fucks at that. The Ars have expired Alphas before, you know the occasional rogue faction member is not uncommon." Jelani moved closer to see what Hiroshi could see.

Two guards, both women. Both decked out in combat-style
fatigues, one leaning on the hut calmly, the other peering about
anxiously. Jelani squinted her eyes to make out their weapons.
It didn't look like either of them held persuaders. Just long,
cylindrical batons.

"Blast," Jelani lamented, "I hate killing women."

"Women? They chose the wrong side," Dezba said, both
asking and answering with her back turned, watching their
rear.

"So, my plan is not so dumb, after all?"

"Of course, it's dumb, boy Seraph. And impulsive. We wait
it out for about another half hour or so. See if they take off. If
they don't, Dezba and I'll put them down, take their uniforms,
fake an emergency, then call the lift down. Shit, we might even
be able to tie you up and act like we captured you."

"I don't think so," Hiroshi said. "Wait—*Shhh*, Searcher.
Something is occurring as I speak." Hiroshi prompted his
hostage hosts over to his vantage. "Someone is coming."

A cloud of dust appeared then neared from the distance,
settling, it revealed an armored soldier. Approaching the
women, they greeted the soldier as a superior.

Hiroshi's mouth fell slack as his eyes made out the familiar
form of a friend. The soldier who had emerged from a cloud of
smoke was undoubtedly High Librarian Ido Xzaven. Hiroshi
could recognize Ido's armor anywhere, and as far as he knew
there was none other like it. Hiroshi made a motion to step
out of cover, but Jelani grabbed his arm before he could expose
them.

"What are you *doing*, kiddo? That's an Alpha. Stay down,
and stay back. Me and Dezba will ground him. We have a little
something we want to try."

An Alpha? They must be mistaken, Hiroshi thought. He examined the armor again, more intent this time. The differences in design were clearer. The Legioneer Alpha was a smaller, lithe, weaponized version of Ido's life saving armor. Amram Donnel's design sense remained as his signature on everything he engineered.

High Librarian Xzaven's suit had always felt strangely out of place among the practical decor of Virtus. Hiroshi had always wondered why Elder Sandhurst allowed Ido to use such ancient and mystic technology when it was against the Syndicate's Code of Valor. He knew how close they were and chalked it up to years of friendship. Even with those concessions, Donnel left the Syndicate of Valor because of Sandhurst's Luddism.

The reunion with Saigo left Hiroshi with many doubts about, and questions for, Elder Sandhurst, 'Hero of Neo-Earth'. Seeing Donnel's Alpha for the first time, Hiroshi felt reassured in his certainty that General Donnel was far too dangerous to be left to his own devices.

Hiroshi chuckled to himself.

"What're you laughing at?" Jelani asked.

"Devices," Hiroshi answered, analyzing the Legioneer Alpha's every movement.

Ignoring his statement, Jelani said, "See how his feet aren't quite touching the ground. That's an Alpha."

That explained the subtle cloud of dust churning away at the imposter's feet as they conversed.

"Those markings on the armor, it means it's an Ace, an Alpha with confirmed kills. Stay back, Seraph, we are moving in," Dezba said.

"Whoa. Okay, our women just activated their batons. The Alpha just pointed over here."

Seeing the Alpha pivot and point directly toward them, Dezba, Hiroshi, and Jelani pulled their heads back. They had been seen, but still hoped to salvage some stealthy entrance into Motopia. Barely releasing three breaths between themselves, the congregation of vegetation providing their hiding spot exploded.

Dezba dashed. Hiroshi rolled. Jelani dived.

All to avoid the brunt of the blast. The charred and broken bits of leaves and stems rained down like brown-green confetti until finally petering to the earth.

The debris cleared around the hovering figure of the Alpha. No longer near the hut, the Alpha was much closer; floating and bobbling in place, gripping its humming persuader.

Hiroshi had encountered many new things since leaving Virtus, but the weapon the Alpha held was unique among them. Scurrying for footing and cover in the aftermath and confusion of the blast, Hiroshi could only wonder if it was the persuader that had created such destruction.

Shifting its weight forward, the Alpha suit advanced at a sixty-degree angle. Spotting Hiroshi, it took aim, the humming stopped, and a blue light leaped from the barrel of its persuader. The dirt was vaporized where the beam touched, where the High Seraph was just a moment earlier, leaving nothing but a crater in its wake. The heat from the beam itself clawed up Hiroshi's nose and singed the fibers of his robes.

Jelani fired three pellets from her persuader; they exploded in the air just above the hovering Alpha. The concussive wave pushed it to the ground. The Ace was stunned but standing, still grasping the humming weapon.

Dezba's curved blades whizzed by on either side of Hiroshi who had ignored the Searchers orders and sprinted toward the grounded Alpha. Her first blade hit the Ace's armor, bouncing off ineffectually and skittering away. The second landed deftly, and stuck. The dagger's tip found a sliver of textile, where the Alpha suit's defense broke for mobility.

Visibly surprised by the accuracy of the throw, the Alpha fumbled at the dagger with clumsy, armored fingers as a maroon stain gathered and spread around the embedded blade. Hiroshi was just as surprised; and equally reassured he hadn't challenged the Searchers earlier.

Skidding to a stop, Hiroshi held Cordis Adolesco unsheathed and ready by his side. Having overtaken the Alpha in the fracas he was now behind his enemy; with the advantage of footing and ready to pounce.

But Hiroshi would not rejoin the fight. Two batons formed an X and blocked his path. The two women from before, who guarded the hut.

"You're not in Virtus anymore, Seraph," the woman on his left said. Squinting, Hiroshi read their name tags. Their uniforms read: *Animal Control Officer* in bold, each with their name written in smaller letters underneath. The woman on his right wore a gray, brimmed cap, pulled snuggle down over her eyes. Her name tag read: *Pamn.* The woman on his left, sported an afro wrapped taut with a gray headband, her name was *Devi.*

"Are those last names? Or do you all just do like a one name thing to keep it easy?"

If either Pamn or Devi appreciated the humor neither of them showed it. Devi swung her baton at Hiroshi's head with impressive speed. Of course, a swipe of his sword deflected her blow. Pamn was quicker. Cracking her baton over his unguarded back; the layers of silk under his robes weren't much for shock absorption—he felt every inch of the scorchfoot long pole rap against him.

A quick spin pushed Pamn back and had him facing Devi, who held her baton like a broom. She twisted its two ends in opposite directions. The business end began to glow and then hum, not unlike the Alpha's persuader. The noise behind him confirmed that Pamn had done the same.

"There isn't any chance I could get you to just put those down, now could I?"

They responded in baton. Pamn and Devi buffeted the High Seraph with the shafts of their sticks. Devi switched from a swing to a thrust. The glowing tip of her baton stopped humming as it made contact with Hiroshi's body.

Devi dug her truncheon deep into Hiroshi's side. Something unexpected occurred. He dropped Cordis Adolesco. No scream. No struggle. Just a moment of brief involuntary and violent shaking, then he collapsed to the dirt.

Jelani and Dezba defeated the Alpha Ace and returned to Hiroshi just in time to assume him dead.

"Now, we definitely gotta' kill these chicks. That was *our* job," Jelani said. Dezba simply made a noise of disapproval as she wiped Alpha Ace blood from her daggers. Once clean, Dezba readied herself for Devi and Pamn, who had rallied and put themselves between Hiroshi's body and the incoming Searchers.

The synchronized hum of their batons cutting the air began their bout. Devi and Pamn made a display of excellent teamwork. High thrusts, mid-swipes, low sweeps, all were executed by the specialists in unison. Pamn and Devi became a two-headed machine, beating forward with four-coordinated feet and arms.

Despite their efforts, the Animal Control Officers could not compete. They would be outmatched in every perceivable way and didn't know it yet.

Two daggers, spinning and shrieking as they glided, were launched at Pamn and Devi: one hit home, throwing their choreography into disarray. The Searchers zeroed in. It was Pamn who had been hit. She kneeled with a crescent dagger embedded in her abdomen. Devi was close enough to inspect her comrade's wound while keeping an eye on the infamous Searchers.

"We do *this* for a living. Don't throw your life away. You already killed the Syndicate's High Seraph. We can't keep them off you, but if you just call the lift down and explain to Donnel we are just here for Hiroshi, *then* we can talk about making sure your expiration date is more of an extraction point, if you get my lingo?" Jelani shouted over to Devi.

"Oh yeah? What about her? I just betray my faction and leave my homegirl to die? Nope. Think I don't know who you two are? I'm not afraid of any woman, man, animal, or Searcher. I've tangoed with creatures persuaders wouldn't budge. Your Seraph friend is not dead. Probably paralyzed, likely brain damaged, but a man his size will regain consciousness in a few days ... These things do have a fatal mode, come any closer and I'll show ya!" Devi shouted back.

"I want my dagger!" Dezba said, almost cutting Devi off.

"Come and get it!" Pamn spat back, blood sputtering from her lips.

Dezba sprang forward. Pamn could barely bat an eye, before Dezba's hot breath was on her cheek.

Dezba smelled the charged air before she heard the hum of Devi's baton. Dezba, already too close and too quick, ripped

179

her dagger free with one hand as she slashed at an approaching Devi with the other. Devi evaded Dezba's blade. But her headband tattered to the ground, cut clean in half.

Pamn pulled her baton towards her body lengthwise, trying to catch Dezba between her arms in an intimate and critical embrace. By hooking Pamn's baton with the freed blade and tugging one end down, she caused the glowing tip on the opposite end to make contact with Pamn's neck. The Animal Control Officer's eyes, now bloodshot, rolled up into her skull and she fell back, still. Pink foam bubbled and popped around her nose and mouth.

With both hands wrapped tightly around the lower grip of her baton, Devi swung at the distracted, crouched Searcher. The shadows cast by the baton's intensified glow allowed Dezba to react and avoid the tip. However, the shaft smacked across her back sending her face-first into the dirt, writhing in pain next to the deceased Pamn.

Jelani watched with her persuader trained on Devi. Her utter confidence in Dezba had erroneously kept her from joining the fight sooner. Alas, Dezba was down, and Devi prepared for the kill.

Jelani licked her trigger with a finger. The explosive flew past Devi. Thumbing the detonator, the round exploded just far enough away from Devi's ear to blow it to shreds.

Squealing and disoriented, she abandoned her advance to Dezba. Jelani stepped up, one foot after the other, never lowering her persuader or breaking line of sight. From where she stood, she could see that Dezba was still breathing. Pamn, however, no longer was. And about seven to ten scorchfeet away lay High Seraph Gunkimono.

Devi stumbled forward. A hateful grimace plastered her face.

She retrieved the pieces of her headband and tied each piece about her fists. Devi gathered her energy and prepared to face death defiantly. She juggled her baton expertly in her hands from left to right, right to left, behind her back, around her neck.

Unsure of Devi's intentions, Jelani didn't fire.

Buying herself time to think, Devi began a retreat just as steady as Jelani's advance. She inched backwards, closer to the hut while looking up at the vanishing point in the sky where those gargantuan chains disappeared.

"What's taking so long?" Devi muttered. Was the General really expecting an Ace and two ACOs to be enough to hold of two Searchers and a High Seraph. The Animal Control Officer thought.

Jelani traced Devi's line of sight and guessed at her intention and destination. Pulling the trigger on her unique persuader, the projectile zipped across the battlefield and landed squarely in the unguarded control panel. The explosion sent bits of metal and wiring airborne.

High above, the locking mechanisms connecting the lift to the Motopia released and the five-scorchfoot-by-five-scorchfoot metal cabin began its freefall.

Looking at the base where the Chains of Motopia were connected to the ground, Devi estimated the radius of the impact and made sure to be nowhere close.

And there was Hiroshi, laying inside the falling lifts impact zone. Dezba was now rising, slowly but surely.

"Dezba!" Jelani called, her companion did not respond or even acknowledge her. Instead Dezba's eyes remained locked on Devi, whose eyes glued to the skies above.

Jelani peered up. Her heart fluttered as a metal box burst

through the creamy cloud line leaving a nearly perfect square outline in its wake. The chain links bucked and thrashed side to side, vibrating and churning up dirt at their base.

Devi knew there was only seconds left before the six-hundred-pound room slammed to the ground. Pamn was down. Hiroshi was down. And both Searchers were up. Knowing escape was unlikely all she could do was keep backing away from the falling lift.

Dezba parroted Devi's movements, backing away from the shaking chains. Jelani considered grabbing the High Seraph, but it was already too late. The cabin collided with the ground with a resounding boom. The shockwave shot out from the epicenter and tore through everything in its radius. The cube shuddered, shivered and threatened to implode under the weight of its own force; but it held.

Jelani, closest to the drop zone, braced with clenched teeth for the brunt of the vibrations from the aftershocks, which rattled her flesh and joints violently as it enveloped her. The cabin was still. The chains oscillated and wailed as they shook and clanged against the cabin ceiling, still energized from the descent.

When the dirt and gravel finally settled and the Chains of Motopia were motionless again, Hiroshi was gone. He left only a dusty impression where he had fallen. Jelani looked about, trying to locate their quarry with urgency. Dezba rejoined Jelani's side.

"You think we're gonna have to bring back a High Pancake of the Syndicate of Valor instead?"

As soon as the 'd' sound of the word 'instead' left Dezba's lips, Devi appeared from around a corner of the grounded lift. Slipping inside, the doors closed behind her.

"We gotta' bring something back, else this shit was point-less," Dezba said to Jelani unenthused. Jelani, nodding in agreement, freed her persuader and approached the cabin cautiously.

There were no windows. The only openings were the two holes in the center of the box and the doors. Flexible metal webbing running from ceiling to the floor provided protected from the passing chain links.

It appeared to be a solid piece of metal that had been bored out, not fitted together. The craftsmanship looked rugged on the surface, but closer inspection showed its meticulous precision. The lift cabin showed signs of erosion at its bottom from countless trips up and down.

Jelani was close enough to touch it. Reaching out with a hand for support, Jelani strafed the cube. Dezba did the same on the lift's far side from the opposing direction. They rounded the last corners and reached the cabin's door together. No motion could be heard inside. Jelani paused as a thought crossed her mind.

"He is not here," Dezba mouthed to Jelani before she could speak.

"Dezba," she whispered, turning to flatten herself out so her back was to the lift, her voice traveled away from it. "Dezba, if we find Hiroshi, we can knock him out—again, and drive the fuck back to Pangaia. Cancel this blasting charade, right now."

Dezba considered it for a moment then nodded emphatically. She then beckoned away from the lift, off into the plains with a dagger.

Jelani nodded and began slinking back around the corner she had only just skirted when a faint click of the cabin door caused her to freeze in place. The doors of the elevator crawled up, then slid open.

Devi stepped out. Her face was battered and beginning to bruise. She held her arms above her head and wore a look of utter defeat on her face. Hiroshi stepped out of the elevator next. His sword drawn and held to Devi's back.

"Greetings. Devi here was kind enough to show me how this thing works."

"Fuck," Dezba muttered, hoping to just be done with Hiroshi's errand. Dezba delivered a punch that tossed Devi back into the lift, knocking the animal control officer unconscious.

"Gotta' aim for the jaw, Seraph," Dezba said, stepping past Hiroshi and over to Devi, grinning. She entered the lift. Jelani returned and entered the lift as well. Hiroshi followed suit.

"Sorry, Searchers. You may have thought I was unconscious or even expired?"

"Maybe. That baton certainly laid you out pretty fuckin' good," said Dezba

"Did it?" Hiroshi asked, cocking his head to the side slightly.

"*Bullshit.* You were faking?" Jelani scoffed.

"Not faking, per se. Those rods do hurt like hell. But what kind of High Seraph would I be if I was incapacitated so easily."

"So, you mean to tell us that you laid on the ground and just waited for us to take care of it."

"When you say it like that it sounds cowardly. Cowardice is not a virtue of a High Seraph. Look, I acquired the lift for us."

"I got us the lift," Jelani reminded him promptly.

"Well, I got us a lift operator," Hiroshi said.

"She kinda' trapped herself in there," said Dezba

"And she would have taken it if I hadn't stopped her," he insisted.

"We have been to Motopia before. And Pangaia is rife with

smaller, albeit similar contraptions. We can operate this shit without her. Seraph, you didn't get us anything but mixed up with the Legioneers. You said you came here to talk. Why the blast are they trying to kill us?"

Thinking of his encounter with Saigo, Hiroshi said, "I cannot tell you everything now. But, like I said, I need to talk to Amram Donnel. Him wanting a fight won't change that. No, quite the opposite, it assures me that my path is indeed righteous and justified. Throw one of your lives down now, if you dare to stop me."

No one spoke. Jelani holstered her persuader and Dezba sheathed her daggers. Hiroshi gave them his back and fiddled at the lift controls.

"You'd think it would just be like 'Up' or 'Down' or something. 'Lobby' or 'Basement'. Why does a lift need so many buttons anyway? Okay, got it." The lift groaned stressfully but didn't move.

"Here we go, Searchers, look sharp."

"What's the plan?" Dezba inquired dryly.

"Follow my lead. I will try to keep us out of any fights. The archives had a few images of Motopia's interior. I have some idea where General Donnel's throne room is located."

The lift rose and began the ascent to Motopia.

Chapter 26

From inside Motopia, the differences between itself and Virtus were immediately apparent. To Hiroshi, with its spherical shape, Motopia looked like the product of an arranged marriage between a factory and stadium. The would-be seats were buildings. In the place of aisles and rows were assembly lines and roads. At the center, where a sporting or event field or control console might be, was a void that extended to the ground below. Motopia was Neo-Earth's largest fabrication center and its smallest city.

Traveling deeper into the compound, Hiroshi painted a map in his mind. Two concentric circles formed the body of the facility. The smaller ring sat slightly displaced above the larger ring. A single sturdy gangway, separated into three segments, ran the diameter, extended across the center gap, around the center support column, connecting the inner edges of the centermost ring, and continued to the outermost section.

A metal doughnut, with a smaller doughnut fixed above its core like a halo, Hiroshi thought. The larger doughnut was sprinkled with massive edifices, potted plants and people. The smaller doughnut was covered by simple and complex machines, tinier buildings and less people. The buildings of the innermost circle appeared reinforced. Hiroshi thought he saw what looked like cannons, each larger than a man, and built with technology to which he held no comparison.

Motopia was Neo-Earth's crown jewel of modernity. Through some magic of engineering, Donnel's Legioneers created the most advanced stronghold of the Factions. Then, as if there were any competition, hoisted it into the sky; to be seen by many and entered by few. Architectural appreciation ended with the butt of a humming persuader ramming into Hiroshi's back.

A squad of six Legioneer Alphas ambushed Hiroshi and his comrades at the lift's egress. Hiroshi, without Cordis Adolesco; Dezba, sans daggers; and Jelani, lacking her persuasive power; were poked and prodded through a succession of hallways—many lined with large bay windows, up a series of stairs to the central gangway. At the end of the lengthy gangway, a right turn then a left, led the group up to then through the doorway of Amram Donnel's throne room.

The General lounged in his ornate throne, knee up and leg rested firmly on a metal ottoman. His head, secure inside the beaked helmet of his full body armor, perched on his massive, armored fist. His eyes never left Hiroshi as the trio were shuffled to the base of the throne positioned at the center of the room.

Two Alphas stepped forward, pushing Jelani and Dezba to their knees. Two more Alphas joined them, placing augmented helmets over the Searcher's heads. The four Alphas then reintegrated into their squad seamlessly. Leaning forward, General Amram Donnel, founder of the Legioneer nation and former High Seraph, inspected his intruders.

Hiroshi examined the alien craftsmanship of the room and

its furnishing. There were no windows and artificial light oozed out of glowing panels on the ceiling. The architecture of the throne and surrounding hall were one in the same: massive slabs of metal meeting at impossibly precise corners with no obvious signs of nuts or bolts or welding. Arching angles joined at flourishing vertices on the ceiling between numerous pillars stretching to the floor, giving the throne room the look of a drained cistern; refit to be airtight. No scuff or scratch, no sign of mistake or misstep.

Hiroshi craned his neck to soak it all in. Legioneer eyes were not much for color though, he observed. War-metal blues and doughnut were Motopia's unbroken motif. The decor reminded him of Span Opticon's Holding Wing and certain odd elements of the Keep. Built twenty years prior, Motopia remained free of the telltale rust and wear of scavenged or recycled materials.

"What's going on? Why is everyone so quiet?" Jelani asked, elbowing Hiroshi.

"It's nothing, Searcher. Excuse the Seraph while he drinks in the magnificence of Motopia." General Donnel answered for Hiroshi, knowing the helmets prevented the Searchers from hearing or seeing. Pride showed through the digital distortions of his own helmet's voice box.

Fixing his attention on Hiroshi, the General continued, "You didn't think you could sneak up here, did you? It's why I built the damn thing, Hiro. Security," Amram said, beckoning to the walls as though they were alive. General Donnel spun with both arms outstretched and raised. "There's no use wasting breath on anything more than why you're here." Amram Donnel's voice boomed and emanated all around the room as he spoke, "I've pondered long in search of words for you—a curious thing to seek out noises meant for the ears of an enemy. Most would have spent their time manufacturing your downfall. Imagining a world free of Zachariah Sandhurst's biting dog. No, no. I've filled my mind with thoughts of your life, not your death. A life where you might be free from bondage, and rid of burdensome, hypocritical Syndicate ideals. I imagine this life for you." Amram was pacing now with arms folded neatly behind his back. "Do you know what else I see? A great ally. A man who accepts fate when it displeases his surrogate father. I see a warrior born of unequaled skill in combat, bowed before a world that deserves more. I see Hiroshi Gunkimono, High Seraph of the Syndicate of Valor, and I see waste."

Hiroshi shifted his weight uncomfortably. The General had his full attention.

"The more I thought, the farther the words I wished to speak to you traveled away from me. The more I prepared, the more effervescent and immaterial my points. And it was then I realized, no words alone can communicate the truths of Neo-Earth. Or the vision of my Legioneers. I know Mr. Galtero, your brother, tried at Holy Lands, but nay—you want to bear *witness* to my motivations to understand for yourself."

General Donnel sauntered to his throne. He did not lounge this time. No, he sat straight up, at the edge of his seat, fully engaged. "Hiroshi, please forgive my cliché preambles. But if you wouldn't mind turning your attention to the display screen on the left." With a motion of his armored hand, what Hiroshi believed to be an inconspicuous wall, was the largest display screen the High Seraph had ever seen. At nine scorchfeet tall and fifteen scorchfeet wide, there was no close contender in his recollection.

"Is this it? A comically large display screen? I did not take you for a fan of the Wave, considering you just snuffed out 'the

189

Illumined One.'" Hiroshi said, scoffing.

General Donnel released a full-bodied laugh.

"The stories about you, hyperbolic as they might be, always leave out your sense of humor." Another wave of his hand and the image on the screen scrambled, then clarified on the still and empty amphitheater at Holy Lands. "What do we have here?"

Hiroshi thought of Paulo Flayr and the regrettable actions preceding his death, then Joan. The dark stains where Ecclesiel and Paulo died were not yet clean; on the General's massive display they stood out like splotches of red copper powder over a white sand beach. Even the image quality was far beyond anything at any of the schools or study centers in Virtus. Hiroshi remained silent.

Another hand-wave. The screen shifted and showed a bird's eye view of the land surrounding the Chains of Motopia. Again, the screen changed and this time it was the inside of Span-Opticon. First Hiroshi's quarters, then an angle from deep inside the Keep.

"Your face tells me you are starting to understand," General Donnel chided. Again, a gesture. A new view, from inside Fortress Pangaia—Celeste's office. Then, to any of the few but widespread screened locales across Neo-Earth. Any place a display screen was installed, the General retained the ability to peer through the screen.

"I can record. Rewatch. Save. I have backups of every sermon Ecclesiel has ever given. After all, it was my engineers, commissioned by Sandhurst's Treaty, that installed them. The 'Illumined One' wanted a way to spread his message, to separate himself from the prophet before him. He was so wanting of acceptance he allowed me to install a small piece of myself in any home that could afford it. There's only one thing to watch and it airs once a week. The power he asked for was approved by Sandhurst and created by me. It only took an intricate network of wiring, radio waves, and geosynchronous satellites to give Ecclesiel the ability to preach technological abstinence across the globe. On one hand, fearing technology and on the other, accepting its obvious utility. I'm tired of the hypocritical lamentations of the technophobes. Neo-Earth is a vacuum of ignorance made stagnant from growth and cultivated solely for stability."

"You mean you watch people from the screens? And you killed Ecclesiel because he was a hypocrite?" Hiroshi asked, his face twisted.

Silence. Amram Donnel lumbered to his feet again. There are no obvious weaknesses to discover in his armor. The few exposed areas on Alpha armor were non-existent or invisible on Donnel's suit.

"*Harrumph.*" The General cleared his throat. "I killed him because I don't *respect* him. Because it was *easy.* Because the Treaty is in turmoil and I'm ready *now.* Ecclesiel was comfortable with the amount of technology that allowed him to control his people. All else is forbidden in the Holy Lands. Don't get me started on Sandhurst's use of Legioneer tech in his study and fabrication centers. Who do you think digitized the Archives? Look at me, at my Impervious Life Suit. It's the consummate improvement on the very same design keeping Ido alive. Zachariah loves tech that fits *his* needs, that keeps his subjects subjective. All else is taboo. Illegal. Contraband. Nonsense. Sandhurst opens the spigot a little wider than Ecclesiel, but his control of its flow is consummate. And the Boundless? Those little fuckin' anarchists wish for enough freedom of information as to render government meaningless. That's what I gathered from their nettlesome movement." General Donnel chuckled. "Not a good week to be Boundless. I didn't plan this, Hiro." Donnel placed his hand on his chest earnestly. "I'm merely capitalizing on the chaos. The Treaty's finished and you know it."

Hiroshi climbed two of the three steps elevating Donnel's throne above the rest of the hall's floor. The Alpha squad tensed.

"The Treaty is ruined because you chose to kill an innocent man merely for offending your sensibilities. You hated the Boundless just as much as the Syndicate or the Vicaarians. They're defunct, and this could have been a shared victory for all of us. But no, you are up here in your flying dreadnought trying to start a spacedamn war!"

"The Treaty is dead because Joan Flayr *isn't!* The reports of her execution at your hands are a lie—well, aren't they? Don't bother denying it. I saw Joan and Paulo together at Ecclesiel's last sermon. They were most certainly among the crowd when your brother took the shot. Ars never killed Paulo Flayr. Alas, Paulo is dead though, isn't he, Hiroshi? Dead at the hands of your human shish kabob technique. Brilliant. I was watching the whole time—even I didn't see you approach. What was that about? You got a thing for Joan? Or did you just shit yourself when you heard a persuader go off? I've re-watched you stick him over and over again and I just can't seem to see clearly which came first, your brother icing Ecclesiel or you perforating Paulo." General Donnel cackled.

Struggling against his bonds, Hiroshi knew he could break them. But his rage settled as quickly as it appeared.

"You think *you* are the hero, don't you? You believe your lies less and your motivations more." Donnel pointed at Hiroshi with a stubby accusatory finger. "You're a killer—Sandhurst's killer. Except you didn't do what you were told. Joan, you let go and let everybody on Neo-Earth think her dead. The Ars, they just fucked up, killed the wrong guy, got greedy. But you. You've been doing whatever you want, killing whomever, whenever you want. It's why I asked Mr. Galtero to invite you here. I hoped you had seen the atrophy of the Syndicate and finally gone rogue."

Hiroshi stepped forward until the tips of his toes and Donnel's touched. "Amram, let me stop you before your 'you and I are not so different' moment. I killed Paulo Flayr, but it was an accident. It is a dishonorable thing to kill a man for no reason at all. No Seraph walks the path perfectly and it's my burden to bear. Joan escaped my custody at Holy Lands in confusion caused by your chaos. My mission might have been a success. If it was your intention to sway me in any way with your gargantuan display screen and your verbose and meandering diatribe, you too have failed your mission. Sure, in the past week I have heard things and seen others that make me question Sandhurst's intentions, but I have done things that would surely make Sandhurst question me. Hearing you now—seeing you as you are—I am resolute. Deep in the heart of your flying dreadnought I find the conviction that I have traveled all of civilization in search of. Clarity that eluded me, even in dreams, is present now."

Smiling, Hiroshi kept on, "Maybe some crust of credit is due to you. When I return to Span Opticon with proof of your treachery, my transgressions will be forgiven." The General squirmed inside his impenetrable armor. "The Elders were right to cast you out of the Syndicate. It was not your love of technology that preceded your fall, it was your love of self that turned you from grace. From up here, above the clouds, I can see the depths of your pride. You *violated* the Treaty! You *assassinated* a human being over the Wave!"

The doors of the room slid open behind Hiroshi. A specter appeared in its doorway then came to rest right next to him at the front of the General's throne.

"Heya, Hiro," Mr. Galtero greeted his younger brother. Hiroshi returned his greeting with a sneer then turned his attention back to Donnel.

"You have stolen fire from the gods," Hiroshi said. "That much is clear. Do you mean to burn down all of Neo-Earth with it? The Treaty brought stability to a time of seemingly endless instability. For seventy years Neo-Earth has known peace. Sandhurst amended the Treaty, allowing your Legioneers to exist. The other factions allowed you to build your 'city in the sky' unimpeded, unmolested; and you return from your self-imposed exile with nothing but scorn for those who left you to your devices. I will not. I cannot walk away from this place in good conscience. To pretend that Motopia is anything but a beacon of war is criminal."

"What about *your* actions, High Seraph? You cut your way across Neo-Earth, barged onto *my* land, into *my* fortress, with two known Searchers. You have some nerve talking to me about declarations of war," General Donnel said.

"When I report back, Sandhurst will no longer show leniency to your actions."

"*If* you report back," Amram Donnel said, slamming his fists down onto the throne's armrest.

"You said you would just talk to him," Mr. Galtero said, butting in.

General Donnel pointed with five fingers towards the massive screen. It flickered then showed an image of a vial of blood. The camera was no longer still. The perspective moved and shifted as if from Hiroshi's own eyes.

"This is called a movie. Maybe you've heard of them. A preferred form of media among the Preneo. I found this moving image and hundreds of thousands of others just like it in a repository deep in the Uncharted Regions years ago. Sandhurst had me make copies and destroy the originals. Of course, I did not. Thus, marked the first time that I disobeyed him. Was Joan *your* first?" General Donnel paused. For a fleeting moment, his shoulders appeared to sag, and his voice retained a somber quality. Suppressing the moment, Donnel spoke.

"These movies were left behind, engraved on quartz and encased in diamond, to make sure that no one could ever hide the truths of Neo-Earth, not for long." Amram was now pointing at the massive display screen with four fingers. "This one here I find really interesting. It explains why certain people, for example Zachariah Sandhurst, might live much longer than others. Why some people, yourself for example, are quicker, or more durable than the average human."

Hiroshi watched, begrudgingly, as Donnel explained. He recognized some of the images as blood cells and various organs of the human body, others for what the Archives described as proteins, molecules, and atoms.

"Pre-Scorch humans had cameras that could look deep into your blood. It's possible to peer so far down that the past is revealed as the present and the future can be viewed in the now. Sandhurst's redacted curriculums teach kids about the basics of DNA. But, the Preneo were masters of it. Artists—sorcerers, twisting and editing DNA just as they molded and reshaped our planet. The Preneo's proficiency in science and technology did not come without a cost."

"What the fuck!" Dezba shouted from inside of her sound dampening helmet. Sensing Dezba's distress Jelani began to yell as well.

"Ahhhhh!"

Turning to his Alphas, Donnel pointed to the ceiling twice with his thumb. They stepped forward and increased the dials on the helmets effectively drowning out their captors.

"Where was I? Ah, yes. The Preneo's constant discoveries pushed the upper limits of our tiny planet's economy, so increased innovation, so increased greed. When the fiat currencies, gold standards and digital bits finally ran out, their godlike grasp on reality dwindled. The humans who scorched the earth, created the great ships and put humanity in space stasis, they did it because they were broke, not because they were smart. Earth ran out of money. Full stop. With the little scraps and energy that remained they manufactured the Scorch Period. Worse than war, it was business as usual. Thousands of years of good science, bad ideas and outdated politics as usual that delivered civilization to its infertile conclusion."

"And all that is in *this* movie?"

The screen flickered to a new movie. "No, Hiro. This one is about the negative effects thousands of years of space sleep can have on human physiology and the techniques used to avoid or counteract them.

"The most common technique being, genetic alteration. You see, when a human, or any mammal really, sleeps for months they grow incredibly weak from atrophy at the muscular level and then deterioration at the cellular level. Preneo scientists wanted humanity to sleep for much longer than a few months. So, they tweaked us, and changed us, with small genetic modifications assumed imperceptible. Taboo techniques and experiments once considered illegal were used on the population, the public, the people of Neo-Earth, to counteract the atrophy and deterioration of their impending, prolonged rest. Alas, there were some unintended benefits. It's theorized to have a less than three percent chance to cause increased lifespan, brain mass, mental acuity, muscle mass, muscle strength, increased bone density, you name it. The Preneo, through their desperation, inadvertently realized what was true only in myths."

"We believe," Galtero added, "as their direct descendants, it's possible that one percent or as many as six percent of Neo-Earthlings have inherited these abilities," Mr. Galtero eagerly added in, moving to a position next to the throne. He leaned on the now empty L-shaped seat with an arm, gripping his briefcase in the other.

Hiroshi cocked his head slightly trying to remember exactly how old Elder Sandhurst was. General Donnel resumed pacing, arms now folded stiffly behind his back.

"Achieving self-sacrifice of the highest order, the Preneo have gone. Undeterred by the ramifications, they made us the unwilling subjects of their grand experiment. The scientists, politicians, economists, the global administrators and custodians, put the world to sleep. It was easier for them to do that than to admit that they were wrong. They bartered for an apocalypse in place of Armageddon. They knocked humanity unconscious and hoped that it might wake up tomorrow unaware of our problematic past. That's the truth of the world. The only truth to find when you ask the obvious questions. What lies beyond the Uncharted Regions?

How do we know just how big they are? What lies across the Perennial Ocean? It's a big planet, Hiroshi. Why are there only five factions? Where do we come from and why do we live concentrated in the western half of a single continent? These questions have answers and Sandhurst keeps these answers buried."

The General made a fist, and the display screen froze; stuck on the image of Preneo scientists packed into an alabaster laboratory engaged in all manner of examinations.

"From this point in history on, there can only be two types of leaders. Those who learn the truth and concede, or those who learn the truth and are inspired. My Legioneers will create a world that can never be put to sleep again. Your brother discovered these same truths, on his own. He sought me out, on his own. You set Joan free, on your own. Fate reunites we three former High Seraphim to forge a brighter future for our planet, transformed from hellish dirt to empyrean earth."

Amram waved his right hand with four fingers pointed up, the display then segmented into four unique perspectives. Four giant clamps were now visible on the screen. Hiroshi surmised he was watching living images, fed directly from outside of Motopia because the constructs on display were quite similar to those he encountered at the base of its chains, and they swayed and groaned realistically. The video feed was complete with the ambient sounds of the passing wind.

Hiroshi followed Donnel with his eyes as he made his way back to his ornate throne and returned to a lounge. A chopping motion from his arm seemed to send a signal through the display causing the clasps to release.

The entire throne room shook and trembled. Hiroshi's stomach plummeted to the plains below. It felt as though all of

Motopia had been dropped into the ocean. Breaking his bonds without exertion, Hiroshi leapt for the nearest pillar and braced himself for the fall.

The room bobbled and jounced about for a minute then stabilized. General Donnel and Mr. Galtero, seeking no support or shelter, stared at Hiroshi and then each other.

"Are—are we moving? What is this, Amram? I have not turned down your offer yet."

"Don't be so naive as to think any part of my plans required you as an ally. Consider me sending down just one Alpha to greet you, mercy. Allowing you an audience in *my* throne room, it *is* mercy, not necessity. I always found you to be a bit of a brat. I suspected before asking, that you might not join my ranks. You're *too* good, Hiro. *Too* disciplined, *too* clean. For you, things came *too* easy. It's unrelatable and *annoying.* You're alive because Mr. Galtero wished it to be so. He thought killing you without giving you a chance would be unjust. Pitying you, I agreed."

Donnel tightened his gauntlets into fists and the display screens reverted back to their dormant, wall states.

Hiroshi released a sigh and shook his head.

"I will not be enticed as Saigo was. It is clear to me you are both mad. I came here to confirm with my own eyes that which would seduce my kin and make him leave his baby brother in the clutches of the man you now want me to betray. You want me to turn my back on the Syndicate, because of a man's flaws? You want me to look past you and my brother's crimes? Crimes against the religious folk of the mountain, crimes against humanity? Confess to me as High Seraph of Syndicate all of your offenses and I will make sure you get Holding when they ask for your head."

"Can I kill him yet?" General Donnel asked Mr. Galtero with an armored fist on his helmet, unmoved by Hiroshi's speech.

Running his hand back through his hair, Mr. Galtero sauntered over to Hiroshi; there was nary a stain or wrinkle on his Preneo uniform.

"Listen—Hiro. Don't you think you're taking this thing a little too personally?" Pausing, "What was Ecclesiel to you anyway? Nothing?" Mr. Galtero was closer to Hiroshi now. Hiroshi felt the warmth of his breath. "Nothing is what's out there for you. Down there. Back there. The Syndicate is crumbling, it's as fragile and brittle as Sandhurst's very own bones. We're taking over. There's no other way to mince it. Sandhurst is on the outs. The Treaty is on the outs. It's time for the Legioneers and whoever chooses to align with us to bring about a new age. An age when contextomy and obfuscation are treated as obvious criminal acts and not the status quo. You see, Hiro. It's not like you think. I gave you a choice just as the General allotted me one." Placing his hand on his brother's shoulder. "I would've stolen you away and brought you with, all those years back when I first uncovered the Syndicate's lies." Mr. Galtero let his suitcase down next to Hiroshi, straightening his suit as he spoke, "But, would that have been fair? I left you there in hopes you would grow and see for yourself the true hypocrisy and dysfunction of the Syndicate. The places I needed to go, the things I endeavored to see, I wouldn't have been able to explain them to you, not yet, nor protect you from the very real dangers of their implications."

During Mr. Galtero's speech, the General had quietly ordered his Legioneer Alphas to escort Jelani and Dezba to the nearest cells. Ensured Mr. Galtero held Hiroshi's full attention, General Donnel activated the combat protocols in his Impervious

Life Suit.

"But—" Hiroshi said.

"—The truth of the world is the powder keg Sandhurst's fragile peace is built upon," Mr. Galtero said. "The Ars would watch it burn for trusts and favors, the Vicaarians would hope it burns in pursuit of some celestial after life, the Boundless would pack as much black powder under our asses as to see an explosion so powerful none of the factions would survive, and the Syndicate and its Seraph's would merely add length to the wick for as long as the simple people would allow. Under tremendous societal pressure to leave the past alone, and woefully unaware of the impending eruption, people have eked out mundane lives. The Syndicate thrives now that the flock is lost and wary of query. To Sandhurst, the past is an effigy, a dead thing to be seen then forgotten. To the Legioneers the past is interactive, a road map to a favorable tomorrow. It's easy to look around and be scared. Worried that the power that created Motopia, if corrupted could destroy the world. Well, I'm telling you, if a change in power and philosophy destroys the world then we might already be living in oblivion. Civilization isn't fragile, it's fickle. It's time for us, the inheritors of Neo-Earth, to walk on our own, to run even. Sandhurst held our hands as we stood. The General wished to create the wind that will teach the world to fly."

The initial lurching of Motopia eased to a constant but subtle tremor when Dezba and Jelani burst back into the throne hall, fierce and covered in what remained of their Alpha escorts. Their signature arms returned to their grasps, but the bindings and the dampening helmets gone.

"Oy! General. We're gonna have to extract you on two counts of Unapproved Detaining of a Searcher, one count of

Conspiracy to Murder a Faction Official, and one count of just, really pissing me the fuck off. We agreed to accompany the Seraph, here, to *talk*. You attacked us. It was one thing to bind us, but those blasted helmets." Jelani tossed Cordis Adolesco over to Hiroshi as she talked, taking a position next to him.

Donnel followed Cordis Adolesco with his eyes as he spoke, "You murdered one of my Ace's and two Animal Control Officers whose research can't easily be reproduced. You didn't exactly come bearing a white fl—"

Dezba didn't join Jelani and Hiroshi, less interested in prattle, she kept advancing. Hiroshi knew what was next.

Two curved daggers whistled across the room cutting Am-ram's remarks short. He smacked one away with a palm and blocked the other with his forearm. Hiroshi was on the offensive. He found Mr. Galtero. Spinning into a crouch with an extended leg, he swept his brother's feet off the ground. Not letting go of his briefcase, he struck the floor awkwardly with a thud and a groan.

A barrage of pellets pelted General Donnel. He didn't bother to dodge or duck. Each missile ricocheted off his suit. Jelani pressed at her detonator hastily, the projectiles exploding midair in an extravagant light show. The concussive waves slowed his advance but did little to no damage to his armor. As the last of Jelani's rounds exploded, Dezba, who had been making a beeline towards Amram, landed an aerial kick, strik-ing his breastplate. The momentum of the maneuver landed her into a crouch on his broad shoulders. Using her muscular legs to push off, she sprang back, barely escaping the General's crushing embrace. Dezba landed out of reach in an expert squat. The wind of Jelani running past cooled her sweaty brow.

Jelani was always there. Every time, and without fail. Dezba followed her sister-at-arms with blades in hand.

"It will take—more than fireworks—and somersaults to see you out of here—alive," General Donnel said between chuckles as he taunted his attackers, pressing the knobs at his neck, the beaked helmet split open along its vertical axis, exposing the grizzled, rosy face of a middle-aged man. "It's time I told you. You will never leave here!" Amram Donnel said. Drunken with madness, his arms flailed about as he spoke. "That motion you felt! That rumbling under your feet! Is *my* feat! The greatest of all!" he boomed.

"Motopia flies! And Hiroshi, young, naive, stupid, Hiroshi, I've set an irreversible course for your Span Opticon fortress. It will be over today, certain and soon!" With each of Donnel's seemingly erratic movements, a section of the smooth metal that appeared to be walls became windows.

Rushing to a window, Hiroshi confirmed Amram's claims with his own eyes. The gargantuan chains that once held the structure up were in fact gone. Just as the 'movie' had shown. He could see them in the distance, limp and coiled upon themselves like some colossal snakes playing dead, hoping to remain undisturbed in the flatland below.

Hiroshi's head spun. Never having experienced the terror of flight, his stomach flipped inside out. The simple oats he ate earlier left his mouth and landed with a moist splat.

He slinked to the floor beside his vomit, plagued by dizziness, panic, a racing heart and blurry vision. All eyes were locked on the last High Seraph, doubled over, in a moment of utter weakness.

The Searchers turned back to an amused General Donnel.

"*Ha!* Galtero, look at your brother. Curled up like a sick dog." Motioning to Hiroshi with a sideways thumb, General Donnel turned his attention to Jelani and Dezba. "Now, you know. Not the half-truths of Neo-Earth, but the truth of human accomplishment. We've stolen fire from the gods! And no one should stop us, *we are the gods!*"

The birdlike helmet snapped tightly shut, sealing him inside his Impervious Life Suit once again. Standing straight up, he assumed his full height of five towering scorchfeet. Clapping his hands together, Donnel became a blur—moving faster than even Mr. Galtero had seen. The General was in one place one instant, and a breath away from Jelani, the next.

The gears and hydraulic pumps inside his suit allowed him to hoist her into the air without effort. Turning the struggling Searcher upside down he drove her head first into the metal flooring.

Dezba's blood baked within her tensed body. Rushing over to Hiroshi, Dezba laid a stern hand on his shoulder and said everything he needed to hear to be shaken from his crippling bout of vertigo.

"Will this be your legacy? Will Donnel tell your story? Well, Sword of the Syndicate? This may be our ultimate bout. Rise and fight with honor or die like the common coward."

Behind them Mr. Galtero and General Donnel circled in on an isolated and immobile Jelani. She moaned into consciousness, the bolts of pain traveling across her body, kept her pinned to the floor. Dezba came to her partner's aid, hurling her body into the armored General. Amram took two steps back, teetering on one foot. Before Dezba could retreat or capitalize, Mr. Galtero was inside his briefcase retrieving a persuader—not his usual.

The moment he had dreaded for a decade, and hoped would never come, had arrived. Mr. Galtero would have to kill his only brother, his little brother, or die himself. Hiroshi's vertigo would likely be his only opening and Mr. Galtero did not plan to die that day.

"No! Not that one!" Amram shouted, but it was too late. Mr. Galtero's finger was squarely on the trigger ready to fire.

Hiroshi, arose. The dignity in his stance returned slowly. Stomaching his nausea, he was High Seraph Gunkimono once again.

Mr. Galtero fired. *Gazow!* Hiroshi was there with a swift knee to knock his brother's shot off course. The cloud of gas and the beam of light that appeared inside of it exploded out of the persuader and tore through the ceiling of the throne room, continuing on far out of sight.

"*Fool!*" Donnel shouted to Mr. Galtero whilst battling an enraged Dezba. Jelani, back on her feet, joined Dezba in keeping the accelerated General busy.

"I know, I know. But all it'll take is just one good sho—" Mr. Galtero shouted back, lining up a point-blank shot. Dezba's soaring blade meant to stop him. Galtero, caught the dagger midair with his free hand. Using the dagger, he slashed at a crouching Hiroshi, shredding nothing but cloth fibers. A sliding tackle kept Hiroshi under the attacks and brought Mr. Galtero down again. The Ghost wasn't grounded for long. A pop-up and a handspring carried him out of Hiroshi's reach—so he thought. Hiroshi was faster than predicted—but was he strong?

"I'm sorry," Hiroshi mouthed, then grabbed Mr. Galtero's wrist above the hand that gripped the persuader. The Ghost tried to pull free, but Hiroshi rendered his brother's arm useless with a bone-breaking, ligament traumatizing wrench. Sweat gathered on Mr. Galtero's forehead but he resisted the urge to wince. A few swipes from Dezba's dagger cause Hiroshi to release Galtero's mangled arm. His hand, still wrapped around the persuader, drooped at the joint, held in place by nothing but skin and connective tissue.

"I have put you out of this fight. It is up to you to decide if that is mercy."

"Have you now? Your combat repertoire has grown alongside your ego," Galtero grumbled, eyeballing his withered appendage. "You know I'm gonna have to fuck you up for this right?" Galtero, succumbing to the pain, put his back to one of the room's many pillars and slid to the floor with not enough will to make good on his threat.

"As opposed to shooting me with that fucking thing!"

Galtero, holding up his arm. "This fucking thing is a Gaser. *Gas—er*, shoots out a cloud of some sort, the properties of which allow for very hot and very powerful beams to be focused and aimed inside. The gas is harmless, cold, but harmless. *Heh.* I saw what Donnel achieved with the Alpha's and made my own version."

The sound of Dezba hitting a wall and the General hitting her shortly after, distracted Hiroshi. When his gaze returned, Mr. Galtero's Gaser was pointed at Hiroshi's nose and had already begun its frigid emissions. The cold air buffeted his face, blowing his hair follicles back. Tiny sparks inside the gas cloud signified an intensifying beam. *Gazow!* The flickering lights coalesced into a purple ray then jumped toward Hiroshi.

Unsheathing his sword and holding it across his chest, the beam hit the sword hilt and deflected away. The vector of energized light would've torn another hole through the command hall if General Donnel had not been there, arms crossed in an X, to absorb the blow. It pushed him back a scorchfeet but didn't leave a scratch on his armor.

Seeing the force of the blast, Hiroshi stared daggers at Saigo.

"Ah. Cordis Adolesco," General Donnel interrupted Hiroshi and Galtero's silent exchange.

"Saigo's idea and my engineering. A beautiful weapon. It is good to see it again. It won't help you. I, of course, designed this suit to be resistant to the very acid that the sword creates. Not only that but I'm faster than any human. Your training, your tactics—meaningless in the face of my innovations."

"Hiro, just join us. Span Opticon won't exist by this time tomorrow," Mr. Galtero offered, struggling to stand and nursing his purple, black and shattered wrist. Ignoring the pain, he pried the Gaser out of its fingers with his good hand, letting the weapon patter to the ground. A few deep breaths later and Mr. Galtero was ready to duel. Tucking what used to be a hand at his side and extending a fist with the other he assumed a fighting stance.

Hiroshi meant to do the same, but a torrent of kicks delivered to his midsection left him no time and no breath. Mr. Galtero mouthed 'I'm sorry' before following up the combination with two straight punches, both to Hiroshi's abdomen: The first with the good hand, the second with the withered one.

The second punch lifted Hiroshi off his feet and sent him into the wall behind him, alongside Dezba and Jelani who had been tossed away by a rampaging Donnel. Hiroshi landed on his feet and closed the gap Mr. Galtero created.

Galtero and Donnel were side-by-side now, waiting for their opponents' next moves. Hiroshi arrived with his sword out and swinging. Mr. Galtero ducked a swipe that would have cleaved his head away and Donnel caught the blade tip in his palms when Hiroshi swung towards him. Jelani appeared, using her persuader butt as a club, she slammed Donnel's hand down, freeing Hiroshi's sword for movement. Hiroshi didn't waste the assist. With all his strength he brought Cordis Adolesco above his head then down on General Donnel's. The vibration of the impact sent painful shockwaves down Hiroshi's arms and back. Amram was stunned. Dezba got on all fours behind him. All he needed was a push. Jelani did the deed by firing one explosive pellet above his head. A step back and Donnel was bowled over by Dezba, who had not just tripped him but grabbed him as he fell. Dezba held Donnel up behind her back. Spinning round with muscles bulging, Dezba slammed his head into a neighboring pillars.

Mr. Galtero, taking advantage of the commotion, grabbed Hiroshi from behind, and wrapped his arms around his brother's neck. Hiroshi tried to call for Dezba or Jelani, but Galtero applied more pressure.

On his feet, Amram made the Searchers pay for his humiliation. Jelani tried to retreat but Donnel was too fast. Using the gears in his suit to accelerate a punch beyond peak human capacity, Donnel drove his fist into Jelani's spine. Blood erupted from her mouth. Dezba was close by—not close enough to stop the maddened General.

Hiroshi flipped Galtero over his head, loosening the choke hold and knocking Dezba's dagger free. The Ghost landed on his back and was up again in an instant. Hiroshi tried to reach Dezba, but Mr. Galtero batted him away with a kick.

Amram Donnel, returning to his quickened state, became nothing more than a gray streak as he darted back and forth hammering Dezba with a punch every time he neared. All the labor went from his movement. He glided across the floor throwing his mass around freely and without penalty. Dezba a dagger up brought a together in time to block one of the General's blows. Lunging for Mr. Galtero's abandoned Gaser, she claimed it and fired. Dezba didn't pull the trigger. She lied down on it.

The gas, then the beam, sped at Amram Donnel. He blocked it as he did before, but the continuous beam brought him to his knees. The purple light flowed into his crossed arms until the heat was too much for him to take. Twisting his body, he had no choice but to allow the light to refract, piercing through the wall again. Dezba stabilized her aim and began to trace an opening in the wall. Mr. Galtero moved to stop her but was batted back by an open palm punch from his brother.

Dezba brought the beam back to its starting position and a chunk of wall fell outwards revealing the skies of Neo-Earth behind it.

Wind roared through the hole as the room depressurized.

Mr. Galtero, knowing of the built-in safety measures, wasn't as worried. He turned his attention to Dezba who had only stopped firing the Gaser because it began to supercool in her hands.

Mr. Galtero charged, elbow down and shoulder tucked with intentions to bowl Dezba over. Dezba flipped the persuader around, so the butt faced up and made a motion to throw the weapon as if it was one of her daggers. Mr. Galtero bought the bluff and braced for impact. But she didn't throw the persuader. She *did* throw one of her daggers, piercing Mr. Galtero's stomach. He winced in pain but did not slow his charge. Dezba threw her second dagger. Aiming for the first she hit her mark and sent the blade deeper into his gut. He doubled over but still didn't stop his advance. The Gaser had cooled down and by the time Hiroshi realized what Dezba had done there was already a sizzling, steaming hole in Mr. Galtero's skull. Inertia brought his lifeless body to rest on her shoulder in an embrace that under other circumstances would've been a hug.

"Nooo!" Hiroshi screamed, rushing to his brother's lifeless body. "I, it was supposed to be—" Tears welled up in his eyes. "Dezba—"

"What have you done!" General Donnel boomed, appearing at Jelani's side. Fearing what he might do next, Dezba reached out. He picked up the dying but savable Searcher and threw her out of the hole the Gaser had created. *Phoop*! And Jelani was gone; dropped from a fatal height with a near-fatal injury.

The fight gone in Dezba. The same for Hiroshi. Dezba mourned her truest friend. Hiroshi mourned his eldest brother. Donnel mourned his closest comrade. Pressing the beads at his neck, his falcon-shaped helmet opened up.

General Donnel was crying. "You fool! You've killed him. And for what? The Syndicate? It won't even be there tomorrow." Turning away from the hole he approached Hiroshi who was kneeling over the lifeless body of Saigo Gunkimono. Dezba was not far away, prostrate, face in her open palms. Unmoving. Unfeeling.

"You know I didn't want this, kid. Not this. I want you to see that. See the truth. The truth of everything that happened here today. And *will* happen *because* of today. You know." Donnel sniffled, wiping tears away. "You gotta' think, Hiro." Donnel raised both his arms above Hiroshi's head. "I'm gonna accelerate my fists to a velocity that will cause your skull to scatter and your brain to emulsify. It's mercy. *They* gutted Mr. Galtero, then desecrated him with his own persuader. All your brother wanted, Hiro—he just wanted you to join us."

Amram did not see, but Hiroshi had Cordis Adolesco drawn and hidden at his side with the lever pressed. The acid had begun to gather and bead at its tip. Donnel barely finished saying the 'n' in 'join' when Hiroshi spun, on his knees, his robe tucked underneath for less resistance. Lunging out with his sword he wanted dearly to impale Donnel through his loud mouth and big head. But the helmet clapped shut as Donnel jerked back avoiding the blade. The sword fell short of its mark. But just enough of the tip was caught in the closing helmet, that a single perforation remained inside, beyond the protection of his armor. A few drops of the potent ooze dribbled onto Donnel's nose. Leaving a red cavern where they landed. In the areas where it made contact, his skin went goopy as the reaction grew.

Instinctively, Donnel tried to wiggle his nose, but those muscles and tendons had joined the steamy broth of blood and acid that dripped down the back of his throat. The acid was his own creation. Observing the collector crabs of the Perennial Plains he reversed engineered the fusing properties of their saliva into a virulent bio acid. Once in contact with any organic, and a lot of inorganic material, the reaction spread until nothing reactive was left. A thimble of ooze had made its way inside his ILS, but it was enough to ensure the fatal liquefaction of a man his size. The armor would be fine, it was designed to survive such an attack, but pieces of the occupant would be collected like soup in the legs of the suit.

General Amram Donnel had two choices—die a horrible death in front of two people who would enjoy it; surrendering his suit to them or jump off of Motopia and die in peace somewhere in the expanse where his Legioneers could recover the ILS at a later time. Turning his attention back to the hole, he lifted his arms and let himself fall backward. Neither Hiroshi nor Dezba bothered to try and stop him.

They sat in silence for a long while until finally, Dezba stood. She retrieved her blades then moved to the throne room's exit. She stood there without speaking for another moment.

"She wasn't dead."

"I know."

"I killed your brother?"

"I know."

"I didn't—"

"—Yeah, I know." A beat.

"What'd we do now, Seraph?"

"What have we done? Motopia still flies, and there's a battalion of Legioneers stationed on it."

Dezba didn't respond. She walked to Central's automatic doors. They slid open, revealing a fresh squad of Alpha's, accompanied by two Aces on the other side. Stepping through the doors, they closed behind her. Hiroshi retrieved Cordis Adolesco, which had been snapped at the tip when it was caught in Donnel's helmet and cast aside before his descent. Moving to Mr. Galtero's lifeless body, Hiroshi lifted him up onto his shoulder. The wound he sustained during his fight with the king collector had been aggravated and reopened. He collected his brother's briefcase and fastened it to his back. When he reached the exit and triggered whatever spooky mechanism that recognized his presence and made the doors open, the Alpha's were dead, with the red waters of life cascading from the few exposed points in their armor.

The Aces, stubborn, still fought. Gliding to and fro as they danced and dodge around the enraged Searcher. Seeing how easily she dispatched their comrades, they dared not get close.

The Legioneers seemed reluctant to use their persuaders. Trained not to fire inside Motopia under any circumstance, or they adhered to an order not to kill Jelani or Dezba; an order that Donnel may not have had time to update before his fall. It didn't look like he had gotten any messages out. No audible alarms could be heard. The beating feet of approaching soldiers absent. The latter would explain why Donnel bothered putting sensory deprivation helmets on the Searchers in the first place. He must've intended to release or keep them as prisoners, but never to kill them.

One Ace was now dead. The other screamed in agony as Dezba sawed his leg off at the knee. The severed leg kept on hovering until it bumped into a wall, teetering over. The Ace to whom it belonged clawed at the ground, desperately trying to escape his rabid attacker. Kicking his severed leg to the side, Dezba trailed behind him, bloody daggers extended to either side of her. She threw them both.

In a surprising effort, the Legioneer increased power in his remaining boot, just enough to propel himself along the ground and out of the way of her daggers.

"GDP. We're being attacked! I repeat. GDP. The prisoners, they're free! The High Sera—" He managed to scream into a communication device built into the wrist of his armor before Hiroshi ran him through with the chipped Cordis Adolesco.

"Not good," Hiroshi said, examining their location for some sense of direction.

Picking up her daggers, Dezba and Hiroshi then retraced their steps back to Motopia's central gangway.

"How many soldiers do you think are on this thing, Seraph?"

Hiroshi paused, trying to recall the entries with the relevant information.

213

"According to our records, Donnel's Legioneers are five thousand. Sandhurst believes three thousand of those five are trained in combat. Of the soldier class Legioneers, there are one thousand known Alphas, and fifty confirmed Aces."

"Two of us against five thousand of them. I like those odds," Dezba said, her eyes shone like glimmering daggers.

"Five thousand!?" Hiroshi scoffed. "The other two thousand are mechanics and engineers. Realistically we only need to beat a thousand of them. The Legioneers have no army without their Alphas ... But then there is the whole legality of this. We did sneak into a recognized faction's command center," Hiroshi said.

"Yeah, we did. On the eve they planned to invade another recognized faction. You really gonna call this hovering atrocity a command center? Here, look." Dezba waved two fingers sarcastically. "With whatever miserable powers entrusted to me by the Treaty of Neo Earth, I sentence all Alphas to expiration with extreme prejudice and excessive bias. Now it's legal. I don't wanna hear any more of your good ole boy shit. They killed Jelani. And if it wasn't for me Amram would've *beat* you."

"And my brother would be alive."

"Your brother died long ago." Spinning, Hiroshi stared down Dezba.

"That's it. Get pissed. Get fucking mad, Seraph. 'Cause there are at least ninety Legioneers behind you and they do *not* look like mechanic and engineer types."

Hiroshi laid Mr. Galtero down gently, unhooked his briefcase, and placed it at his side just as tenderly. Turning back to Dezba he said, "Let us do this."

Chapter 27

A shadow like billowing smoke reached the eastern boundary of the Holy Lands. If the Vicaarians were not preoccupied in mourning, they would have noticed Motopia's approach. And, like the people of the plains, they might have sought shelter to wait out the passing, skyward phenomena. The shade from above did little to affect the climate of the already downcast Vicaarians.

With its body nestled among the clouds and mostly obscured, Donnel's masterpiece looked down at the lasting devastation from its creator. From a courtyard atop Holy Land's mausoleum, Joan Flayr stared back.

The flying disc wrapped in clouds matched Motopia's profile in sight and size, but Joan knew it could not be. Motopia was chained, isolated miles to the east, far beyond the plains, and closer to the ocean than the mountains.

"Is that a planet?" a child no taller than two scorchfeet asked, tugging at Joan's sleeve. Her attention broken; Joan recoiled at the touch of a sudden stranger. Releasing a sigh of relief upon realizing it was only a curious young one, she searched the surrounding courtyard for the parents.

"Mommy says sometimes planets can be seen even in the

daytime. Did you know that?"

"I did," Joan said, finding enough joy and wonder in the child's round face to settle her grief in the moment. "Do you mind my asking where your parents are?"

"Mommy is at work and Daddy is … right over there." The child pointed to a neighboring congregation of important looking Vicaarians with a stubby finger.

"Which one is *your* father?" The child appeared confused by Joan's question at first, but still laughed a response

"Nadir. Our last name is Ming. Nadir Ming, he's right there. Everyone knows my dad." The child shifted its look of infinite curiosity from Motopia to Joan. Joan searched the group of two women and three men for the Vicaarian's Master of Logistics.

"Is that him there, with the notepad in his hand?"

"Daddy never goes anywhere without his papers. 'Don't draw on my super important work stuff okay, Mittens?'" The child mocked her father's tone and mannerisms as she quoted him. Joan tried her hardest not to laugh by returning her eyes back to the sky.

Motopia, having traversed the width of the mountain range in minutes and continuing its westward course, no longer flew directly above the courtyard. The evidence of its presence was a wake of clouds arranged in odd, artificial patterns as if the fragile, indestructible fabric of reality had been combed or raked.

When Joan turned back to the child they were no longer alone. The mourning Vicaarians had taken notice of Motopia. Gathered around Joan at the courtyard's edge, they watched Motopia leave the skies of their territory.

Finding his child in the crowd, Nadir Ming eyed Joan suspiciously as he grabbed the young one's hand and walked away.

Joan heard Nadir ask a question as they departed.

"The sad lady?" the child said, looking over her shoulder. "She was nice to me." Their pace hastened and the conversation decreased in volume and clarity. This time it was the young one who appeared to ask a question, pointing at the sky with her free hand.

"It was an omen." Joan heard Nadir say, and quite clearly, "A sign from the Fallen that we have failed. Now we must—" The rest of his sentence was lost to the wind as Motopia shrank in size and Joan found another secluded corner of the courtyard to resume her solemn grief.

* * *

Motopia was a scene of scurrying madness and streaming bodies.

"What's going on?" Alpha Ace Geeza Londo said, stopping one of the many Alphas pushing past him. "Where is everybody going?"

"Sir. The deadman's signal in Donnel's ILS has been triggered. The Gloam Dawn Protocol is in full effect. You didn't get the ping?"

"My communication unit just stopped working. I'm on my way down to Engineering to see what those eggheads have to say."

"Listen, Lon, I mean, sir, I gotta' go. My squad is about to leave."

"Wait, wait, the Gloam Dawn Protocol? Donnel's dead and the invasion is still on?"

"Just as he always said it would be," Alpha Jaelynn said, moving away. Geeza grabbed the Alpha by the elbow.

"Wait. What of Leadership?"

"The intruders are blocking the main gangway, so all the top officials have pulled back from the conflict and are congregating in the cargo bay, waiting for transport." Geeza didn't meet the Alpha's gaze or attempt a response. "Are you alright, sir?" Alpha Ace Londo nodded yes and loosened his grip on his comrade. Shaking off the confusion of the encounter, the Alpha scurried off to join her crew.

Thoughts of his own crew blossomed in his mind. If he had not received the Gloam Dawn alert, then his crew was also unable to reach him.

Setting off in the opposite direction of the crowd, Geeza arrived at the War Games room across from the Barracks. From inside of War Games, he headed for the locker rooms at the back of the combat simulation center.

Two Alpha's and three members of the Legioneer infantry waited there. Seeing their leader tardy and sweating, they greeted him with pseudo sarcastic cheers.

"Maurie, Ona, Rob, Nadine, Meyers ... Good to see you all," Londo said, meeting their eyes, from Alpha to infantry, as he said their names. "I didn't get the alert. My comm is busted."

"We figured," Alpha Maurie Bond said, fidgeting with his humming persuader before slinging it over his shoulder.

"Here, lemme' get a look at that thing," Technology Specialist and Alpha Ona Kita said. Geeza Londo held out his arm as his team's mechanic unfastened the bracer and began her silent inspection.

"Okay. Here's the situation," Geeza Londo said, clapping his hands together. "General Donnel is dead or sustained a mortal injury at the very least. That means we have lost the benefit of his leadership during this assault. It won't be what we envisioned or wanted, but that's life."

"Sounds like High Seraph Gunkimono backs up what is said about him," Intel Specialist Meyers Hamzara said, arms crossed over his own wrist communication device which, modified to operate at longer distances, was significantly larger than most.

"Relax, Meyers. You speak too soon or too true, either way it hurts," Alpha Maurie Bond cut in.

"Hiroshi is just a man. Weak to the same things Donnel is—was," Geeza said, shooting Meyers a quick glance.

"So, it's gonna be a recovery mission? Secure Donnel's ILS suit, get it off Motopia?" Tactics Specialist Niviar Nadine asked amid the sounds of her cracking her knuckles.

"The ping came from the ground ..." Meyers confirmed.

"The ground?" Geeza said, seeking clarity.

"Yeah. And, I don't mean below us. The last ping was from the Perennial Plains. Wait. An incoming message? That's weird ... Mhmm, okay. Leadership has successfully evacuated Motopia, along with any other critical personnel."

"Just us fighters left, huh?" Tactics Specialist Rob Dinimarajan said amid a chuckle. "You think we will be enough for just—" he continued, while counting on his fingers. Reaching three, he pretended to lose count and threw his hand up in exasperation. "Three, intruders?"

"Those '*intruders*' are top notch warriors, from no-nonsense factions," Alpha Kita answered.

"Who may have just murdered the General," Geeza said, piggy backing off Ona Kita's point.

"So, what's the move, Lon, sir?" Tactics Specialist Nadine asked, looking up for the first time since lacing up her inner boots and slipping into armored ones.

"We join the fight! Meyers, where's the conflict located, now?"

"The data suggests the fight is centralized on the upper ring, on the segment of the gangway nearest Donnel's throne hall. We are currently taking casualties. Heavy. Sir, I'm only seeing two assailants," Intel Specialist Hamzara said.

"How the fuck is that possible?" Dinimarajan scoffed between puffs of a lit cigarette.

"Numbers are our best advantage ..." Meyers began to explain.

"... And they're using positioning to make numbers work against us," Tactics Specialist Niviar said.

"Not to mention the fucking moratorium on persuader use inside of Motopia," Dinimarajan said, in a way the others knew exactly how stupid he thought the idea was.

"Damn. Donnel's dead," Alpha Kita echoed, still tinkering with Geeza's communication device.

"His safety measures aren't," said Tactics Officer Nadine, crushing the cigarette Dinimarajan passed her way on the bench they shared.

"Motopia is built to withstand more than a few persuader shots," Alpha Maurie pointed out, focused on the charred marks on the bench.

"It can sustain immense damage from the outside. Much less from within," said Alpha Ace Londo. Geeza moved over to his locker and removed the articles to complete his Alpha Ace uniform and armor.

"Those measures won't be very *safe* if everyone dies before we get to Virtus," Alpha Bond countered.

"Maurie is correct. I hate to say it, but the Searchers and the Seraph are endangering the larger operation."

"That's Leadership's issue," Meyers grumbled.

"'That's Leadership's issue, sir.' Stand up straight."

"Sorry, sir ... Sir?"

"What is it?"

"Another ping. The highest-ranking Ace is dead. That makes—"

"*Me* the highest-ranking Ace, and I'm not even in the fight. Are you all ready? We're hitting the gangplank. And I'm not accepting any casualties." Laying a heavy arm on Ona Kita's shoulder, Londo continued. "You fix that wrist unit?"

"Couldn't fix it, sir. But I was able to confirm that it's broken," Alpha Kita said.

"Hilarious. Everyone, fall in. We're moving out."

Slipping on his Alpha Ace boots, Geeza Londo hovered out of the locker rooms, away from War Games, and towards the conflict, with his hand-picked squad of Alphas and Specialists close by.

Encountering the stairwell that would bring his squad directly up to the frontlines of the battle, Geeza hesitated. Instead, they took the stairwell down, traversing a longer route in hopes of accessing the gangway at their intruders' rear.

* * *

Keano gulped down steamy bits of meat and rice as Altazar watched from across the restaurant table, sustained by the feeling of reuniting with his friend.

After the confrontation with the Seraphim, Depot had remained closed with a sign outside that read: *Renovations.* Altazar remembered returning to his home at the base of the tallest ruin in Virtus. There he removed his savings from underneath a floorboard, then made way to Pangaia. With no small amount of effort or trusts, he had persuaded the Ars Femina to release Keano into his custody.

Keano stopped eating to take a breath in between bites. Noticing Altazar's staring, he spoke; but not before releasing a belch into his hand.

"Spacedamn that's good. I labored at that prison castle for six days and most of seven. Didn't eat anything. Not a cracker, crust, or nut." Keano reached for his cup and drank. "Sipped a cap of water when they let me ... I knew I was going to die there, I just felt it." Tears pooled in and streamed down the creases in his face. "When I saw you, Zar I didn't know what to think. I was just happy to see someone familiar."

"I couldn't let you go out like *that.* Took me longer than it should to know what needed doing. I'm sorry," Altazar said, holding back tears of his own.

"Sorry? Zar, did you hear me? I was a dead man 'til you busted me out. I had made my peace and everything. I'm the luckiest octogenarian this side of those mountains. You don't have *shit* to be sorry about. Not to mention you brought me to my favorite joint and they still have outdoor seating. It's incredible."

"I won't beat myself over it if you won't let me," said Altazar, clasping his hands together behind his head as he sunk into the comfort of his chair. "Yeah, this place is great."

"You ever consider putting outdoor seating up at Depot? Pshh. I could get a crew together and have something up for you in days."

Altazar laughed off Keano's preposterous offer. Looking about the small restaurant from one of two tables on its outside patio, he was uninspired but impressed by its simplicity and cleanliness.

"One heck of a story though." Keano grinned and dropped his utensils to either side of his plate. "I think my stomach shrank. You want the rest of this?" Keano motioned to his plate, where a third of the meal he had ordered remained.

"Nah. I'm good. I've been eating a lot lately."

Keano leaned in, resting his hands and forearms on the table then said, "I don't know what it cost you to get me out. A younger version of me wouldn't have cared. You did what you did knowing I can never repay you—I respect that, but damn me to space if I'm gonna let you treat me like a charity assignment. That's a premium cut. Still has meat on it and everything. On the side, got your long grain rice and roasted greens. I don't think I could trust a man who would turn that down no matter what hole in hell he'd sprung me from."

"You don't have to ask me twice." Altazar picked up the unused utensils on his side of the table and put them to work. His fork became a shovel, and his knife was his spear.

The warmth of a smile wider than the walls of Pangaia, expanding across Keano's face melted the glacial wrinkles in his facial continent. As the smile faded, the ice of age returned.

Altazar, hunched over their plate, polished it as best as he could manage with the tools at hand. Over his shoulder, far to the east. Keano's eyes, owl-like in sharpness and wideness, spied motion above the mountains in the previously static background.

An object larger than any old Keano had ever seen and moving faster than he thought possible, cleared the mountain range. Though the object was an unalarming distance from their restaurant and enveloped in a cloudy shroud, Keano could see enough to know that their late lunch was over soon.

"Just when I thought my luck was looking up," Keano grumbled, staring spiteful daggers at the ominous disc in the distance. "Altazar? Wanna hear a story?"

"Absolutely," Altazar said, cleaning his chops with a quick combination of tongue and back hand.

"This one is about two friends, best friends. They're out to lunch when the sky opens up to swallow them." Keano's eyes did not move away from the inspiration for his tale.

At first, Altazar raised an eyebrow. Then he offered an eager grin. It was not long until the smile succumbed to a frown of understanding.

"The story is unfolding now? Behind me?"

"It is."

Chapter 28

Dezba darted past Hiroshi. The gangway filled with dozens upon dozens of Legioneers, but it was only so wide. Enough for five or six soldiers to hold the front line at a time. The railings of the gangway were reinforced with sheet metal panels. Wind whistled through gaps in the sheets allowing the gangway to bend with and not break under stress. In their haste the Legioneers had created a bottle neck at the opposite end of the gangway and were handing themselves over as sacrifices to the fearsome warriors at its opposite end.

Barging into the first row of Legioneers, Dezba managed to knock members of the infantry off their feet, as far back as the third and fourth rows of their formation. Hiroshi joined the fray, leaping over Dezba and landing atop the downed soldiers in the third row. Cordis Adolesco flashed and flickered as Hiroshi slashed and hacked his way through the horde.

Adjusting their tactics, the Legioneers began to pile onto the gangway from both its ends. Hiroshi lost sight of Saigo' body amid the battle tide, but he heard Dezba behind him. Grating steel against armor, then flesh. He felt the dead weight of Legioneers piling up around her and her daggers. The mobility provided by their specialized armor was meaningless in close quarters. The advanced and humming persuaders; their greatest weapons, were not in use. The soldiers had them but refused to fire them.

Dezba and Hiroshi, supporting one another back-to-back, formed a two-pronged vector of death. Anybody who dared to come within sword reach or dagger grasp was dispensed, and quickly. Ace, Alpha or infantry. If any soldier slipped by Hiroshi, they were eviscerated by Dezba, if any Alpha escaped her reach, they were swiftly impaled by him. As collaborating artists, they painted a scene full of dismembered and disembodied humanity.

Unique storylines and personal plots ended, family's torn asunder, businesses dismantled abruptly, as whole squads were erased. Without thought, the Seraph and the Searcher fought. Legioneers kept appearing, pouring out of and up from the barracks, plazas and malls of Motopia's larger ring.

Hiroshi stepped away from Dezba to confront a pair of Alphas. Feeling a presence behind him, but hearing no feet, he knew it was an Ace. The High Seraph about-faced with a twirl and extended sword. The Legioneer bobbed his head under then away from the swipe and managed to slap Cordis Adolesco free from his grasp with a deft hand. Another wise infantryman, whose asymmetric wrist bracer caused him to resemble a lanky collector king, approached from Hiroshi's blind spot and kicked the sword out of reach. The High Seraph repelled his attackers with fists and legs.

"Be still!" Alpha Ace Londo boomed. "All in the back, clear the gangway! Persuaders hot!" The surrounding Legioneers stopped throwing themselves blindly at their enemy and took up a protective formation around their ranking officer. The Legioneers who had entered the gangway from the side closest to Donnel's throne scurried back, disappearing around the corner where they could be heard but no longer seen.

Gazow. The telltale blue beam of an Alpha persuader left the barrel and stretched across the entire length of the gangway. Hiroshi and Dezba dove to either side to escape the scorching blast.

Gazow. Gazow. More rays fired as Ace Londo's unit closed in on Dezba and Hiroshi.

"Persuaders up!"

The second line of soldiers raised their weapons while the front lines took knees to refresh. Dezba spun. Gaining centrifugal force, she flung her curved knives as hard she could.

"Fire!"

The Searcher might have taken down at least one of the Alpha pair, but Ona Kita blasted the daggers out of the air. There was no blue light from her missiles. Smoke rose from the barrels of two smaller persuaders, similar in style and make to Mr. Galtero's silent persuader. Alpha Kita's akimbo firearms were anything but silent. The twin barrels joined again at the location of the daggers.

Two more shots pushed the weapons under and through the gap in the sheet metal paneling sending them careening off the edge of the gangway, lost to the larger ring below. Hearing no sound of petering below, Hiroshi looked to Dezba. Dezba looked over the edge and shook her head with a fervor that destroyed any desire in Hiroshi to do the same.

"An Alpha might survive that fall. Not us," Dezba shouted to Hiroshi, before dipping under a scorching beam of blue light.

"We're not getting across. We have to go back!" Hiroshi said. Dezba nodded in agreement. Hiroshi faced the encroaching wall of Legioneer infantrymen, Alphas, and Aces. Flinging off his robe he tossed it in their direction.

Alpha Ace Londo and squad let fly in unison, leaving six smoldering holes in the black and red garments. The robes settled to the floor in tatters as Hiroshi and Dezba sprinted back down the gangway.

Alpha Bond narrowed his eyes on Dezba's leg then let his persuader hum. The electric blue bolt began a short journey. It arrived at its destination, much faster than an arrow would have, slower than a bullet might, but the devastation and damage delivered were beyond either.

Returning to their original rally point, Hiroshi skidded to a halt at Mr. Galtero's corpse, which had been knocked over and trampled upon in the fray. Dezba collapsed to the ground in front of them both, contorted by agony. Unfastening her knee and shin guards hurriedly, she inspected the wound.

To Dezba's surprise the entry didn't look like much. Just a small dark circle, three times the size of a pinhead, right in the middle of her kneecap. The energy beam created by the humming persuader was thinner in diameter than it appeared to the naked eye. Running her hands underneath her knee she braced for the pain of contact. Her fingers dipped deep into a small fleshy cavern where most of the joint should have been. The humming persuader had burned a clean cone through her leg and left the surrounding tissue cauterized and in shock. Dezba looked at Hiroshi.

"How bad is it?" Hiroshi asked, propping his late brother up.

"I'm fine." She lied.

Hesitating for a moment, Hiroshi grabbed his brother's briefcase then tossed it to Dezba. Wincing, she caught it, opened it and took out the Gaser and another one of Galtero's toys. Hesitating herself for a moment, Dezba nodded then tossed the case back, along with three-grenade shaped devices; each larger than the last.

Another volley of suppressive blue burst down the platform. Luckily for the duo, the gangway was separated from the rest of the Motopia by a short hallway and stairwell.

Dezba hit the deck shooting. No noise was created when the persuader fired. The only thing Hiroshi heard was the shuffle of her armor and the squeeze of her leather half-gloves around the handle of the sidearm.

Three Alphas collapsed to the grating, bleeding from silent holes in their armor. Then four more. Additionally, two more Legioneers succumbed to their wounds and spilled over the edge of the railing, joining Dezba's daggers some distance below. Alpha Ace Londo and his squad ceased their advance, momentarily distracted by the noiseless mayhem.

"What *is* that?" Hiroshi asked, mouth agape.

"Silent Persuader. Your brother's favorite. It's Preneo tech."

"Right. What if you silently persuaded the soldiers behind us so we can get back around the corner and find a way out of here? Or we could wait 'til—"

"On my signal, Seraph. Arm one of those and toss it at the Legioneers." She pantomimed a twisting motion with her hands.

"Not my style."

"Death suits you better?" Dezba asked, returning to Galtero's briefcase to reload the nigh empty persuader.

"It does."

"I said, 'no boy scout' shit."

"You said, 'no good ole boy shit'."

"Arm the fucking grenades, Seraph."

"High Seraph."

"And throw 'em behind them. It should just blow the platform. Wait for my signal."

Hiroshi didn't argue. Dezba rolled her eyes behind Hiroshi's back as they inched around the corner that would release them from the battle zone of the scaffold bridge. The squads, ordered to that position by Ace Londo to escape the persuader bombardment, were caught off guard.

Thus, the scene was set. Arms out, gripping two unique and devastating weapons, Dezba steadied her breathing and cleared her mind. She thought of the cumulative and often nonconsensual persuader lessons Jelani had imparted over the course of their partnership. Dezba breathed in a big breath. Letting it out, she shouted to Hiroshi, who was standing directly next to her, "My signal!"

Hiroshi armed the smaller two of the three grenades with a couple of twists.

"Chuck em', past them. Now!"

Hiroshi, with his back to the wall, peeked back around the corner and lobbed beeping bombs as far as he could. They careened through the air. Tactics Officer Dinimarajan, spotting the missiles, motioned to destroy them with his persuader. As they grew near, he understood his attack would only cause the bombs to detonate.

"Get down!" he shouted to his comrade. "Those are Ghost Grenades!"

Two simultaneous explosions blew the middle segment Motopia's main gangway to smithereens. The blasts larger and more powerful than Dezba expected, or Hiroshi predicted. Most of the Legioneers' attacking force was consumed by the explosion. Those who weren't thrown clean off the city were left behind in the form of charred limbs and dismembered torsos.

The remaining Legioneers fumbled at their weapons, but Dezba was ready. Initiating with her fingers a transaction of death, she pressed the triggers for three uninterrupted seconds. Twenty living soldiers became twenty lifeless or dying bodies littered about the metal hallway. Shining red splattered over the surrounding matte silver completed the morbid display.

Dezba returned to Galtero's briefcase, to reload the persuaders without a second's thought.

"You—you said it would just be the platform," Hiroshi stammered, stepping in between the Searcher and the briefcase. "You said—" Before he could finish, Dezba shushed him with a finger over her lips.

"More, head this way," she said, motioning with her head to fresh soldiers pouring out of the barracks below them.

"They are even closer than that. I can hear them in the stairwell."

"More will die, High Seraph. It's them or us."

Hiroshi stepped aside. Dezba reloaded the Gaser and silent persuader, then returned to their corner vantage. Hiroshi was there next to her. Placing himself between his brother's body and the oncoming voices and feet, the Seraph and the Searcher braced for the next wave. Two squads, composed entirely of Alpha Aces. They bobbled about, hovering just slightly above the floor, aiming their humming persuaders. Dezba aimed her own back at them, while Hiroshi toyed with the last and largest of the Ghost Grenades, hating himself for what he would do next.

Chapter 29

Celeste tilted the wooden front legs of her chair off the sticky floor and downed a fifth beer. She awaited the arrival of an Ars Femina operative from the shadowy corner of E. M. Brace, a small lounge located at the base of Span Opticon Plateau. E.M. Brace was a cozier, ritzier alternative to saloons like Depot. Where the retro bars offered anonymity, the lounges offered privacy to trusted patrons.

"*Powsers*! You all are gonna wanna' see this shit. There's a castle in the sky! Can't say if it's flying or falling," said a man dressed in the garbs of a fabrication center executive, bursting through the front door.

Hearing his excited claims, E. M. Brace's inhabitants streamed, shuffled and bumbled into the streets of Virtus. Grumbling the whole way because her contact was late or a no-show, Celeste was the last to leave the lounge. She trailed just behind the barkeep.

Outside, she couldn't immediately see what everyone else fixated on. Her view was blocked by awnings, street signs, and towering ruins. Finding a relatively secluded area near a locked kiosk, Celeste looked to the sky. Once her eyes adjusted to the distance, she rubbed them to make sure what she saw was real.

She had drunk her drinks quicker than usual, maybe she was inebriated. The image did not change.

Motopia, free of its chains, had descended from the sky, down through the clouds, and hovered over Virtus. The Floating City glided in from the east and Holy Lands could be seen in the distance. A trick of perspective made Motopia appear as though it balanced atop the tip of Benben Observatory.

The inhabitants mixed with other Virtans who took to the streets. Their chatter and excitement grew to a fever pitch, pointing and seeking new vantages as Motopia descended and advanced. To Celeste, its path was clear.

Children that laughed and joked, pretending to be the invading city itself, ran around with their arms out simulating the miracle of flight as they played. No one seemed to understand the danger they were in. Motopia flying was an unbelievable fact itself but Motopia traveling to Virtus implied something much worse than ambition. If Motopia was mobile and currently above Virtus, it was sound to assume that Ecclesiel's murder was part of a larger plot to upset the delicate balance between factions.

Still no word heard from her network of Jelani or Dezba's return. Celeste unwillingly accepted the possibility that she had moved too slowly. The body discovered in the Level 7 Armory provided valuable clues, if only she found it sooner.

The gathering, filled with people watching their approaching doom, and growing in number, gasped. Motopia had stopped moving. Perched, suspended impossibly in midair, it held position above Span Opticon Castle.

Celeste pushed through the swelling crowds slowly at first, then increased to a jog as she became more aggressive with her relocations. Sprinting full speed, shoving hapless civilians out of her way as she sliced a path to Span Opticon.

There had been talk for more than twenty years suggesting Motopia was much more than Donnel claimed. When the General said he would create a floating city it inspired disbelief, mockery and panic alike. When construction was complete, it was clear that Donnel meant 'suspended' in place with chains when he boasted 'floating'. The panic died down.

Celeste never imagined Amram Donnel's grasp of flight beyond the hovering capabilities of his Alpha's boots. Yet, Motopia had traveled far across Neo-Earth, splashed through the milky cloud line and parked itself above the Syndicate of Valor's stronghold.

Could this mean checkmate? Celeste mused as she juked lamps posts, ducked under light installations, spun around traders and vagrants, skirting only those too large, too small or too old to shove. Any box or bundle in her path she vaulted over. Trash cans were tossed aside and overturned as she charged ever certain toward uncertainty.

The plan was to remain inside the borders of Virtus, gaining intel until an appropriate window to kill Sandhurst. Donnel's surprise invasion made the waiting part of the plan pointless. Celeste slowed down but never stopped running as a thought solidified in her mind. Her plan to capture Hiroshi would prove needlessly risky for Dezba and Jelani if Donnel meant to take control himself. At Donnel's behest, the battle to determine the future of all Neo-Earth would start or culminate in Virtus. Not sure which one, Celeste increased her pace anyway, hoping to reach Span Opticon before anything major took place.

Increasing bedlam spilled into the streets as she neared the Syndicate's fortress. It seemed not everyone was excited by the sudden appearance of Motopia. For every group of observers gathered at a corner, there was another running amok through back-alley trade areas. Curious minds witnessing a miracle on one block and enterprising opportunists scavenging or looting on the next.

Sandhurst's illusion of order shattered; undone in minutes what took many years to build. General Donnel achieved this without laying a single boot on the ground. With her eyes fixed on Motopia, Celeste traversed Span Opticon Plateau, navigating the winding road up with the confidence of a High Seraph.

Arriving at the front gates of the Span Opticon Castle, Celeste met with the fallout Grase created days earlier. Areas of the outer gate roped off and in various stages of repair. The makeshift construction site looked recently abandoned. Considering the current situation, Celeste didn't blame them. Only the most dedicated workers would spend the next precious and unknowable moments at work and not with their families.

The sight of Motopia, swollen stomach and open maw, waiting hungrily to swallow Virtus bit by bit, inspired strong emotions, but dedication was likely not one. Not a soul stood guard at the massive gate. Smirking, she knew none of her Ars would buckle in such fashion, even under the pressure of invasion, even if from the sky.

Making sure Cinder was securely fastened to her back, Celeste eyeballed the route she would take to make it to the nearest window or balcony. Using the scaffolding from the construction site as a runway and springboard, Celeste reached a network of eaves with a vault. Hanging by her arms, she made her way around the side of Span Opticon. With one arm she freed Cinder from her back and threw it up and over onto the balcony. Rocking back and forth she gained enough momentum to do the same. Dusting herself off, she prepared to infiltrate. From her current position it would be easy enough for her to find the Chamber of the Elders, Celeste concluded.

"Psst!"

Celeste dropped down and out of view, persuader in hand.

"Celeste. It's me, Armma," the voice whispered loudly from below the balcony's lip. Peering over the edge, Celeste and Cinder confirmed the voice belonged to her contact.

"Armma, the fuck are you doing here?"

"Nobody was at E.M. Brace. I got there and saw you run off. Cinder was on your back, even under that tarp I can recognize it. I made sure nobody was tailing you. Then, I followed you here."

"Damn it all to space, you could have just LCL'd me."

"A long-distance communication link? In public? You're serious? Anyway, you looked like you were in a hurry. I figured it would be best to see where you were going."

"Armma, I almost blew you in half." The telltale concern that had won the loyalty of all of her subordinates was evident in Celeste's voice.

"Nah. At this range, I don't even think *you* could hit me with a thing like that," Armma said with a smile across the entire length of her face. Her arms were at her hips, and she shifted her weight onto one leg as she craned her neck up. Her red hair and freshly straight-razored crew cut faded on the sides of her head. Her Ars Femina armor shined like new. Smiling back, Celeste knew she was only half-joking.

Armma was five years young in the Ars, but she was already one of Celeste's silent favorites. Lacking a passion for any specific weapon, Armma routinely completed extractions and expirations without taking requisitions from Level 7. She would find or fashion a weapon in the field. Her resourceful-ness and ability to think on her feet gained her favor, making her an obvious choice for clandestine affairs.

Celeste beckoned Armma up with a nod. Following Celeste's lead, Armma climbed the scaffolding, ran the runway, navi-gated the eaves, then finally hoisted herself up onto the stone balcony. Finding a spot next to Celeste, who had returned to her hidden position, Armma addressed the elephant in the sky.

"So, Motopia, it flies? Like, for real, for real? That's it above us now?"

Celeste nodded gravely.

"You knew about this?"

"There were rumors, but I wasn't buying that horseshit. Look at her now," Celeste said after whistling. "We have to get to the roof. I can't see shit from this balcony."

"Agreed."

Celeste and her operative slipped into the room attached to the balcony. Quietly incapacitating any member of the Syndicate unlucky enough to encounter them, Celeste and Armma made their way to the top of Span Opticon. A ladder at the top of a spiral staircase brought them through a hatch and to the highest battlement. From there, the colleagues shared a simple moment taking in the sight.

Motopia pitched a sharp shadow across a large swathe of Virtus, entirely engulfing Span Opticon Castle. The floating city was frozen at an uncanny thirty-degree angle with one of its rounded edges hovering just forty-five scorchfeet above Holding Wing.

Three explosions tore through Motopia's exterior; two smaller blasts then seconds later a third, sending bits of people and paneling showering down to the battlements below.

Celeste and Armma split up to avoid the largest pieces of the crashing debris. When the smoke and chafe cleared, Motopia's insides laid exposed. The installation bobbled around its central axis before returning to a stable flight position. Regrouped and safe for the time, the Ars Femina infiltrators examined the fallout of the detonations. Nearly a third of the smaller ringed city had been destroyed and a hefty slice of the larger ring had been blown wide open.

"What the hell is that thing? I don't know anything that can take that kind of damage and still function, let alone fly," said Celeste, her gaze fixed squarely on Motopia.

"I figured something like that would've plummeted to earth," Armma said.

Looking through the magnifying scope of Cinder, Celeste spotted a curious group deeper within the city. There were three people. One carrying the other and a woman trailing behind, limping. By adjusting the settings on Cinder, she was able to increase its magnification and confirm the injured woman was Dezba. Armma, squinting, utilized her spookily accurate eyesight. "Is that Hiroshi? Looks like he's carrying a body."

Celeste, stunned at the clarity of Armma's vision, whipped her head around in disbelief. "Not only is that Hiroshi, but that's Dezba behind him. She's injured."

"We gotta' get to her! Where's Jelani?"

"I don't know. And I don't know how to get up there. I don't think we should try. We are here for Sandhurst."

"What and we're gonna find him on the roof?" Armma responded, her statement watered with sarcasm.

"Dammit, Armma what do you want me to do?"

Celeste traced the line from Armma's eyes back to Cinder.

Twisting her lips into a crooked pucker and tilting her head from side to side as if weighing her options, she turned to Armma with a wink.

"Aight. I'll see what I can do. I'll need a spotter."

"Spotted."

"Who?"

"Looks like a few Alphas coming up behind them pretty fast."

Aiming Cinder at Motopia. "There?" Celeste asked.

"No. Yup ... Right there! You see 'em?" Armma said.

Celeste responded with the muffled sound of three projectiles leaving the barrel of her long-distance persuader. The closest Legioneer fell to the floor, still, another spun around and over a railing—toppling out of the hole in Motopia, hitting the battlement below, he slid over the edge and landed in a messy bundle on the ground.

"What about the others?"

She did not watch what happened next. No, instead, lowering the persuader, she simply stared at Armma who was still surveying the scene. Over on Motopia, a hanging panel fell from its delicate position near the ceiling, landed in a pile of debris and caused a chain reaction that sent burnt and twisted scraps of metal tumbling across the hallway, effectively blocking the path of Legioneers. Armma, smiling, slapped Celeste on the back.

"I don't miss a mark." Before they could enjoy the victory another group of Legioneers appeared, this time ahead of Hiroshi and Dezba.

"Hey, hey! They're taking aim." But so was Celeste. This time, five projectiles made the journey from Span Opticon's rooftops to the outer edges of Motopia. Each missile found its fatal home deep within the body of its target. Cinder made short work of their Alpha armor. The five eager troops who showed up to save the day were now still, their previous ambitions laid to rest.

Seeing their attackers thwarted so abruptly and without obvious cause made Hiroshi halt, Dezba who had been moving slower and slower collapsed behind the High Seraph.

"Dezba is down," said Armma

"Now I get to see what the boy is made of."

Still searching his surroundings for a reason to explain the sudden deaths of eight Legioneers, Hiroshi scooped up an unconscious Dezba and hoisted her onto his other shoulder. Carrying both Saigo and Dezba, Hiroshi struggled forward, balancing their added weight.

"He could've left her. He should've left her." Armma could not believe her eyes.

"I had my suspicions about him when we first met. Turns out I might have been right. We may be able to work with this Hiroshi."

"*If* he makes it."

"If he makes it," Celeste echoed. "As long as I can see him, I got them covered. But we can't help him get down."

"I'd find a way down," Armma said, only half joking.

"I know you would. That means he's got a chance."

"Celeste, we have company. Seraphim are starting to make their way up here."

Shouldering Cinder once again, Celeste and Armma inched around the octagonal panels of Holding Wing and out of view of Sandhurst's arriving Seraphim. The Syndicate's response time seemed slow but they more than made up for it with numbers. Three to four hundred Seraphim filed out of various hatches and doors and took defensive postures at various positions on the roof and battlements.

"I can still cover them from here. But I need you to watch my back while I watch theirs. If we end up inside Holding, we'll have bigger problems than getting Dezba off Motopia," said Celeste.

"Fuck. I lost him while we were moving. I see a few more dead Legioneers, but no High Seraph. No Dezba."

The shape of a lone Legioneer Alpha Ace exited from a freshly created hole in the outer shell of Motopia. The Ars Femina infiltrators might have missed it if not for the blue hot sparks and the tumbling scorched metal cut out. The Ace stepped into the light of day, revealing its cargo to Armma and Celeste. He held on one shoulder a man who looked like a defeated Hiroshi and on his other shoulder was a still unconscious Dezba. The Alpha leapt from Motopia with his cargo secured by each arm.

The little understood processes that granted the ability to hover above ground were now working triple time as the Ace used the simple thrust to slow his rapid descent. The Alpha's boots failed repeatedly—winking in and out as they struggled under the additional weight. Celeste and Armma lost sight of the Alpha, his pair of sputtering boots, and his passengers as they disappeared in front of Span Option's looming Holding Wing. Seraph Guiles was first among the crowd to recognize the corpse of former High Seraph Saigo Gunkimono.

"That is the former High Seraph Gunkimono!" Seraph Guiles shouted, ushering his comrades to his side to receive the falling Alpha safely. Hiroshi released his baggage to the surrounding Seraphim then removed the Alpha Ace helmet.

Celeste and Armma didn't see the Seraphim swarm the Ace's impact location. They did hear jubilant and triumphant cheers overtaking the battlements. Hiroshi was bleeding and battered to near exhaustion but alive. Refusing assistance from his troops, Hiroshi peeled off the remaining pieces of armor, and gave them to Seraph Guiles along with a field promotion to Squad Leader. Next, Hiroshi explained that rope would be needed to board the city and where the mechanism to release Motopia's Lift could be found if still intact.

"What about the Searcher? And your brother, sir?"

"They are coming with me. I need to speak to Sandhurst."

Chapter 30

Hiroshi staggered into the Chamber of the Elders. Holding himself up against the worn stone of Span Opticon with one shoulder and balancing the weight of Saigo and Dezba on the other. Stopping in the darkness to catch his breath, he waited for the hovering lights that signaled the approach of the Elders. They appeared, but this time the razor thin twine used to achieve the dazzling effect of the light show could be seen. The shadows created by the performance grew and shrank comically instead of menacingly. The chairs, now empty, once seeming to emerge from nowhere, dropped from visible compartments hidden in the room's obvious ceiling. The machines manufacturing the simple illusion jerked and creaked spastically, abandoned by the small crew needed to operate them. Hiroshi recognized the Legioneer aesthetic, already present in Donnel's early creations as a High Seraph.

"Sandhurst!" Hiroshi called out into the void. Nothing but his own voiced answer back at first. *Sandhurst!* But then came the soft shuffling of feet, the subtle rustling of heavy robes, the creaking of ancient bones. Elder Sandhurst stepped out of the shroud of darkness into the light of Hiroshi's gaze. Hiroshi slid Dezba and Saigo off his shoulder gently, then wiped soot and blood from his face. His hand carried even more dirt than it removed.

"My son has returned," saying this, the Elder moved to the still body of Saigo Gunkimono, bent over and gently kissed his forehead above the fatal wound. "Who did this?"

Motioning to Dezba with a nod. "The Searcher." Sandhurst stroked his sparse gray whiskers, pausing to order his words choicely, "You brought her here ... to face justice?"

Hiroshi met the fire in Zachariah's eyes with his own intensity. "The Searcher—Dezba, is under *my* protection."

"*Your* protection?"

"I do not know if you saw, but Donnel's invasion was thwarted in its infancy. Our Seraphim believe I am why there was no clash of armies here today and they are not all wrong. Dezba and I, upon defeating Donnel in his throne room, set sights on their elite units. We carved a path through their stronghold, with the intention of weakening their forces as best we could. If it was not for the sacrifice of the late Jelani and Dezba, Donnel might have survived to see his attack through. Donnel was mad. He wished to destabilize the Treaty by assassinating faction leadership. I killed him in hopes of preventing an all-out war, not because *you* declared him your enemy. I killed him because it was right. Sandhurst, your reign is over. This will no longer be an organization that lives out the will of one man. The rule of the Elder is over. I am, upon my own moral authority, casting you and any who are loyal to you out of the Syndicate of Valor. As we speak the Seraphim are rounding up any stragglers left on Motopia and bringing them to Holding—to await trial."

"Trial? They are all would-be murderers guilty of treason. The punishment for which is death, as outlined by the Treaty of Neo-Earth."

Hiroshi didn't immediately respond, instead he fished inside his pockets and retrieving a rolled-up canvas. Sandhurst followed Hiroshi's hands with his eyes nervously. He couldn't stop himself from recoiling.

"You see—that's how this all started." Hiroshi shook his head with disappointment. "You demanded that I make an example of Joan Flayr, before bothering to ever explain the implications or repercussions of the action. Sure, I have led a dozen live missions, participated in a handful of inter-faction combat exhibitions, and achieved unheard of feats on both. But it was never me you saw. All you see is a piece—a prosthetic as useful as the withered limb it is intended to replace.

"You would not leave your post as the gatekeeper of progress until a suitable, callous heir is found—or manufactured. You groomed me—spoiled me, all in hopes that I would become your best pet yet. You treat your loyal subjects as a neowolf breeder might treat a litter of mutts. Amram was your first attempt, an exemplary dog, no doubt, but he soon felt no need for a master. So, when he shed the name you had given, stopped responding to your beckon and call, and ignored the rules of your house, it was time for him to go elsewhere. Next was Saigo, my dear brother. He was your second attempt at domestication. This time you were much more personable and loving. Having experienced abandonment for the first time with High Seraph Donnel, you wrapped your arms around Saigo so tightly you only let him out of your sight to play fetch. Except it became his favorite game, the only thing to keep his tail wagging. So, as soon as he found a stick worth the chew, instead of returning it to your hand he took it and ran far away. Far from you, but to something familiar. And now me, your best, last hope to pass the baton, Hero of Neo-Earth. In me, you fostered excellence, obedience, humility—all the ingredients needed to grow your most loyal hound. Keeping me in isolation, filling my head with lies and exaggerations. Where you tried to make Donnel your companion, and Saigo your child, you made me your subject. Spreading stories of how dangerous your Hiroshi was. How you could beat him on the nose with the same paper he had just retrieved, and his tail would never stop wagging. For a time, it must have seemed you had done it, crafted the premier pup. But you have failed. As you have failed repeatedly. The manipulative, abusive, master who blamed his pack for his own myopia."

Hiroshi's grip tightened reflexively over the canvas. Sandhurst caught the edge of his chair, still suspended a scorchfoot above his head and pulled it down to the floor, then sat. Without the crew of Seraphim at the controls, it didn't spring back up into the air. It simply rested on the floor, as obvious and unnecessary as the leader who sat in it. Everything Hiroshi had been enamored by during his last visit was now an eyesore. How could he have been so foolish as to blindly follow such a charlatan?

As if hearing Hiroshi's thoughts, Sandhurst began a defense for the silent accusation.

"Spare your childish accusations of dishonesty. You do know, I know, you lied to me. Have been lying ever since I asked you to complete a simple task. You disobeyed *me* and dared come back *here*, with malice, to tongue lash *me*? The stories always forget to mention your sense of humor. It is true that I have not been completely honest with you, Hiroshi, as you have not been completely forthcoming with me. Do you blame an old man for holding onto the dreams of his youth? If that man had lived two hundred years and he was sure it was the dream keeping him alive? As long as I am shepherding this planet's lost flock, I will draw breath. Am I wrong to cull when it is time, to shear when wool is needed?"

"It is not some dream keeping you alive. It is some mistake in your blood—a tweak in the DNA of those of us who were meant to survive the Scorch Period. Mistakes like it are rare, but mistakes indeed. The evidence sits above us hidden within Motopia's archive. You are no deity or demigod. Your age gives you no right to rule. The gift of life was bestowed upon you at random and you meant to use it for good. But you no longer walk an enlightened path. You cling to control as if it were your very lifeblood. It is not. I too am likely the product of their mistakes. But my gift is strength. With it, I give you permission, no, I require you to let go now. Allow me to steer the Syndicate back to the light. But go you must. I will explain your absence to the Seraphim and the people of Virtus. I will tell them you left willingly and dissolved the Council of Elders before you did. And if that means death in your eyes, then spend the remainder of your days thinking of how it was mercy *your* Hiroshi returned to Span Opticon with, and not malice."

"Hiroshi, my son."

"I am not your son! For all I know, Saigo and I's parents were killed in one of your suppression raids like Joan's were. You created the Boundless when you decided you could single-handedly control the narrative. You created the Legioneers by declaring the pursuit of certain technology illegal. We could have had their members as our own, if we ran a more reasonable operation. And you excluded the Feral-men from any rights afforded by the Treaty. They aren't even allowed inside the boundaries of Virtus. Why could that be? Is it because the Feral-men are the direct descendants of the Preneo? Never subjected to space sleep like the rest of us? But why would that breed contempt from you? Unless, it is the Feral-men who despise *you* and choose not to participate in your global charade on their own. Zachariah, it does *not* cease there. Why would the Feral-men hate *you*, Hero of Neo-Earth?" Hiroshi unraveled the canvas he had been abusing during the confrontation.

Sandhurst's eyes rolled across the document from top to bottom—squinting as he scanned. His eyes widened as the realization of what he was looking at struck him.

"What? Where could you have gotten such a thing?" he asked in excited disbelief.

"I found this in Saigo's carrying case. It has the same quality and detail of an academic image. The wear on the paper and inking. The way they are smudged and not faded, suggests it is not a recreation."

"It is no facsimile, Hiroshi. That document your holding is about one hundred and seventy years old. It was treated with a resin known to the Feral-men to preserve a canvas picture for much longer than anything possible here in Virtus. Ingenious really how they—"

"Enough about the canvas! What does it depict? That looks like you in the middle."

"It is me."

"And these men and women around you look like the Mansamusas from the Eight major Feral-men tribes."

"They are."

"But you are all smiling here, posing for the artist to capture your collective accomplishment. What was it? What did you and the leaders of all the Feral-men achieve on that day?"

"They hate that term. Did you know that?" Sandhurst rapped

his fingers against the arm rests of his fallen throne. Hiroshi paced to and fro, eyes locked on Sandhurst's own. "I should know, I am the one who made it up. After I—I betrayed each and every one of them. They helped me uncover the pieces that put together a more complete history of the world, but they had no desire to help me put the world back together. I told them then I wished to unite the various factions and tribes under one singular document of peace, my Treaty of Neo-Earth. And they told me to leave." Elder Sandhurst, sitting straight up now, held his head high as volume and confidence returned to his wavering voice.

"Fifteen years in the wilderness. And at the end we had created a map of the world. Not just the civilized and habitable areas we call Neo-Earth, but most of the globe. When I told them my plans to create a syndicate that stood for valor and a country that stood for virtue, they took the map and exiled me from their territories. They embarrassed me, threw me aside because of my ideals. They were perfectly content digging up trinkets and tech until I wanted to heal the world with them. That photo is of the day we finished the map. That is why all the Mansamusa's and I are so happy. This photo was taken right before I told them of what I meant to do with what we had achieved. My dearest friends, the Feral-men, who took me in at the age of ten, showing me their culture and customs, and for a time treating me as one of their own, I did not think they were capable of stealing my work."

Hiroshi noted genuine sadness in the elder's tone.

"You see, it was not just me who yearned for simplicity. They were left behind by us, the Preneo. Why should they help me rebuild the same empire that callously abandoned them? It took me nearly two hundred years to see their point of view.

But it was too late. My younger self was spiteful and vindictive. That is why no Feral-men are allowed inside our borders. If they wished to cast me out, taking that which was partially mine, then I would do the same. *I* defeated the anarchists and the opportunists and rallied and made sovereign those people who listened. Before *my* Treaty, Feral-men traveled as they pleased. No longer. If they took my map, I meant to take their globe. With every new addition, the Treaty further shrank their territories and grew our own. Virtus was founded on the graves of those who preferred discord over order. To maintain that order, I obviously withheld secrets. You would tell your Seraphim everything?"

"I already have."

A look of genuine bewilderment took over Sandhurst's face.

"I told our men that in your old age you transferred leadership of the Syndicate to me. I told them that what appeared to be a surprise invasion was actually part of your plan. I told them the events of the past few weeks were part of your final campaign."

"Drivel. Never once has there been a change in leadership."

"No, not in seventy years. Which is why they will ask no questions. They cheered and offered up booming applause. Not a single Seraphim looked sad or confused. To them, I will always be *your* Hiroshi. But you are released, no longer a hostage to your title or chair. Be plagued no more by thoughts of your flock. I will protect them from wolves—having been raised by one. If you leave peacefully, I will."

"And if I do not?"

Hesitant, Hiroshi continued, "Go anywhere. Just go now, and far enough for Neo-Earth to escape your shadow. There will be no punishment for your past crimes, and I won't ask you to confess. I have learned all I needed to know from my brother. This is all the restraint I can muster. Go to your friends—the Feral-men and confess to them. Maybe *they* will take pity on an ancient man. Makes little difference to me—the Syndicate will be safe, *is* safe."

Hiroshi placed a firm hand on Sandhurst's fragile shoulder. "The work is done."

Zachariah Sandhurst, former Hero of Neo-Earth, slid out of his seat, his feet dangling for a moment before making contact with the chilly stone floor. His robes entered free fall for an instance before snapping back to the brittle foundation of his bony body. He gathered his robes about him with as much dignity as a parent scolded by their child could. Moving to the entrance, inching past his former subordinate, he ran his fingers over a tiny knife tucked away in the folds of his sleeves.

"I wouldn't," Hiroshi said. Caught, he let the knife fall back into its resting place.

"I could have come with a saber in arm, instead I came armed with your secrets. You cowered from this canvas just the same. You ask me to behead Joan Flayr—I should have taken your head for ordering her parents killed."

Sandhurst didn't slow his exit, he simply shouted his responses over his shoulder, "They were party to an illegal settlement of dissidents!"

"And you had that settlement erased! Instead of welcoming refugees, you declared dissenters outlaws and aggressively policed taboo technology. It was your brashness that strengthened the Boundless Movement." Hiroshi didn't follow his master as he called out. He knew if he did, he might cut him down in anger. "When Saigo discovered images of flying machines, you made him cover it up. You sent him down the fatal path! I could have your head for that!"

Sandhurst said nothing, almost at the door.

"And when I was a child and needed my older brother dearly, you told me he died. I should have your head for that!"

Zachariah reached the exit, stopping in the doorway just long enough to repeat Hiroshi's words, "The work is done."

Hiroshi could not see the smile on the Elder's face. And even if he had, he was in such a mood it was best that he did not.

Elder Sandhurst stepped out of the dimness of the Chamber of Elders into the relative brightness of Span Opticon's hallway lights. Being as old as he was, it took more than a few moments for his eyes to adjust to the change.

The blurry masses at the center of his vision came into focus. He was not alone. Somebody had been listening to them—waiting just outside the room. Sandhurst rubbed his eyes to encourage a quicker clarity. It was two people. The last people a disgraced patriarch would want to encounter on route to exile.

Blocking his path were Celeste and Armma. Celeste with Cinder tenderly in her grip, Armma held a solid, de-broomed stick. The smell of gunpowder was in the air. Looking past them, he saw blood slowly traveling into the hallway from Elders Cherveyo, Apopthis, and Lilleane's quarters.

Sandhurst's stubborn heart skipped a beat. Clutching his chest, he tried to defend himself with their sympathy. But there were no buyers interested in what he was selling. Only takers. Only takers.

Celeste locked eyes with Armma then nodded toward Sandhurst before continuing on into the Chamber of Elders.

Ignoring his helpless charade, Armma cracked him over the head with the sturdy pole. It did not break but Elder

Sandhurst's skull did—just like an egg. Two hundred years of memories spilled out like runny yolk.

A face of confusion and desperation was all he could manage. He couldn't moan or scream as his faculties shut down, bit by fragile bit. He clawed with inaccurate, stiffened fingers at the Searcher's leg as she stepped over him.

Thwap! Another blow from the broomstick stopped all uncertainty in its tracks. Wiping sticky bits of hair and bony gristle off and onto the wall, Armma returned to Celeste. Zachariah Sandhurst, architect of the Treaty of Neo Earth, self-appointed father of emergent civilization, and the oldest man to yet live, was dead.

Epilogue

Marble and Aikiki came to the spot where hours before, something had fallen from the sky and settled in a dust cloud. Aikiki looked back at their settlement in the distance. The night breeze jostled her beaded locks. A chill caught her spine. The fires had all but gone out and smoke danced above the tents and bled into the starry backdrop.

"Come." Marble beckoned with a nod, standing triumphantly, both hands on his hips, at the rim of the small crater. Aikiki hesitated for a tick then moved to his side.

Mouths ajar, they shared silence.

"It's a man, I think," said Marble.

"Or a woman," Aikiki said.

"Well, it's a person for sure. Right?"

"I've never seen a person look like *that*."

"I see an arm," Marble proclaimed, moving closer still. He surfed a small landslide, created by their movements, deeper into the crater's basin.

"Its leg is over here!" Aikiki called out to Marble, descending to inspect their discovery.

"Here's its head," he said.

"It ... looks like a bird or some kinda' ..." Aikiki trailed off.

"I've never seen a bird made out of metal," Marble replied bemused.

"Never seen a person made outta metal either."

"True. And we've seen a lotta' stuff out here."

Stepping back to view their find in full, the children then inched forward until they stood over the still form of what appeared to them to be a giant, mechanical, bird-person.

Amram Donnel, the last-first General of the Legioneers had been released from the burdens of the living when he hit the ground. No amount of engineering would save him. His Impervious Life Suit became his tomb.

An eager Aikiki found the release pins at the neck. The ILS helmet snapped open. Locating the inner release pins, she methodically and unceremoniously separated corpse and broth from the suit like briny meat from an oyster. Marble, known for his cunning, didn't dare. He retreated to the crater's edge, as limb by lifeless limb, Aikiki pried man from machine. She struggled at the torso, unable to lift the dead weight.

"Help me."

"What're you gonna do?" Marble called down.

"Help me and you'll see."

Marble mustered his fabled courage and rejoined Aikiki. Together the children lifted Amram Donnel's remains, rolling them aside.

Aikiki reached into the gauntlets to separate the gloves. Finding and depressing them, the armored hands fell free, stiffened into open palms.

"Grab one. We gotta' bury him," Marble obliged. Each, with a massive, armored hand as a shovel, began to dig a grave fit for a general.

They slid him into his resting place, dead at the center of his own crater; an inverted mausoleum dug out with his own hand. Tucked into his death bed by his own machinations.

"Well. What now?" Marble inquired, nudging his best friend with an elbow. Aikiki unveiled a mischievous smirk and proceeded to wipe down the suit of armor with her sleeves. Marble shook his head disapprovingly, but his eyes showed all the encouragement she needed. A few quick wipes and she was ready to slide in and suit up.

"Wait!" Marble blurted out, grabbing her arm. "What if it's rigged?" Her furrowed brow was all the response he needed.

Aikiki had already taken the late general's place inside the suit. The smell of freshly sizzled flesh and the stale breath of a large man slinked into her nostrils. She gagged but suppressed the reflex quickly. The smell was alien but with it came a peculiar brand of deja vu. Aikiki felt a tingling sensation run across her body. Some invisible force inhabited the thin space between her skin and the suit's inner lining. She felt the force probing, prodding, adjusting to her size and shape as she squirmed to get comfortable.

It happened suddenly but she was sure of what it was. The inspecting force accepted her. The armor was now an extension of her natural body, as responsive and flexible with the added durability of a machine. She shifted to her knees. The suit responded perfectly to her tiny body. Marble was in awe. Aikiki and he ventured off on secret expeditions countless times before, and still he struggled to believe what he saw. Aikiki Fennec, his best friend, daughter to the Mansamusa's Orisha and Grover Fennec, was practically royalty. The princess in all but name became a hulking tower of metal and mass. A monster hiding the frame of a child. An awesome enormity, tangible and friendly. It was all too much. Marble started feeling faint. In all the excitement he forgot to breathe.

A breath.

Aikiki made it to her feet and took her first steps. Marble had never seen a suit of armor like the one before us. Avoiding the General's Alpha patrols was lesson one for scavengers in his camp, so Marble was confident this was no Alpha armor. The Alpha armor curved, Aikiki's new armor jutted. Marble neared and ran his hands up the cool metal surface, along the rivets and edges of the layered plating. It was undamaged from its fall.

Aikiki paused, then knelt and extended her large arm to Marble.

"Hop on."

Marble scurried up her arm and found a comfortable perch on her shoulders.

"Lookit this thing, Marb. This changes everything. Our whole clan will be rich once we scrap this thing."

"I guess," Marble said.

Aikiki set her sights on their settlement. She cleared the crater's edge in one step. Giant armored foot after giant armored foot, the pair made their return.

They trekked north through the Perennial Plains back to the crescent of tents that was their home. She trudged up to the outskirts of the settlements, passed her own tent, and went directly up to the Mansamusa Marquee. Three of Orisha and Grover's guards stood at the ready outside the tent.

Before they could recover from shock, Aikiki revealed herself, speaking through the suit, "It's me, daughter of the Mansamusas. Me and Marble saw something fall from the sky and this is what it was. Lookit me? Isn't this amazing?"

Whatever features that allowed the helmet to amplify its wearer's voice also distorted it slightly. But the guardsmen who had worked for the Mansamusa's since Aikiki was a baby, recognized hers instantly. They beckoned her in, grim disbelief on their faces and disapproval in their body language.

Orisha stirred in her sleep. Grover rolled over to comfort her. It was then he felt the rumble of approaching footsteps. He also heard the shuffling feet of his guards, no alarm in their gate.

"Orisha, wake up. I believe we have an important guest," Grover whispered into the ear of his betrothed. She awoke. They quickly threw on their garments and sat in wait at the edge of their royal-sized bed for the approaching party.

Orisha could hear the sighs and whistles of functioning machinery now. They could see the shadows of their visitors cast on the burgundy cloth of their private partition. Grover, tensing his muscles, reached out for Orisha.

"It's the General," Orisha said close to inaudibly. Grover nodded in agreement, nothing but serious business on his face.

Two large gun metal fists reached in and pushed the doorway flaps aside. Torchlight poked through any holes it could, illuminating the large figure as it neared.

"Marble!" Grover exclaimed.

"Where's Aikiki!?" Orisha joined, eyes wider than the bulk of the armor in front of her. Marble guiltily searched for a response on the floor with his eyes.

"It's me, mom. Pops? I'm here. Isn't it cool? We found this armor in the plains, it fell out of the sky. Some guy was in it. He was dead so we buried him—just like you taught us. I know I said me and Marble would stop sneaking out after dark but we just knew it would be worth it—the danger and trouble. Look at this thing." Aikiki flexed her metal muscles playfully. "We could sell it and never have to scavenge again. My *kids* would never have to scavenge. Their *kids* would live lives of leisure as well. What? Why do you look like that? Aren't you happy? We're rich!"

"Oh, *shit!*" Grover exclaimed

"It's over," Orisha concluded.

Their guards had already strung together the implications and began preparing their settlement for war. Not the territorial skirmishes characteristic to the Feral-men way of life, but all-encompassing war that would touch the farthest reaches of their scorched and fallow Neo-Earth.

* * *

A strong wind lifted the blue half-cape on Joan's Vicaarian robes, but not her spirits. It blew in from the Perennial Plains and crashed up the steep peaks of the Holy Land's mountain range. Finding Benben Observatory, it made way to the top and collapsed on Joan's shoulders as a gusty updraft.

Joan shivered as she watched Neo-Earth through a quartz crystal window. The distorted image scrolled with her every movement. Darkness showed to the east and the faint light of civilization glowed to the west. Joan savored the peace. The completion of her objective would draw the attention of those eager to interrupt her solitude.

Meaning no disrespect, she took out the last bit of Paulo that remained above ground in Holy Lands, a book of matches. Igniting every stick, she lit the gargantuan blue candle reserved only for the Vicaarian Lighting Ceremony.

If the candle stayed previously unlit out of reverence for Ecclesiel, Joan didn't care. This was for Paulo. People as far as Pangaia would see the light and assume it for the Illumined One, but they would be reminded that someone important had died. That is what mattered.

Flickering and crackling, the fire warmed Joan's body and displayed shimmering shadows on her face. Turning her back to the cozy flame, her gaze struck Span Opticon and its newly acquired and badly damaged satellite, Motopia. Snarling, Joan hissed a name through clenched teeth.

"*Hiroshi.*"

* * *

As Celeste and Armma confront the High Seraph, elsewhere within the walls of Span Opticon, a child is born in the tender embrace of an ancient Librarian. Their bond, instant. Her adoption, automatic. Her given name, Baronica Jeffroy-Flayr. Her heritage, daughter to the rugged Grase Jeffroy and the rogue Paulo Flayr. Her legacy, our future.

-Ido Xzaven, High Librarian of the former Syndicate of Valor

About the Author

J. E. Caesar was born in Boston, Massachusetts to his Trinidadian mother and Jamaican father. He spoke his first words earlier than most and was among the last of his classmates to learn to read. When his joy of telling stories met his new found skill in reading them, his love of writing was born.

Inspired by his surroundings, peers, and unique upbringing as a first generation American in the heart of a historic city, J. E. Caesar wrote numerous poems and short stories before he began work on Empyrean Earth.

Also by J.E. Caesar

Seven Arms of The Squid

Coming Soon...

Made in United States
North Haven, CT
26 April 2023